Emotions and Contingencies in Conrad's Fiction

Yoko Okuda

Emotions and Contingencies in Conrad's Fiction

palgrave
macmillan

Yoko Okuda
Atomi University
Tokyo, Japan

ISBN 978-3-031-66722-0   ISBN 978-3-031-66723-7   (eBook)
https://doi.org/10.1007/978-3-031-66723-7

© The Editor(s) (if applicable) and The Author(s), under exclusive license to Springer
Nature Switzerland AG 2024

This work is subject to copyright. All rights are solely and exclusively licensed by the
Publisher, whether the whole or part of the material is concerned, specifically the rights
of translation, reprinting, reuse of illustrations, recitation, broadcasting, reproduction on
microfilms or in any other physical way, and transmission or information storage and
retrieval, electronic adaptation, computer software, or by similar or dissimilar methodology
now known or hereafter developed.
The use of general descriptive names, registered names, trademarks, service marks, etc.
in this publication does not imply, even in the absence of a specific statement, that such
names are exempt from the relevant protective laws and regulations and therefore free for
general use.
The publisher, the authors and the editors are safe to assume that the advice and information in this book are believed to be true and accurate at the date of publication. Neither
the publisher nor the authors or the editors give a warranty, expressed or implied, with
respect to the material contained herein or for any errors or omissions that may have been
made. The publisher remains neutral with regard to jurisdictional claims in published maps
and institutional affiliations.

This Palgrave Macmillan imprint is published by the registered company Springer Nature
Switzerland AG
The registered company address is: Gewerbestrasse 11, 6330 Cham, Switzerland

If disposing of this product, please recycle the paper.

For Mother

Acknowledgements

In writing this book, I have benefited greatly from the advice and support of many scholars, colleagues, and friends. First of all, I would like to express my gratitude to the late Professor Charles H. Peake, the late Dr. Paul Kirschner, and the late Dr. John H. Stape for their attentive guidance at the beginning of my career as a Conrad scholar.

For this project, I am grateful to Atomi University for granting me a year's research leave as a Visiting Fellow at Clare Hall, University of Cambridge (April 2017–March 2018), without which it would not have been possible to plan and start this project. I would like to express my deepest gratitude to Dr. Hugh Epstein for reading the early drafts of the chapters with great patience, raising questions for me to clarify and offering apt advice as well as moral support. I would like to extend my sincere gratitude to the members of the Joseph Conrad Society (UK), the Joseph Conrad Society of America, and the Joseph Conrad Society of Japan, in particular Professor Robert Hampson, Professor John G. Peters, Professor Jeremy Hawthorn, Professor Allan Simmons, and Professor Tetsuo Yoshida. I am also very grateful to Professor Patrick Colm Hogan of the University of Connecticut and Professor Trudi Tate of Clare Hall, University of Cambridge, for their valuable advice. Apart from literary scholars, I am deeply indebted to Dr. Karen Ottewell of Lucy Cavendish College, University of Cambridge, for offering me illuminating insights

viii ACKNOWLEDGEMENTS

into writing English-style essays and to Mr. Roger Northridge for reading the manuscripts and pointing out grammatical mistakes and awkward expressions. My thanks are due also to the librarians of Atomi University Library, Cambridge University Library, and the Chuo Library of Musashino, Tokyo.

I am very grateful to Dr. Eileen Srebernik and Ms. Uma Vinesh, editors, and Dr. Melvin Thomas, production supervisor, at Palgrave Macmillan, for their advice and assistance.

Portions of this book were first published as articles in the following journals:

> 'The Emotional Sub-Text of "The Duel".' *Conrad Studies* (Japan) 2 (2011): 57–75.
> '*Nostromo*: Nature, Identity, and Emotions.' *Conradiana* 48-1 (2016): 47–63.
> '"The Perfect Communion": The Significance of the Body in "The Secret Sharer".' *Yearbook of Conrad Studies* (Poland) 12 (2017): 101–111.
> '*Lord Jim*: Always "the Unexpected".' *L'Epoque Conradienne* 42 (2019): 83–104.

I would like to thank the editors of the above journals for kindly granting me permission to reproduce my articles in their partly revised form: Dr. Nathalie Martinière of *L'Epoque Conradienne*, Dr. Andrzej Juszczyk of *Yearbook of Conrad Studies* (*Poland*), Professor John G. Peters of *Conradiana*, and the Editorial Committee of *Conrad Studies* (*Japan*). I would like to extend my thanks also to the referees of these articles for their helpful comments and suggestions.

An earlier version of Chapter 2 was presented at the conference 'Transnational Conrad: between Texts and Theory' held by Société Conradienne Française in Limoges (France) in September 2017, Chapter 3 at the Colloquium of Clare Hall, University of Cambridge in October 2017 and also at the 45th Annual International Conference of the Joseph Conrad Society (UK) held in Chelmsford, Essex, in July 2018, Chapter 4 at the 43rd Annual International Conference of the Joseph Conrad Society (UK) held in London in July 2017, Chapter 7 at the international conference 'Joseph Conrad: 'Twixt Land Sea' in Olsztyn

(Poland) in November 2017, and part of Chapter 8 at the 5th Conference of the Joseph Conrad Society of Japan in November 2021. I would like to thank the participants of these conferences for their comments.

I wish to dedicate this book to my mother, Mrs. Akiko Okuda, who passed away in August 2013, for all the encouragement and emotional support she had given me.

Tokyo
May 2024

CONTENTS

1	**Introduction**	1
	Part I The Power and the Subtlety of Emotion	
2	**Always 'the Unexpected': *Lord Jim***	23
	Always 'The Unexpected'	25
	A Momentary Lapse or a Prolonged Habit?	27
	An Awakening Sense of Insecurity	31
	The Final Question	33
3	**Emotional Reactions, the Idea, and a Lie: 'Heart of Darkness'**	39
	Emotional Reactions	40
	The Idea	49
	A Lie	54

xii CONTENTS

Part II Common Subjective Tendencies

4 Nature, Identity, and Emotions: *Nostromo*   61
Nature and Its Power Over Humans   63
The Two Bases of Personal Identity   64
Identity Founded on a Fixed Idea: Charles Gould   65
A Reflection of Nature: Emilia Gould   68
Humility Before Nature, Audacity Before Men: Dr.
Monygham   72
A Sign from Nature: Decoud   74
The Power of Nature: Nostromo   77

5 Surprise, Anger, and Obsessive Thought: *The Secret*
Agent   83
Irony and the World of Contradictions   85
Indolence and Intransigence: Verloc and the Professor   87
Security and Insecurity: Heat and the Assistant Commissioner   92
Selflessness and Selfishness: Stevie and Winnie   97

Part III Maturing in Adversity

6 A 'Pilgrimage of Emotions': 'The Duel'   109
Shifting Emotions   111
Compassionate Love: Léonie and Feraud   114
Passionate Love: Adèle   118
Not 'the Why' but 'the How'   121

7 'The Feel of the Ship': 'The Secret Sharer'   123
The Body's Potential to Express and Communicate   125
The Body's Potential to Learn   126
The Mind's Eye Versus the Bodily Eye   131
The Art of Handling Man and Ship   134

Part IV Emotion and the Body

8 The Body, the Theatre of Emotions: *Under Western Eyes*   139
Impressions and Consciousness   142
Conversation and the Body   149
'Person,' or the Living Body   160
Words, The Foes of Reality   163

9 Conclusion   171

References   177

Index   185

Abbreviations

CL   *The Collected Letters of Joseph Conrad* (Vols. 1–9), ed. Frederick R. Karl, Laurence Davies, Owen Knowles, Gene M. Moore, and J. H. Stape. Cambridge: Cambridge University Press, 1983-2007.

CR   *Joseph Conrad: Contemporary Reviews* (Vols. 1–4), ed. Allan H. Simmons, John G. Peters, Mary Burgoyne, Katherine Isobel Baxter, and Richard Niland. Cambridge: Cambridge University Press, 2012.

CHAPTER 1

Introduction

In a letter addressed to Edward Noble, dated 28 October 1895, Conrad tells the aspiring novelist:

> [...] you must treat events only as illustrative of human sensation – as the outward sign of inward feelings – of live feelings – which alone are truly pathetic and interesting. You have much imagination; [...]. Well, that imagination (I wish I had it!) should be used to create human souls; to disclose human hearts – and not to create events that are properly speaking accidents only. (*CL* 1: 252)

Conrad, in this letter, conveys a notion that he is to hold throughout his writing career: what makes a novel truly poignant and appealing is 'sensation' illustrated in the framework of events, which are not much more than 'accidents.' In English, the word 'sensation' commonly signifies 'a physical feeling; specifically a mental state resulting from a stimulus operating on any of the senses or from a condition of part of the body' (*OED*1.a.); however, Conrad here uses the word in the sense of 'a mental feeling, an emotion; the feeling characteristic of a particular circumstance or situation' (*OED* 2.b.).[1] The tone of the letter carries a sense

---

[1] Richard M. Berrong indicates that the equivalent French word 'sensation' ['feeling'] 'doesn't translate well into English' (*The Conradian* 35.1: 39), so Conrad may have used the word in the French sense.

© The Author(s), under exclusive license to Springer Nature Switzerland AG 2024
Y. Okuda, *Emotions and Contingencies in Conrad's Fiction*, https://doi.org/10.1007/978-3-031-66723-7_1

of conviction that is rather strong for a writer who had published his first novel—*Almayer's Folly*—only 6 months earlier. Yet the same sense of conviction resonates in a letter written more than twenty years later to Barrett H. Clark. In this letter, Conrad claims: 'Some critics have found fault with me for not being constantly myself. But they are wrong. I am always myself. I am a man of formed character. Certain conclusions remain immovably fixed in my mind [...]' (*CL* 6: 210). The enduring notion expressed in his letter to Edward Noble may well be regarded as one of these conclusions that has remained 'immovably fixed' in Conrad's mind.

It stands to reason that Conrad should stress the role of emotion in a novel as, not only the novel but literature in general 'tends to appeal to the recipient's emotions through the emotion-laden acts and experience of the characters, and the value we attribute to literary works is largely a matter of our emotions' (Hogan: 2018b: 2). Conrad depicts the acts and experience of such characters as Jim, Nostromo, and Razumov in order to convey their emotions. However, according to Keith Oatley, literary criticism has not paid very much attention to this appeal to emotion made by literature:

> [...] emotions have preoccupied writers almost from the time writing was invented. In Europe the novel continued the tradition begun by Erasmus and Shakespeare of understanding the emotions that lie beneath the surfaces of social life. Curiously, however, apart from Aristotle's ideas that tragedy induces pity and fear in the audience, and makes for *katharsis* of these emotions, [...] the Western tradition of literary theory has not much to say about emotions. (2004: 152)

It seems that historically in the West, emotions have been of more interest to writers than theorists of literature, whereas, according to Patrick Colm Hogan, poetic theory in ancient India, for example, was 'particularly suffused with emotion' (2018a: 1).[2] Nevertheless, this state of affairs in the West seems to have changed in the last few decades:

---

[2] According to Hogan: 'In traditional Indian poetics, there are two key features of literature, one semantic, the other affective. The semantic feature is *dhvani*, suggestion, the cloud of associations that accompany word, image, scene, character, or other aspect of a work. The affective feature is *rasa*, sentiment, the emotion felt by a reader or audience member, usually an empathic form of an emotion felt (as we imagine) by its character or narrator' (2018a: 1).

1 INTRODUCTION 3

[...] emotion received relatively little attention in much of the criticism and theory that dominated Western universities in the middle decades of the twentieth century. This began to change toward the end of the century, and there has been a flowering of work on emotion and literature in the past 15 years – inspired in part by a slightly earlier flowering of work on emotion in cognitive science and related disciplines. (Hogan 2018a: 4)

The study of emotion in literature is part of Affect Studies, which are 'sub-disciplines in literary studies and have developed a wide range of approaches to, and interpretations of, affect, covering such areas as aesthetics, ethics, and political economy to name only a few' (Buzzard and LePan 2014: 8). Annette Federico notes that scholars 'want to bring the experience of embodiment back to the discussion, and especially the experience of affective life—what it *feels* like to move through time, to be in the world, to act, think, and respond to stimuli' (2016: 103; Italics original). Literary theorists are finally catching up with literary writers.

*

This book is the first book-length critical study of emotions in the works of Joseph Conrad. Its primary purpose is to call attention to Conrad's unique insight into the workings of human emotions that are implicit in his works. It is not an attempt to read his works in the context of psychoanalytical, philosophical, or religious ideas extrinsic to the text. Conrad is, '[by] common consent, one of the most original' of the early twentieth-century writers (Evans 270), and, therefore, it would not be surprising if his ideas of emotions were also quite unique. There are two distinguishing features in Conrad's perception of human emotions. One is that he directs his attention not only to the nature of separate and independent emotions, such as love, anger, or fear, but also to the diversity of emotional reactions they induce in the characters' minds and bodies. The other feature is that Conrad explores emotions in the framework of his distinctive world view.

In English, the term 'emotion' is a relatively recent term:

'Emotion' is a newer term, scarcely used until 200 years ago. Before that there were passions, sentiment, feelings, affections. Such words occupied a cluster that included sin, will, grace, soul. By contrast, 'emotion' is a term

4   Y. OKUDA

from literary and scientific clusters that became prevalent only during the nineteenth century. (Oatley 2004: 135).[3]

'Emotion' is a difficult term to define and has been defined in various ways, according to how it is addressed. Affect Studies in literature may be divided roughly into two traditions: one which approaches emotion/affect from a theory-based philosophical perspective and another which approaches it from an experience-based psychological perspective.[4] The primary purpose of theory-based affect studies in literature is to understand how some philosophers and theorists, such as Gilles Deleuze and his successors, or the contemporary theorists of feminist criticism, queer theory, and cultural materialism, draw on literary studies to construct their theories on emotion/affect, commonly with a characteristic emphasis on the body that originates in the philosophy of Baruch de Spinoza. Conrad criticisms which predate Affect Studies have also drawn on the theories of such philosophers as Arthur Schopenhauer and Friedrich Nietzsche, or psychoanalysts such as Sigmund Freud and Carl Gustav Jung, but the focus of their concern was not to elucidate the nature of emotions. On the other hand, the primary purpose of experience-based affect studies in literature, which approaches emotion from a psychological perspective, is to understand emotion itself, sometimes by integrating literary insights with the findings of other disciplines, such as philosophy, linguistics, and neuroscience.

The distinction between the philosophical approach and the psychological approach is borne out by the definitions of emotion provided by *The Oxford Companion to Emotion and the Affective Sciences* (2009). The entry on 'emotion definitions' is divided into 'philosophical perspectives,' 'psychological perspectives,' and also 'neuroscience perspectives.' The definition from philosophical perspectives begins with a discussion on

---

[3] Oatley says that 'to denote the wide range of phenomena that the term "emotion" covers, some writers have revived the terms "affect" and "affective," which had been used in English in the early seventeenth century. More commonly nowadays, however, the terms "emotion" and "emotional" are used to denote this range' (2004: 3). This book adopts the words 'emotion' and 'emotional' rather than 'affect' and 'affective,' because 'emotion' and 'emotional' are the words which Conrad uses customarily in his novels, short stories, essays, and letters; and also because the word 'emotion' conveys the dynamic sense of emotion as the life energy that compels us to action or inaction.

[4] Hogan classifies affect studies into affective science and affective poststructuralism. (2018a: 22).

the etymology and the meaning of the words 'the emotions,' and goes on to consider the features associated with particular emotions, such as physiological changes and the types of cognitions and attitudes that give rise to the emotion. (142).

On the other hand, the definition from psychological perspectives holds that it is 'virtually impossible to arrive at an agreed-upon definition of the category and what [mental and bodily] states or processes are to be included in it' (142). Then it goes on to argue that the determining features that define emotion are that emotions:

> (1) are focused on specific events, (2) involve the appraisal of intrinsic features of objects or events […], (3) affect most or all bodily subsystems […], (4) are subject to rapid change due to the unfolding events and (5) have a strong impact on behaviour […]. (Sander and Scherer 2009: 143)

The use of the word 'event' in conjunction with 'emotion' is reminiscent of Conrad's assertion that events are illustrative of feelings, and suggests that, like the psychological approach, Conrad's approach to emotion is experience-based.[5] After all, Conrad calls his memoir, *A Personal Record*, 'a bit of psychological document' ('A Familiar Preface' xx).

Although emotions are discussed more often in terms of their separate and distinct nature than their comprehensive effects, Conrad's interest in emotions seems more focused on the so-called 'reactive emotion.' According to Oatley, reactive emotions commonly occur somewhat suddenly (2004:3):

> Reactive emotions occur when the appearance of the world as we assume it to be is pierced by reality. In our assumed world, objects and people take on the colors of our understandings, of our hopes, of our desires, of our likes and dislikes. A reactive emotion occurs with the unexpected; it is a meeting of what we assumed with what we did not assume. […]. The world suddenly intrudes through the layers of our assumption. (2004: 4–5)

It may be said that Conrad's interest in emotions lies primarily in what makes a character react in such a way when a reactive emotion occurs, and if possible to consider the ethical values their reactions carry. What

---

[5] Cognitive science occasionally suggests affinities with Conrad's idea of emotions.

compels Jim to desert the *Patna*, Kurtz to mistreat his native followers, Verloc to exploit Stevie, and Razumov to betray Haldin? They are all driven by their emotions reacting to the world that has '[intruded] through the layers of [their] assumptions'; if so, what is this world which intrudes so penetratingly?

*

In a review in the *Daily Telegraph*, dated 12 August 1908, W. L. Courtney maintains that there is 'one characteristic which every reader of Joseph Conrad will appreciate': 'He has a certain quality about him which makes him a thing apart, almost elemental. He sees the world as a whole, and is under no misapprehension as to the insignificant part played therein by humanity' (*CR2* 451). What does it mean to see 'the world as a whole,' and why is the part played by humanity 'insignificant'? These questions are notable because they are concerned with Conrad's fundamental view of the world and his sense of identity.

Conrad's world view has attracted the attention of reviewers and critics, especially among his contemporaries. John Galsworthy in his disquisition refers to Conrad's 'cosmic spirit' and praises him for having a 'feeling for the whole' and not being 'departmental' (Galsworthy in Watt 1973: 91). It suggests that even a novel like *The Secret Agent*, which occasioned the writing of the disquisition, and whose setting is limited to just a few square miles of London, can evoke a sense of the cosmos or the universe. He calls Conrad 'a lover of the Universe' and says that 'on his canvases the figures he has loved pass and repass across a background that he has loved as much or even more; they step forth and sink back into the great Scheme from which all came and into which we all return' (Galsworthy in Watt 1973: 90).

Galsworthy's disquisition called forth a similar response from Courtney. Although he finds Galsworthy's eulogy 'a little extravagant,' he nevertheless maintains that 'when we come to a writer like Conrad, we are conscious that though he is interested in his puppets, they are not half so interesting to him as the vast forces of nature, the obscure dominion of fate, and the unyielding tyranny of circumstance, which crush the feverish activity of men as their plaything' (*The Daily Telegraph*, 12 August 1908, p.4; *CR2*: 451–53).

The phrase 'the vast forces of nature' reminds us of the review of *Nostromo* written by Edward Garnett in 1904:

[Conrad] has a special poetic sense of *the psychology of scene*, by which the human drama brought before us is seen in its just relation to the whole enveloping drama of Nature around, forming both the immediate environment and the distant background. In Mr. Conrad's vision we may imagine Nature as a ceaselessly-flowing infinite river of life, out of which the tiny atom of each man's individual life emerges into sight, stands out in the surrounding atmosphere, and is lost again in the infinite succession of the fresh waves of life into which it dissolves. (*CR* 2: 204; Italics original)[6]

Likewise H. L. Mencken, in his *A Book of Prefaces* (1917), calls Conrad 'a cosmic artist' and says: 'What he sees is [...] the overwhelming sweep and devastation of universal forces, the great central drama that is at the heart of all other dramas [...]' (Mencken in Watt 1973: 64).

It is easy to dismiss such broad perspectives as 'cosmic' and 'universal' as exalted and outdated, but it may be that we have simply lost that sense of the universe or the cosmos that these contemporary reviewers shared with Conrad; and moreover, it may be that it is the weakening of such a sense that is partly responsible for the current ecological problems we face. Ian Watt, who is one of the few postwar Conrad critics to use such words as 'universe' and 'cosmos' in his writing, comments on Galsworthy's disquisition in these words:

To the modern reader Galsworthy's eulogy may seem of largely historical interest. It certainly reminds us of how much loftier was the Edwardian notion of critical style than that customary today. Galsworthy, in this much like Conrad as a critic, writes in terms of such cosmic generality that we find it difficult to be sure that he is actually talking about anything in particular. Yet if we can penetrate the surface of his special rhetorical decorum, Galsworthy is essentially dealing with some of the basic critical issues raised by Conrad and *The Secret Agent*. (Watt 1973: 60)

Here Watt seems to be suggesting that some of the basic critical issues of *The Secret Agent* require an awareness of 'cosmic generality' that the criticism of the middle decades of the twentieth century lacked.

---

[6] This passage is curiously reminiscent of the opening lines of a Japanese classic, Kamo-no-Chomei's *Hojoki* (1212): 'On flows the river ceaselessly, nor does its water ever stay the same. The bubbles that float upon its pools now disappear, now form anew, but never endure long. And so it is with people in this world, and with their dwellings' (Kenko and Chomei 5).

Interestingly, however, a resurgence of that broader perspective can be detected in the literary criticism of the twenty-first century. In a chapter entitled 'The Novel as Planetary Form,' Joseph Keith maintains that the so-called 'planetary turn' has been 'inspired and ethically informed by a growing awareness and concern with ecological crises […] which are planetary in their scale and threat and which require, in turn, an ability to think the "big picture" in response' (Keith in Bulson 2018: 278)[7]; but he also wonders 'whether the "problem" of scale that the planetary poses is genuinely a new one for the novel' and whether we might not read 'Joseph Conrad's *Heart of Darkness*—and its formal innovations— as a much earlier effort to address what is ostensibly a contemporary problem of scale' (Keith in Bulson 2018: 280). Likewise, Nidesh Lawtoo, in *Conrad's Shadow*, observes that 'it is arguably Conrad who can best help us navigate past the fallacy of anthropocentrism that must be avoided in the twenty-first century' (2016: xxxi), for 'Conrad is well positioned to use "the mirror of the sea" to reflect, and to help us reflect on, the new ethical riddles emerging from catastrophic scenarios that now threaten the planet as a whole' (2016: 43).

Strictly speaking, the concept of 'planetary' differs from the concept of 'cosmic,' not just in spatial terms but also in terms of human involvement. However, it does signify thinking on a bigger scale than in the criticisms of the second half of the twentieth century. In a chapter in *Conrad and Nature*, a critical anthology, Hugh Epstein asserts that '[w]hatever Conrad's own beliefs, his fiction exacts from its protagonists an encounter with natural forces which necessitates the imposing of a conception of human existence upon worlds both material and immaterial that know nothing of our conceptions nor our existence' (Epstein in Schneider-Rebozo et al. 2019: 191), which may be a view closer to those of Conrad's contemporary reviewers. Moreover, these reviews and criticisms suggest an answer to the question posed earlier in this Introduction—what it means to see 'the world as a whole.' Conrad is interested, primarily, in the universe or the cosmos, which makes the part played by humanity insignificant from the cosmic perspective. Ian Watt maintains that '[…] the ties which most obviously "bind" mankind to the visible universe are really the shackles which the laws of the cosmos impose upon

---

[7] *The Conradian* 46.2 (Autumn 2021) is devoted to Conrad and the planetary.

1 INTRODUCTION 9

human aspiration, the iron conditions within which men must attempt to live' (Watt 1973: 97).

*

What is so notable about Conrad's view of the universe that it attracts the attention of his contemporary reviewers? One clue is the word 'accident,' casually mentioned in the letter to Edward Noble. In Conrad's narrative world, an event is an 'accident,' a contingent occurrence which could not have been foreseen, 'an event that is without apparent cause' (*OED*). Conrad mentions the word 'accident' several times in his letters written between 1895 and 1897. In a letter to T. Fisher Unwin, dated 22 August 1896, he says: 'Our captivity within the incomprehensible logic of *accident* is the only fact of the universe' (*CL1*: 303, emphasis added). Again, in a letter to R. B. Cunningham Graham, dated 20 December 1897, he enlarges on the phrase 'captivity within the incomprehensible logic of accident' by adopting the metaphor of the Victorian industrial knitting machine:

> There is a – let us say – a machine. It evolved itself (I am severely scientific) out of a chaos of scraps of iron and behold! – it knits. I am horrified at the horrible work and stand appalled. [...]. I feel it ought to embroider – but it goes on knitting. [...]. And the most withering thought is that the infamous thing has made itself; made itself without thought, without conscience, without foresight, without eyes, without heart. It is a tragic *accident* – and it has happened. You can't interfere with it. [...]. In virtue of that truth one and immortal which lurks in the force that made it spring into existence it is what it is – and it is indestructible! (*CL1*: 425, emphasis added)

He uses the metaphor of the knitting machine to convey his strong sense of being confined in a universe whose distinguishing feature is 'contingency,' defined as 'the quality or condition of being subject to chance and change, or of being at the mercy of accidents' (*OED*: 3d); 'it has happened' and 'it is' without apparent cause, independent of the tragic sense it induces in the human heart. The machine is, in its essence, dynamic, as it 'goes on knitting' and constantly 'knits us in and knits us out' (*CL1*:425), and it does not possess human attributes such as 'thought,' 'conscience,' 'foresight,' 'eyes,' or 'heart.' The passage suggests that the world perceived by Conrad is impermanent and impersonal.

10   Y. OKUDA

The impermanence of the world, once acknowledged, can affect the view of one's own identity, as it seems to have affected Conrad's idea of his personality, as expressed in his letter to Edward Garnett, dated 23/24 March 1896:

> If one looks at life in its true aspect then everything loses much of its unpleasant importance and the atmosphere becomes cleared of what are only unimportant mists that drift past in imposing shapes. When once the truth is grasped that one's own personality is only a ridiculous and aimless masquerade of something hopelessly unknown the attainment of serenity is not very far off. Then there remains nothing but the surrender to one's impulses, the fidelity to passing emotions which is perhaps a nearer approach to truth than any other philosophy of life. And why not? If we are 'ever becoming – never being' then I would be a fool if I tried to become this thing rather than that; for I know well that I never will be anything. (*CL1*: 267–68)

The phrase 'life in its true aspect' is suggestive of life in a contingent world, which lies beyond the ken of human knowledge. Human beings make up an insignificant part of such a world, and therefore, when life is looked at in its true aspect, even 'one's own personality' is an illusional manifestation of the unknowable impermanent world, which is 'ever becoming—never being.' The two phrases are in quotation marks, but the source has not been identified. In the phrase 'ever becoming,' the verb 'become' is in progressive form, and therefore it is suggestive of mutability, whereas in the other phrase, 'never being,' the verb 'be' is participial, and therefore suggestive of stasis. This indicates that Conrad regarded his own personality to be subject to constant change. Consequently, the only palpable things are 'impulses' and 'passing emotions' which compel us to respond to the world in one way or another according to the immediate circumstances that we find ourselves in. For example, Jim jumps off the *Patna* and Kurtz abruptly returns to the Inner Station after coming down three hundred miles, both surrendering to an irresistible impulse; on the other hand, Marlow shows fidelity to the passing emotion of his remote kinship with the indigenous people and Razumov remains true to his newly awakened sense of Natalia Haldin's physical presence. In his letter to F. Warrington Dawson, dated 20 June 1913, Conrad states: 'For me the artist's salvation is in fidelity, in remorseless fidelity to the *truth of his own sensations*' (*CL5*: 238; Italics original).

The passage quoted above from the letter to Garnett seems to suggest the dual nature of Conrad's perception of personal identity: one which identifies him with 'a ridiculous and aimless masquerade of something hopelessly unknown,' as part of Nature in a constant state of flux, and the other which identifies him with the illusion resulting from 'the surrender to one's impulses' and 'the fidelity to passing emotions,' the self-image forged in the mind under the pressure of emotions. The two senses of identity, one real but forbidding and the other illusory but flattering to one's ego, are not, however, presented as contradictory to one another; they are presented more like the two sides of the moon. The front side, bright with borrowed sheen, represents oneself as the illusory image created in the mind through the pressure of emotions; this illusory image is nevertheless necessary for survival. On the other hand, the reverse side, the dark side, represents oneself as part of Nature, the side that some people might be vaguely aware of but find it rather hard to come to terms with. In *Lord Jim*, Jim's powerful emotions enable him to act out, if for a brief period, the self-image which he has created for himself, because he is totally unconscious of the reverse side of his identity; whereas Razumov, who at first tries to preserve an identity founded on what the silver medal promises, later discovers the true nature of identity. Conrad explores the nature of both illusory identity and real identity through the characters in the framework of an impermanent world, but he carefully refrains from judging one character against the other.

Narratology tells us that a narrative story 'by definition involves change' and characters are 'not enduring but time-bound' (Margolin in Herman 73). However, in Conrad's works, contingency as a sign of impermanence is not just an element in the narrative, but the context in which he explores the emotion-laden acts and experience of the characters. As Paul B. Armstrong states: 'Victims of bewilderment in Conrad experience with devastating force the absence of any guarantee to the order, meanings, and beliefs they had taken for granted. The dislocations in his fictions reveal the frailty of the constructs we ordinarily trust without thinking much about them—our beliefs about our identity, our situation, or the nature of the world' (110).

Conrad's approach to emotions ranges widely from work to work: 'My attitudes to subjects and expression, the angles of vision, my methods of composition will, within limits, be always changing—not because I am unstable or unprincipled but because I am free. Or perhaps it may be more exact to say, because I am always trying for freedom—within my limits' (To Barrett H. Clark, 4 May 1918; *CL6* 210). The theme of emotion figures as an important and consistent theme throughout Conrad's works, yet the letter suggests that the subjects and expression, the angles of vision, and the methods of composition may vary from work to work, because he is 'always trying for freedom.' But in what sense is he free? W. L. Courtney's conjecture suggests one answer: Conrad 'has probably no theories about his art, and writes in obedience to the obscure promptings of his genius. Now and again, when he has a subject which suits him, he writes a little masterpiece' (*CR* 2: 452). Conrad tries for freedom, but that freedom has its limits, as it is confined to the world governed by the law of impermanence; and incidentally, a sense of impermanence is at the core of Eastern religions.

*

When the late Professor Charles Peake[8] of London University suggested to me, decades ago, that I should discuss Conrad from a Japanese perspective in my MA dissertation, my first reaction was that of blank dismay. What did I know about my own literary traditions— *The Tale of Genji*, the *Noh* drama, *Kabuki*, or even *haiku*—well enough to be able to apply their ideas to the interpretation of Conrad's novels and tales? I did not realize then that all these traditions shared the background of Buddhism,[9] which I practiced and occasionally read books on. Buddhist books, particularly Zen books for lay people, often allude to the emotional problems that people face in everyday life and during meditation.[10] It so happened that one evening, in the study room of a hall of residence, I put down the book on Zen Buddhism which I had been browsing and started to read over *Lord Jim*, when I came across Marlow's words: 'Whether they knew it or not, the interest that drew them there was purely psychological—the expectation of some essential disclosure as

---

[8] Charles H. Peake is the author of *James Joyce: The Citizen and the Artist* (Edward Arnold, 1977).

[9] Hogan says that 'Lady Murasaki's eleventh-century *Tale of Genji* places emotion at the foundation of the production of fiction when she writes that "the storyteller's own experience … not only what he has passed through himself, but even events which he has only witnessed or been told of—has moved him to an emotion so passionate that he can no longer keep it shut up in his heart"' (2018a: 2).

[10] Meditation in Zen Buddhism is similar in some respects to the mindfulness meditation in which you focus on what you are sensing from moment to moment, without being drawn into thoughts or judgment which are often induced by emotions.

1 INTRODUCTION   13

to the strength, the power, the horror, of human emotions' (*Lord Jim* 56); and it suddenly occurred to me that Conrad and Buddhism shared an abiding interest in human emotions. Buddhism, therefore, played the role of a catalyst for a change of direction in my critical study of Conrad.

There are some curious similarities between Conrad's world view and that of Buddhism, both of which give prominence to contingencies. There is, for instance, a Buddhist tenet called the Three Signs of Being. The first sign is *Change*. Buddhism assumes:

> [...] an impersonal universal law, inherent in all things. This law has all the attributes of divinity, but is immutable, not personalized as in the theistic religion; not being apart from created, manifested things, it is their principle or nature; it does not antedate them and has not created them; it does not *do* anything – it *is*! (Schloegl 1; Italics original)

This assumption is analogous to the assumption underlying Conrad's metaphor of the world as a knitting machine that 'has happened' and 'is' (*CR* 1: 82). The second sign, *No-Self*, presumes that, as all things are impermanent, so are human beings in mind and in body. We are, as Conrad observes, 'ever becoming—never being' (*CL* 1: 267), and our identity changes subtly as the circumstances change. The second sign is closely connected to the third sign, *Suffering/Emotions*.[11] In an impermanent world every moment is unique, so one is forever encountering unexpected events that, more often than not, contradict one's assumptions; one learns to focus on the immediate circumstances through meditation, so as not to be distracted or swept away by a sudden onslaught of emotion, which may induce the loss of self-possession, so highly valued in Conrad's works.

While it is arguable whether Conrad was influenced by Buddhism, it is possible, even probable, that he was acquainted with some of its aspects. Buddhism was brought to Britain at the beginning of the nineteenth century by Christian missionaries, scholars, and imperial civil servants in the wake of the British colonization of such Buddhist countries as Ceylon, Burma, and China. According to Philip C. Almond's *The British Discovery of Buddhism*, the 'discovery' of Buddhism took place in two distinct

---

[11] The Sanskrit (or Pali) word *dukkha*, according to Walpola Rahula, has 'a deeper philosophical meaning and connotes enormously wider senses' than just 'suffering' or 'pain' (1982: 17).

stages: the first stage took place in the first four decades of the nineteenth century and the second stage in the Victorian period. During the first stage, Buddhism was cited as an example of a religion '"out there" in the Orient, in a spatial location geographically, culturally, and therefore imaginatively *other*,' but in the second stage, the primary location of Buddhism was the West, 'through the progressive collection, translation, and publication of its textual *past*'; and so Buddhism by 1860, had come to exist, not '"out there" in the Orient, but in the West' (Almond 1988: 12–13; Italics original). Then in 1879, Edwin Arnold published *The Light of Asia*, a life of Gautama Buddha in blank verse in eight volumes, which went through more than a hundred editions in England and America, and its popularity brought about 'an enormous upsurge in awareness of, and interest in, Buddhism in late Victorian England' (Almond 1988: 1), especially among the middle and upper classes, but also to an extent among the working class (Almond 1988:33).

Although Conrad probably encountered Buddhism for the first time as a seaman when he visited such countries as Siam (Thailand), if there was 'an enormous upsurge in awareness of, and interest in, Buddhism in late Victorian England,' it is possible that Conrad's intellectual interest in Buddhism was aroused, after he settled in England, by the English newspapers and journals which often took up Buddhism as a current topic of interest, and also by the English friends he made, such as John Galsworthy, Edward Garnett, and Ford Madox Ford[12]; it suggests that Conrad must have been acquainted with Buddhism before he read Schopenhauer at the turn of the century, which would explain why he makes the frame narrator of 'Heart of Darkness' compare Marlow's sitting posture to the pose of a meditating Buddha. However, it is equally possible that Conrad acquired such an outlook on the world during his seafaring career on sailing vessels, which entailed being constantly exposed to the elements; and in that case, Buddhism may have aroused Conrad's sympathy and evoked a favourable response in him, because he recognized in it a world view similar to his own. Nevertheless, the following discussions of individual novels and shorter stories by Conrad are not offered as 'Buddhist' readings, even though they may reflect in some ways my own religious and cultural background.

---

[12] Ford Madox Ford's father is said to have been a student of Arthur Schopenhauer, who acknowledges that his philosophy has been influenced by Buddhism.

1 INTRODUCTION 15

*

This book sets out to demonstrate that one of Conrad's major themes is emotion, and that this thematic issue is explored in the framework of a narrative world governed by impermanence. I wish to reveal how prevalent the word and the concept of emotion is in Conrad's fiction, and to explore the emotional subtext underlying his fiction, not by drawing upon extrinsic theories, but by attempting to identify the concept of emotion characteristic of Conrad, keeping close to the subtly changing attitude, the angle of vision, and the method he holds to from work to work.

Half a century ago, Paul Kirschner wrote:

> Critics who interpret Conrad's fiction in the light of psychoanalytical theories often seem more inspired by Freud or Jung than by Conrad himself. [...]. I have found it more rewarding to regard Conrad as a great psychologist who knew what he wished to say, and to approach his work as the deliberate expression, in art, of his ideas about human nature. (1968: vii)[13]

Today, the names of Freud and Jung might be replaced by other names of more recent philosophers or psychologists; however, I too find it more interesting and rewarding to regard Conrad as 'a great psychologist' and to share the perception of human emotions that is implicit in his works. There are, of course, inspiring criticisms that elucidate literature by drawing on philosophic, psychoanalytic, and political ideas extrinsic to the text, and even those that do so by drawing on ideas culturally alien to the literary work, such as Paul Foster's *Beckett and Zen,* which reads Beckett's works in the light of Zen Buddhism. However, it is not my purpose to write a book on Conrad and Zen, as the purpose of this book is to draw the attention of the reader to Conrad's own unique insight into the workings of human emotions.

For this reason, this book attaches prime importance to a close reading of Conrad's texts. Annette Federico maintains that close reading requires that 'we temporarily put away our own habits of thinking, our opinions and certainties, and make space for another's ideas, look through another's eyes' (2016: 9). In a frequently-quoted passage in the 'Preface' to 'The Nigger of the *Narcissus*,' Conrad states, 'My task which I am trying to achieve is, by the power of the written word to make you hear, to make

---

[13] Incidentally, Kirschner suggests that '[a] closer affinity with Conrad may be seen in the "individual psychology" of Alfred Adler (1870–1937)' (1968: 279).

16   Y. OKUDA

you feel—it is, before all, to make you *see*' (x; emphasis original). More often than not, critical attention has focused on the phrase 'to make you *see*' rather than on the phrase 'by the power of the written word.' What does Conrad mean by the phrase 'the power of the written word'? In a letter to H. G. Wells, dated 30 November 1903, Conrad confides to him: 'for me, writing—*the only possible writing*—is just simply the conversion of nervous force into phrases. [...]. For me it is a matter of chance, stupid chance. But the fact remains that when the nervous force is exhausted the phrases don't come;—and no tension of will can help' (*CL3*: 85; Italics original). It seems that Conrad conceived even writing in terms of emotions and contingencies. Several days later, he writes in a letter to Kazumierz Waliszewski, dated 5 December 1903, just a few lines after the frequently quoted sentence 'Homo duplex has in my case more than one meaning': 'I never sought for a career, but possibly, unaware of it, I was looking for sensation,' and adds: 'I write with difficulty, slowly, crossing out constantly' (*CL* 3: 89). Even in 1907, Conrad confides to Marguerite Poradowska, 'English is still for me a foreign language whose handling demands a fearful effort' (*CL3* 208).[14]

For Conrad, writing was a craft, a task which demanded the skill of a writer, just as the task of a seaman demanded the skill of a seaman. He believed that the task of a writer demanded 'absolute sincerity [of intention],' which was always possible, no matter how difficult it was 'to depict faithfully in a work of imagination that innermost world as one apprehends it, and to express one's own real sense of that inner life' (*CL3*: 89). In a letter to Hugh Clifford, dated 9 October 1899, Conrad expresses his faith in 'the power of the written word' and the craftsmanship in writing:

> [...] words, groups of words, words standing alone, are symbols of life, have the power in their sound or their aspect to present the very thing you wish to hold up before the mental vision of your readers. The things 'as

---

[14] As to why Conrad adopted English to compose his works, he writes in his letter to Hugh Walpole, dated 7 June 1918: 'When I wrote the first words of *A. F.* [*Almayer's Folly*] I had been already for years and years *thinking* in English. I began to think in English long before I mastered, I won't say the style, (I haven't done that yet) but the mere uttered speech. Is it thinkable that anybody possessed of some effective inspiration should contemplate for a moment such a frantic thing as translating it into another tongue? And there are also other considerations: such as the sheer appeal of the language, my quickly awakened love for its prose cadences, and a subtle and unforeseen accord of my emotional nature with its genius' (*CL6*: 227; Italics original).

they are' exist in words; therefore words should be handled with care lest the picture, the image of truth abiding in facts should become distorted – or blurred.

These are the considerations for a mere craftsman – you may say, and you may also conceivably say that I have nothing else to trouble my head about. However the *whole* of the truth lies in the presentation; therefore the expression should be studied in the interest of veracity. This is the only morality of *art* apart from *subject*. (*CR2*: 200; emphasis original)

Here he proclaims his commitment to the words in his texts as a writer. Words can convey 'the image of truth abiding in facts.' If they are handled skillfully by a craftsman who has the moral tenacity to find the right words to convey that image, those words will indicate with exactness the things 'as they are.' They will acquire the power to present what Conrad holds up 'before the mental vision' of each reader.[15]

*

This book explores the emotional subtext underlying the following seven works written by Conrad between 1898 and 1911: four novels— *Lord Jim*, *Nostromo*, *The Secret Agent*, and *Under Western Eyes*; two novellas—'Heart of Darkness' and 'The Secret Sharer'; and one short story—'The Duel.' The works written during this period have a special significance from the point of view of emotions and contingencies. In 1898, Conrad began writing *Lord Jim*, and for the first time foregrounded the issue of contingency, laying the ground for subsequent works. In these works, he explored the emotions of a broad variety of characters that range widely in age, gender, position, and nationality, in the framework of an impermanent world. This exploration culminated in *Under Western Eyes*, published in 1911, in which he integrated the major emotional issues he had addressed in preceding works. In contrast, in the novels written after *Under Western Eyes*, such as *Chance* (1914), *Victory* (1915), and *The Rover* (1923), Conrad tends to narrow the scope of his exploration to the emotions of a middle-aged or elderly man and a harassed young woman in whose life he becomes involved. For this reason, it may be said that it is in the works written between 1898 and 1911

---

[15] Conrad maintains that 'the shape and ring of sentences' could assume 'plasticity' and 'colour' (Preface to *The Nigger of the 'Narcissus'* ix), which suggests that words can also belong to the visible and tangible universe.

that Conrad makes his most extensive as well as intensive explorations of human emotions.

Structurally, the main part of the book is divided into four parts, and each part comprises two chapters, with the sole exception of the last part which is devoted to a single work. Each part presents a different approach to emotions, reflecting Conrad's deepening understanding of the issue. Interestingly, the seven works, taken up roughly in the order of their composition, fall almost spontaneously into these four categories.

The book begins with Chapter 1, Introduction, which previews the key concepts –emotion, contingency, and identity—in the light of Conrad's letters to various correspondents, in anticipation of the exploration of these issues in individual works.

Part I analyzes the emotional expressions manifested by diverse characters and attempts to assess their ethical significance. Chapter 2 on *Lord Jim* highlights Marlow's world view through the key concept of 'the unexpected,' which is a manifestation of impermanence, and explores the stressful power of Jim's emotions in terms of another key concept, 'the sense of insecurity.' Chapter 3 on 'Heart of Darkness' builds on Chapter 2 but shifts its emphasis from the stress to the subtlety of emotion. It elucidates how Marlow's emotional understanding is cultivated by what he witnesses on his journey, and demonstrates that Chinua Achebe's accusation of Conrad's insensitivity to the indigenous people is unsupported by the text; the emotional understanding leads finally to Marlow's illuminating insight into Kurtz's complex emotionality.[16]

Part II expands the critical field of vision from the emotions of the individual to the collective and discusses the emotional propensities shared by a group of characters. Chapter 4 on *Nostromo* raises the universal issue of reconciling one's sense of personal identity with the consciousness of being part of Nature by examining how emotions are involved in forging one's personal identity. On the other hand, Chapter 5 on *The Secret Agent* looks at the typical concatenation of emotions manifested by a number of characters when their unwarranted assumptions and expectations are threatened by an unforeseen event in a world of contradictions.

---

[16] *OED* defines the term 'emotionality' as 'emotional character, disposition, or component of behaviour,' and the 'Glossary' to *Understanding Emotions* defines it as 'way in which individuals differ from one another in experience and expression of emotions; the emotional component of personality' (Oatley et al. 2006: 415). In this book, the term is always used in the above sense.

Between Chapter 5 and Chapter 6 there is a dividing line. The earlier four chapters address emotional issues in stasis, so to speak, emphasizing specific emotional traits of certain characters; in contrast, the last three chapters address the emotional issues in motion, emphasizing the gradual change that takes place in the emotional attitude of the protagonists. Part III focuses on the effects of the strain placed on an individual by one-to-one involvement with an opponent or an accomplice. Chapter 6 on 'The Duel' attempts to elucidate the stages of D'Hubert's emotional maturation in the short story by thematic and stylistic analysis of the narrative, whereas Chapter 7 on 'The Secret Sharer' traces the maturing process that the captain undergoes by introducing, as an exceptional case, a Zen Buddhist principle, foregrounding the thematic issue of the body for the first time, in anticipation of the final chapter.

Part IV is comprised of a single chapter on *Under Western Eyes*. The chapter demonstrates that the novel provides a framework for synthesizing the major emotional issues addressed in Parts I, II, and III, and that Razumov's final discovery of the true nature of identity is made possible by his newly awakened sense of his own body and that of others.

The book concludes with a brief discussion in Chapter 9 on Conrad's dual perspective and the moral vision implicit in his memoir, *A Personal Record*, which contains some of the most memorable summations of his outlook.

Basic emotions are familiar and universal, yet it is often these emotions, such as surprise, anger, and even love, that stand in the way of our solidarity with others. The issue of emotion, in one way or another, underlies all the problems we face today, social, political, and ecological. Literature is immediately relevant to solving these problems because it is literature that presents 'the largest body of works that systematically depict and provoke emotion' (Hogan 2011: 1), enabling us to become more conscious of our dispositional emotionality; and in this endeavour I have always found the works of Joseph Conrad both essential and inspiring.

PART I

The Power and the Subtlety of Emotion

CHAPTER 2

Always 'the Unexpected': *Lord Jim*

What is it by inward pain makes him know himself?
What is it that for you and me makes him – exist? (*Lord Jim*)

Part I of this book takes up two works from the early period of Conrad's writing career—*Lord Jim* (1900) and 'Heart of Darkness' (1899). These works lay the basis of Conrad's exploration of human emotions and look forward to the subsequent works in which he continues his exploration. *Lord Jim* and 'Heart of Darkness' partly overlap in the period of their composition: Conrad began writing *Lord Jim* in 1898, but delayed it for a year while he wrote 'Heart of Darkness' and collaborated with Ford Madox Ford on *The Inheritors*. It is therefore not very surprising that there are some affinities between *Lord Jim* and 'Heart of Darkness.' In both these works, Marlow is a homodiegetic narrator, that is to say, a narrator but also a character who becomes involved in the situations and events he recounts; he manifests a strong curiosity in the emotional reactions of Jim and Kurtz and responds sensitively to the emotions they express. However, there are also some differences between the two works. In *Lord Jim* Marlow focuses his attention more or less consistently on Jim and observes the propensities of his emotionality, whereas in 'Heart of Darkness' he directs his attention to the emotional reactions of a variety of characters before focusing it on Kurtz.

© The Author(s), under exclusive license to Springer Nature
Switzerland AG 2024
Y. Okuda, *Emotions and Contingencies in Conrad's Fiction*,
https://doi.org/10.1007/978-3-031-66723-7_2

Lord Jim, begun as a short story entitled 'Tuan Jim: A Sketch,' later developed into a novel which was published by Blackwood in 1900. Criticisms of the novel often direct their attention to its psychological aspect: Albert J. Guerard calls it 'a psycho-moral drama' (126) which '[creates] in the reader an intricate play of emotion and a rich conflict of sympathy and judgement' (127), and Tony Tanner maintains that the theme of the novel is 'the experience of total darkness' which carries 'a profound moral and psychological significance' (Tanner in Moser 459). More recently, Robert Hampson in *Conrad's Secrets* (2012) turns his attention to the dimension of psychological medicine and argues that 'in *Lord Jim*, we see the beginning of Conrad's fictional engagement with trauma' (152), while Nidesh Lawtoo in *Conrad's Shadow* (2016) directs his attention to the specific emotion of panic that Jim experiences: 'Panic is not a much-discussed affect in Conrad studies as yet, but Conrad repeatedly returns to diagnose its contagious effects along lines that anticipate contemporary theories of catastrophe' (69).

Of all Conrad's works, it is *Lord Jim* that features the thematic issue of emotions most prominently: as soon as Marlow takes over the narration in Chapter 5, he declares that what attracted the sailors and the waterside business to the *Patna* inquiry was 'the expectation of some essential disclosure as to the strength, the power, the horror, of human emotions' (57). He observes Jim's inarticulate struggle with what Keith Oatley calls 'reactive emotions': 'the sudden emotions that occur when assumptions about the world are pierced by reality' (4–5). H. M. Daleski asserts that '[t]he essence of the test is that it is always unexpected' (81), and Paul B. Armstrong maintains that '*Lord Jim* […] pivots on the surprise and shock of baffling unexpected events' (109). Both Daleski and Armstrong stress the aspect of the 'unexpected.' What the Conradian universe highlights is the nature of the world in which impermanence is inherent in all things; Marlow describes it as 'the world whose events move, men change, light flickers, life flows in a clear stream' (330). It reflects Conrad's own world view discussed earlier in the Introduction, and prepares the ground for his exploration of emotions in the subsequent chapters.

This chapter first identifies the characteristics of Marlow's world view, and then examines Jim's shifting sense of security and insecurity and his untimely death in the framework of Marlow's world view.

Always 'The Unexpected'

The first half of the novel, centred upon the *Patna* affair, introduces Marlow's view of the world as governed by 'the unexpected' in opposition to Jim's unconscious view of the world in which everything can be anticipated and prepared for in advance.

Marlow's initial encounters with Jim at the beginning of the narrative are marked by unexpectedness. When he first catches sight of him walking along the quay with the other officers of the *Patna*, he is astonished by his deceptive appearance: his face looks neither guilty nor ashamed, but innocent and decent, in spite of the offence he has committed as a seaman. Moreover, when the skipper of the *Patna*, presumably, tells his former officers that their certificates have been cancelled, Jim, to Marlow's chagrin, retains an appearance of impudent unconcern. Marlow is again surprised by Jim when he finds himself in an 'unexpected predicament' concerning a misunderstanding over the word 'cur.' In the event, Jim apologizes to him, but mutters moodily: 'All these staring people in court seemed such fools that—that it might have been as I supposed' (76). On hearing this Marlow says: 'This opened suddenly a new view of him to my wonder. I looked at him curiously and met his unabashed and impenetrable eyes' (76). What arouses Marlow's curiosity is Jim's strong conviction of his own assumptions that is implicit in those words. Marlow is so fascinated by this that he decides to invite Jim to dine with him on the spot, so that he can probe him further.

The unexpectedness which marks Marlow's early encounters with Jim carries a broader significance for him than these one-off happenings might suggest. During the conversation at the Malabar House, Marlow uses the phrase 'It is always the unexpected that happens' to convey to Jim his beliefs and sentiments about reality. It is strongly reminiscent of Conrad's view of a world governed by impermanence, and indicates that therefore, in principle, nothing can be foreseen or prepared against, because every single moment is unique. Similar expressions are found in Conrad's letters from round about 1900, when *Lord Jim* was published, such as, 'the unforeseen always occurs' (22 June 1891, *CL*1: 83) and 'It is always the unforeseen that happens' (4 September 1892, *CL*1: 262) in the letters to Marguerite Poradowska, and 'The unexpected always happens' (22 February 1896, *CL*1: 262) in the letter to Edward Garnett. As Joanna Skolik points out, this is a proverb (33): 'The unexpected always happens. A paradox similar to "Nothing is certain but the unforeseen"' (*Oxford*

Dictionary of Proverbs 333). When Marlow mentions the proverb during their conversation at the hotel, he mentions it 'in a propitiatory tone' (95) because Jim has just shown a sign of irritation at Marlow's seeming stolidity. In fact, Marlow had put on a stolid face in order to hide his amusement at Jim's absurd naivety in asserting in earnest that 'he had been preparing himself for all the difficulties that can beset one on land and water' (95). Marlow may have mentioned it to Jim just to remind him that his naïve assumption went against what was generally believed to be true. But it is in any case a strong counter-argument to Jim's assumption, and therefore Jim's exclamation 'Pshaw!' expresses his annoyance and contempt for what he considers the insensitivity and obtuseness of, not only Marlow, but also the general world that the proverb circulates in.

Marlow's belief in a world governed by impermanence is manifested also in some of the replies that he makes casually to Jim during the conversation at the hotel. For instance, when Jim tells Marlow that he had made up his mind not to put up with any insulting words from anyone concerning the *Patna* affair, Marlow abruptly says, 'so that bulkhead held out after all' (83). 'After all' in this context means 'in spite of what was expected.' Marlow is implying that what Jim has decided not to put up with is not the insults from others which reproach him for evading his responsibility to the passengers, but the fact that the bulkhead held out unexpectedly so the *Patna* did not sink as he and other officers had assumed, and as a consequence he is held responsible for failing to meet the contingencies of the accident. Similarly, when Marlow says, 'It is unfortunate you didn't know beforehand!' (85), he is insinuating sarcastically that Jim has been speaking as if he should have been forewarned of the accident. Marlow says, 'a law regulates your luck in the throwing of dice,' and that 'it is not Justice the servant of men, but accident, hazard, Fortune [...] that holds an even and scrupulous balance' (320). Accident, hazard, and Fortune cannot be foreseen, and therefore they presuppose that 'It is the unexpected that always happens.' We may call this 'the logic of the unexpected' on the model of Conrad's expression 'the logic of accident' which he uses in the letter to T. Fisher Unwin. Marlow associates the world with the contingent and maintains that:

> [...] we are only on sufferance here and got to pick our way in cross lights, watching every precious minute and every irremediable step, trusting we shall manage yet to go out decently in the end. (35)

Marlow believes that 'It is always the unexpected that happens,' but does he always act in accordance with his belief? Marlow has invited Jim to dine with him at the Malabar House so that he can satisfy his curiosity about Jim's emotional reactions. However, in the course of the conversation, Jim's powerful and complex emotion unexpectedly rekindles in him an 'illusion that he had thought gone out, extinct, cold' (128), and he finds himself unwisely professing his trust in Jim: 'I am trusting you. [...] I make myself unreservedly responsible for you. That's what I am doing' (183). The word 'trust' means, as Marlow indicates, a firm belief in the reliability or ability of someone; however, it also means acceptance of the truth without proof; therefore in this scene Marlow commits himself to a belief in Jim's reliability in the unforeseeable future. Moreover, the word 'trust,' in its archaic form, means 'confident *expectation* of something' (*OED*, emphasis added), and therefore Marlow's trust in Jim goes against his belief that 'It is always the unexpected that happens.' The commitment may have been given in full knowledge of the impermanence of the world, in concession to a world in which trust signifies that one's fellow human being will act with what moral rectitude he is capable of when the unexpected situation arises. Nevertheless, it was imprudent of Marlow to declare his trust in Jim, because it has the effect of unexpectedly intensifying Jim's illusion, and condoning his defiance of the impermanent world.

A Momentary Lapse or a Prolonged Habit?

Throughout the first half of the novel, while Marlow takes 'the logic of the unexpected' for granted, Jim continues to defy it obstinately:

> He would be confident and depressed all in the same breath, as if some conviction of innate blamelessness had checked the truth writhing within him at every turn. He began by saying [...] that he could never go home now; and this declaration recalled to my mind what Brierly had said, 'the old parson in Essex seemed to fancy his sailor son not a little.' (79)

Marlow is aware that Jim's 'conviction of innate blamelessness' is rooted in his struggle to save 'his idea of what his moral identity should be' (81). For Marlow, such an idea may be no more than 'a notion of a convention, only one of the rules of the game, nothing more,' but for Jim, it is 'terribly effective by its assumption of unlimited power over natural instincts,

28   Y. OKUDA

by the awful penalties of its failure' (81). Then what is Jim's idea of 'what his moral identity should be,' an idea which exercises so much power over his instincts and even threatens to impose penalties? An important clue to this question is a letter from his father, 'the old parson in Essex,' who fancied his son 'not a little.' In a letter which Jim received just before the *Patna* accident—the letter described by Marlow as 'yellowed by time and frayed on the folds' towards the end of the narrative (338)—the old parson tells his son that 'his dear James' will never forget that 'who once gives way to temptation, in the very instant hazards his total depravity and everlasting ruin' (343). According to Marlow, Essex, where his father lives, is a 'corner of the world as free of danger or strife as a tomb'; he and his family live there 'breathing equably the air of undisturbed rectitude' (342)[1]: 'Nothing ever came to them; they would never be taken unawares, and never be called upon to grapple with fate' (342). 'The unexpected' may reign alike in Essex, the Arabian Sea, and Patusan, but there is a considerable difference in the degree of insecurity inherent in them. Jim declares to Marlow that he could never go home, because he is intuitively aware that his father, 'who would never be taken unawares,' would not understand the adverse circumstances he is struggling with. It implies that Jim *does* have some insight into the threatening changeability of the world, perhaps as a result of the *Patna* accident. What prevents Jim from admitting that he jumped off the *Patna* on the instant is his conviction that, if he admitted it, it would be tantamount to admitting that he had given way to temptation, and therefore, in his father's words, condemned himself to 'total depravity and everlasting ruin.' John Lester maintains:

> Conrad's Protestant clergy [...] are generally inadequate and unworldly. [...]. The most extended example of an inadequate clerical parent comes in *Lord Jim*. [...]. Marlow's picture of the old man [...] reveals how out of touch the parson is with the harsh realities confronting Jim, who, indeed, believes his father 'wouldn't understand.' (1988: 81–82)

---

[1] Marlow suggests, ironically, that the morally correct behaviour has been assured by Jim's father's possession of 'such certain knowledge of the Unknowable as made for the righteousness of people in cottages without disturbing the ease of mind of those whom an unerring Providence enables to live in mansions' (5).

2 ALWAYS 'THE UNEXPECTED': *LORD JIM*   29

However, the real cause of Jim's jump from the *Patna* has nothing to do with moral depravity; for it is the natural consequence of his ingrained habit. Jacques Berthoud points out that courage is 'not exhibited in the spectacular and isolated deed, but in "habit"' (70). What impels Jim to jump off the *Patna* is his confirmed habit of daydreaming. Reading 'light holiday literature' engenders in him a desire for adventure, and it becomes his habit to indulge in daydreams that soothe his frustrated feelings. On board the training ship 'he would forget himself, and beforehand live in his mind the sea-life of light literature' (6), but he is whisked back to reality by the collision between the coaster and the schooner; however, his mind, habitually indulging in reveries, cannot react to reality alertly enough. How Jim behaves in reality is in striking contrast with how he imagines himself to behave. In his imagination Jim's mind and body respond freely and effectively to the imagined circumstances, enabling him to act heroically, but when faced with reality, something deprives him of control over both his mind and body. In an imagined world, everything is familiar and nothing unexpected impinges on your emotions, but in reality it is otherwise, so powerful emotions of surprise or fear can easily overwhelm you both mentally and physically.

Jim's conduct on the *Patna* is also suggestive of his habit of daydreaming. After he recovers from an injury inflicted by a falling spar during a storm, Jim decides to take a berth on the local steamer *Patna*, rather than a berth in the home service. This indicates that he too, like the majority of the seamen that he associated with in the port, 'craves for peace,' and shares with them 'the soft spot, the place of decay, the determination to lounge safely through existence' (13) indulging in a sense of security. During his last watch on the *Patna*, dissatisfied with the apparent security, he seems at first glance to be seeking insecurity in his imaginary adventures, but in fact it is the reverse: 'made audacious by the invincible aspect of the peace,' he is seeking the 'adventurous freedom of his thoughts" (2) in which he can indulge in a sense of security. Far from being 'an example of devotion to duty' and keeping an alert watch, he keeps watch perfunctorily, and almost falls asleep during the last ten minutes: 'He was a little sleepy [...], and felt a pleasurable languor running through every limb as though all the blood in his body had turned to warm milk' (21).

In *The Mirror of the Sea*, Conrad says:

30   Y. OKUDA

> [...] a sense of security [...], even the most warranted, is a bad counsellor. It is the sense which [...] precedes the swift fall of disaster. A seaman labouring under an undue sense of security becomes at once worth hardly half his salt [...]. It is the sense of insecurity that is so invaluable in a seaman. (30)[2]

A seaman indulging in a sense of security is unguarded against 'the unexpected,' whereas a seaman with a sense of insecurity is constantly on the alert against the unforeseen, taking for granted that 'It is always the unexpected that happens.' Indulging in a sense of security 'precedes the swift fall of disaster,' and therefore it is not surprising that Jim, with his ingrained habit of seeking a sense of security in an imaginary world should find himself unwittingly jumping off the *Patna* into the lifeboat when the accident happens:

> [...] there can be no guarantee against surprise, for, by definition, that which is foreseeable can no longer be surprising. [...]. The kind of foresight that consists in trying to draw unexpectedness out of the unexpected is nothing more than a preparation for failure. Jim's eventual jump is no merely impulsive mistake, but the result of a prolonged habit of self-deception. (Berthoud 1978: 73)

Ian Watt also suggests that Jim's 'error' is 'not a momentary lapse, but the outcome of a conflict rooted in his own personality' (73), that is to say, his habit of indulging in the sense of security born from unbridled imagination. However, as Nathalie Martinière suggests, '[i]t [the unexpected] overturns habits or expectations' (45),[3] and this long habit seems to have been broken by the unexpected experience of the *Patna* accident, for Jim is never shown to be indulging in adventurous daydreams in the second half of the narrative.

---

[2] In William Shakespeare's *Macbeth*, Hecate says: 'He [Macbeth] shall spurn fate, scorn death, and bear/His hopes' 'bove wisdom, grace, and fear;/And you all know security/Is mortals' chiefest enemy' (III. v. 30–33).

[3] In her article, Martiniere considers the 'unexpected' from a narrative point of view.

An Awakening Sense of Insecurity

In the second half of the novel, the verity of Marlow's world view is confirmed by 'the sense of insecurity' pervading Patusan. Patusan is the chief settlement of a remote district in a native-ruled state. However, as it can be inferred from the fact that the name Patusan is evocative of the name *Patna*, it 'is not essentially different from the great world; it is merely cut off from it' (Berthoud 1978: 90), because Patusan, like the rest of the world, is governed by the law of impermanence. Patusan is a place where 'utter insecurity for life and property was the normal condition' (228), which suggests that the place is thoroughly governed by the law of 'the unexpected,' and therefore it has the beneficial effect of fostering a sense of insecurity in Jim. This is indicated in the way he escapes from Tunku Allang's courtyard, soon after he arrives in Patusan:

> It was apparently when thus occupied in his shed that the true perception of his extreme peril dawned upon him. He dropped the thing [nickel clock] – he says –'like a potato,' and walked out hastily, without the slightest idea of what he would, or indeed could, do. [...]. He strolled aimlessly beyond a sort of ramshackle little granary on posts, and his eyes fell on the broken stakes of the palisade; and then – he says – at once, without any mental process as it were, without any stir of emotion, he set about his escape. (253–54)

With his newly awakened sense of insecurity, Jim manages to escape safely from the courtyard 'without any mental process as it were, without any stir of emotion' (96).

The importance of the capacity to live with a sense of insecurity is highlighted in Marlow's interview with Stein, although Jacques Berthoud complains that Stein's advice to Marlow 'has, unfortunately, so often been discussed out of context that it is now difficult to recapture its original effect' (86). Stein's own dream appeared to him unexpectedly in the form of a rare butterfly sitting 'on a small heap of dirt' (210); just as 'a sign—a call' (315) from home comes to Jim unexpectedly in the shape of Brown on a knoll above 'the muddy bank of the creek' (360). Stein's advice to Marlow indicates that the key to 'how to be' lies in being alert to 'the unexpected,' in whatever form it may come—a chance to fulfill a dream or 'a menace, a shock, a danger' (385); such circumstances—whether adverse or favourable—must be encountered with an awareness of the insecurity of things. To convey to Marlow his idea of 'how to be' in such a circumstance, Stein speaks figuratively of 'a man that is born' who 'falls into a dream like a man who falls into the sea':

> If he tries to climb out into the air as inexperienced people endeavor to do, he drowns – . [...]. The way is to the destructive element submit yourself, and with exertions of your hands and feet in the water make the deep, deep sea keep you up. (214)

The words 'the destructive element' are suggestive of the danger and insecurity inherent in an impermanent world. Trying to climb out of the destructive element implies seeking false security, whereas submitting to it indicates retaining a sense of insecurity. Opportunities to realize our dreams present themselves unexpectedly, and they are by nature insecure, and therefore one must adapt oneself to the demands of the moment, and make the best of the situation.

Stein's vision of the deep sea fraught with danger conjures up in Marlow's mind a similar vision: 'a vast and uncertain expanse, as of a crepuscular horizon on a plain' at dawn or dusk, with 'pitfalls' and 'graves' (215). The vision corresponds with a vision which he has later in Patusan. Marlow finds himself 'unexpectedly [...] waylaid' by Jewel (307), who, on account of her knowledge of the miseries that her mother suffered in her marriage, refuses to acquiesce to Marlow's assurance that Jim will never leave Patusan:

> 'My mother had wept bitterly before she died. [...]. The tears fell from her eyes – and then she died,' concluded the girl in an imperturbable monotone. [...]. It had the power to drive me out of my conception of existence, out of that shelter each of us makes for himself to creep under in moments of danger. [...]. For a moment I had a view of a world that seemed to wear a vast and dismal aspect of disorder. (313)

At first, these two visions may seem to belong to different contexts, but when they are read in the light of the following vision which Marlow has when he is talking to the French lieutenant, the three visions combine to evoke a pervading sense of an insecure world that one disregards most of the time.

> [...] he [the French lieutenant] pronounced, "*Mon Dieu!* How the time passes!" Nothing could have been more commonplace than this remark,

but its utterance coincided for me with a moment of vision. It's extraordinary how we go through life with eyes half shut, with dull ears, with dormant thought. [...]. Nevertheless, there can be but few of us who had never known one of these rare moments of awakening when we see, hear, understand ever so much – everything – in a flash – before we fall back again into our agreeable somnolence. (143)

The words 'before we fall back again into our agreeable somnolence' suggest that this vision must also have been disturbing enough to 'drive [him] out of [his] conception of existence': the real world suddenly intruding into his assumptions. The passage is also reminiscent of what Conrad says in the 'Preface' to *The Nigger of the 'Narcissus'*: 'My task which I am trying to achieve is, by the power of the written word to make you hear, to make you feel—it is, before all, to make you *see*!' (xlii). That is to say, the task of the writer is to give the reader the chance to experience such 'moments of awakening when we see, hear, understand ever so much' about the insecurity inherent in the impermanent world.

THE FINAL QUESTION

Jim, however, never experiences such moments of awakening. His own particular sense of insecurity derives, not from his insight into the insecurity inherent in the impermanent world, but from the circumstances of 'utter insecurity' pervading Patusan, in which he has to '[think] nothing of poison' when he is offered a cup of coffee by the old Rajah (250). Yet, ironically, according to Marlow, '[t]he unexpectedness of his coming was the only thing [...] that saved him from being at once dispatched with krises and flung into the river' (251). Patusan fosters in Jim a sense of insecurity which, for a time, prevents him from being taken unawares emotionally; he therefore manages to escape safely from Tunku Allang's courtyard 'without any stir of emotion,' and subsequently succeeds in defeating Sheriff Ali with 'no fears as to the result' (267). However, by the time Marlow visits him in Patusan, the place has ceased to be insecure, but 'peaceful.' When, one evening, Marlow and Jim are watching the settlement in front of his house, Marlow says that:

He confessed to me that he often watched these tiny warm gleams go out one by one, that he loved to see people go to sleep under his eyes, confident in the security of to-morrow. 'Peaceful here, eh?' he asked. (246)

34   Y. OKUDA

This confidence in 'the security of tomorrow,' on shore as well as at sea, precedes disaster and forbodes an unexpected event which might occur and take Jim unawares.

There are three crises which Jim encounters and recounts to Marlow in the course of the narrative: in the first episode, the *Patna* accident, he inadvertently jumps off the ship because he has been indulging in a false sense of security, but in the next two episodes, that is, when he escapes from Tunku Allang's courtyard and when he defeats Sherif Ali, he is supported by his newly awakened sense of insecurity. In the letter addressed to 'the privileged man,' Marlow relates two more such episodes. In the first of these episodes, the unexpected invasion of Patusan by Brown and his henchmen, Jim is taken unawares because he has again been indulging himself in the apparent security of the place. The words Brown utters threaten Jim's sense of security by reawakening his memory of the *Patna* affair and shaking his 'conviction of innate blamelessness' (5), so that his usual calmness deserts him and consequently he misjudges Brown's character. Yet he is so sure of his decision that he even dares to declare to the Bugis that he is 'ready to answer with his life for any harm that should come to them as a result' (409). Brown, incited by Cornelius, launches a surprise attack on the island and kills Dain Waris, and Jim therefore has to atone for his mistaken judgement with his life.

When Tamb' Itam tells him that it is no longer safe even for his servants to go outside the fort, suggesting that the Bugis no longer trusted him, Jim for the first time becomes aware of his precarious position in Patusan. Marlow says, 'I believe that in that very moment he had decided to defy the disaster in the only way it occurred to him such a disaster could be defied' (400); yet before leaving for the town, Jim stays in his fort for another 'hour or so' arguing with Jewel (410) and leaning on the gun-carriage looking at the river (412). Marlow suggests in his letter that it was 'about this time' (412) that something unexpected happened in Doramin's campong. Dain Waris's body is brought before his father, and the white sheet covering the body is removed at a sign from him. Before this incident, Doramin has been sitting for a long time in his arm-chair 'one hand on each knee, looking down,' (410–11), then he moves his eyes slowly over the crowd, 'as if seeking for a missing face' (411). These gestures are not suggestive of bitter revenge in any way. There is a reason for this: although Jim's mistaken judgment is partly responsible for Dain Waris's death, Doramin is also partly responsible for his son's death, because Doramin's word 'would have been decisive' for an immediate attack. In Marlow's opinion, Doramin did not give his word because 'well aware of his son's fiery courage, he dared not pronounce the word' (362). Instead, he orders his son to go down to the island 'guided solely by his wish to keep his son out of harm's way' (364). According to Marlow, Doramin is 'one of the most remarkable men of his race [he] had ever seen' (259), thus it is unlikely that Doramin would have acted unfairly to Jim by laying all the blame on him for his son's death. It is only after his son's body is brought into the campong and he sees the silver ring held up by a bystander that he becomes infuriated at Jim.

> His [Doramin's] eyes searched the body from its feet to its head, for the wound maybe. It was in the forehead and small; and there was no word spoken while one of the bystanders, stooping, took off the silver ring from the cold stiff hand. In silence he held it up before Doramin [...]. The old nakhoda stared at it, and suddenly let out one great fierce cry, deep from the chest, a roar of pain and fury. (411)

Doramin regards the talisman ring as a proof of Jim's betrayal of 'eternal friendship' (233), and therefore he now waits for Jim's arrival 'with the pair of flintlock pistols on his knees' (414), somewhat reminiscent of the time when he sat in his armchair on one of the twin summits exposed to an attack from the Sherif Ali's camp 'with his little fierce eyes—a pair of immense flintlock pistols on his knees': 'Magnificent thing, ebony, silver-mounted, with beautiful locks and a calibre like an old blunderbun. A present from Stein [...] in exchange for that ring' (202). Ironically, the ring and the pistols, which had once been symbols of friendship and trust have turned into symbols of enmity and betrayal.

The final episode poses a conundrum to the reader because this incident of the unexpected reappearance of the silver ring is inserted between the report of Brown's attack on the island and Jim's arrival at Doramin's campong an hour later. Does Jim surrender his life assuming that he has 'come ready' (415), that is to say, assuming that he has come completely prepared to lay down his life so as to take on his responsibility for unwittingly betraying the Bugis' and Dain Waris's trust in him? Is that why he says, 'I have no life' (409)? If so, has he been successful in demonstrating that 'nothing less than the unconceivable itself could get over his perfect state of preparation' (95), and proving that the proverb 'It is always the unexpected that happens' is false. Or does he surrender his life in recognition of what the silver ring stood for then—the scheme of the universe that haphazardly opens and closes 'the door of fame, love, and success':

> People remarked that the ring which he [Doramin] had dropped on his lap fell and rolled against the foot of the white man, and that poor Jim glanced down at the talisman that had opened for him the door of fame, love, and success [...]' (415).

In that case, does he die with an alert sense of insecurity which enables him to accept the sudden change of circumstances? Paul B. Armstrong maintains that what Jim's last 'proud and unflinching glance' (416) suggests is left for each reader to judge:

> The privileged reader hears 'the last word of the story,' but the inconclusiveness of Jim's 'proud and unflinching glance' when he dies frustrates the expectation of finality. The promise of completion is offered, only to be withheld as the ambiguity of Jim's death leaves open a variety of readings [...]. (1987: 122)

However, 'the inconclusiveness' of this episode that '[frustrates] the expectation of finality' is not altogether inconsistent with the indeterminacy inherent in impermanence.

Does Jim die defying or yielding to the logic of the unexpected? Does he die trying to climb out of the destructive element or does he finally submit himself to the deep, deep sea? These are no doubt important questions, however, the crux of the novel lies not in these questions but in the two questions posed by Stein at the end of his interview with Marlow:

> What is it by inward pain makes him know himself?
> What is it that for you and me makes him – exist?

It is only when he hears these questions that Marlow feels that Jim's 'imperishable reality came to [him] with a convincing, with an irresistible force!' (219). What makes Jim aware of himself, and what makes him exist for others? The clue to the one and only answer to both these questions is found in Marlow's words: 'I don't know how much Jim understood; but I know he felt, he felt confusedly but powerfully. [...]. *The thing is that in virtue of his feeling he mattered*' (222, emphasis added). What makes Jim know himself and what makes him exist for others is his capacity to feel and to express 'the strength, the power, the horror, of human emotions.' It seems to suggest that what is important is our awareness of the power of our emotion and the readiness to respond to the given circumstances, either adverse or favourable, under the emotional stress.

Lord Jim foregrounds the inherent nature of the world as Marlow perceives it by introducing the key concepts of 'the unexpected' and 'the sense of insecurity,' and depicts the strains of living in accord with the scheme of the universe under the stress of powerful emotion. Jim's resistance to the impermanent world evokes in him diverse reactive emotions, such as acute fear or a craving for security, which Marlow observes attentively. In 'Heart of Darkness,' Marlow shifts his attention from the strength and the power to the subtlety and the duplicity of emotions. In contrast to *Lord Jim*, Marlow in 'Heart of Darkness' begins by observing the emotional reactions of various characters, ranging from the indigenous to the European, which prepares him for his subsequent encounter with Kurtz through whom he perceives the danger inherent in being blind to one's own emotionality.

CHAPTER 3

Emotional Reactions, the Idea, and a Lie: 'Heart of Darkness'

> This man suffered too much. He hated all this, and somehow he couldn't get away. ('Heart of Darkness')

'Heart of Darkness' was first published in *Blackwood's Magazine* from February to April 1899, and then in a book form in *Youth: A Narrative, and Two Other Stories* by Blackwood & Sons in November 1902 and by McClure, Phillips in February 1903. It may be said that the novella has been considered critically from every conceivable perspective—philosophically, psychologically, and historically, to name only a few. For instance, in the 1950s, Albert Guerard called it 'a *Pilgrim's Progress* for our pessimistic and psychologizing age' (1958: 33). In the 1970s, Chinua Achebe accused it of being a racist work, attacking the novella, or rather Conrad himself, calling him 'a bloody racist'[1]; Achebe protested that 'even after due allowances have been made for all the influences of contemporary prejudice on his sensibility, there remains still in Conrad's attitude a residue of antipathy to black people which his peculiar psychology alone can explain' (14). In the 1990s, Edward Said, in his

---

[1] In the Penguin version, the word 'bloody' has been replaced by the word 'thoroughgoing.'

© The Author(s), under exclusive license to Springer Nature Switzerland AG 2024
Y. Okuda, *Emotions and Contingencies in Conrad's Fiction*,
https://doi.org/10.1007/978-3-031-66723-7_3

39

40   Y. OKUDA

Culture and Imperialism, pronounced that 'Kurtz's great looting adventure, Marlow's journey up the river, and the narrative itself all share a common theme: Europeans performing acts of imperial mastery and will in (or about) Africa' (1993: 25). Graham Bradshaw[2], however, questions Said's view that imperialism is 'at the core of his writing,' and maintains that 'Conrad's preoccupations in "Heart of Darkness" go well beyond the destructive aspects of imperialism' (2018: 16–17).

One of the major themes which Conrad addresses in 'Heart of Darkness' is that of emotions, and yet the novella has not often been considered in terms of the emotions it portrays, so the theme still needs to be discussed extensively and in detail. This chapter first explores the significance of emotion in the novella by considering how Marlow seeks to identify the emotions of others and responds to the emotional tenor circulating around him. Following this, it examines the nature of Marlow's imaginative understanding of Kurtz's emotionality and his insight into how it is related to the idea fixed in Kurtz's mind. Finally, it concludes that Marlow's lie to the Intended reflects his compassionate sensitivity to the emotions she expresses.

Emotional Reactions

In 'Heart of Darkness' the objective reality is often affected or obscured by the emotional condition through which it is observed. At the beginning of the novella, the frame narrator, a member of the audience of Marlow's narrative on a cruising yawl, the *Nellie,* warns the reader that Marlow's yarns are not typical of seamen's yarns, because Marlow seems to consider that the essence of the story is not contained in its core, but on its outer edge, and he does so by expounding his view with multiple layers of similes:

> [. . .] to him the meaning of an episode was not inside *like a kernel* but outside, enveloping the tale which brought it out only *as a glow brings out a haze, in the likeness of one of these misty halos* that, sometimes, are made visible by the spectral illumination of moonshine. (48; emphasis added)

---

[2] Graham Bradshaw is the author of *Shakespeare's Scepticism* (Harvester Press, 1987).

The extensive use of similes in this sentence suggests that he is making a subjective assertion. Susan R. Fussel and Mallie M. Moss maintain that, generally speaking, the 'subjective nature of emotional experiences appears to lend itself to figurative expression' (1). If so, the passage quoted above suggests that the frame narrator is trying to convey the emotional impression he has received from Marlow's yarns. The subjective statement has the effect of drawing the reader's attention towards the place of subjective emotions in Marlow's tale. The passage is somewhat reminiscent of the advice Conrad gives to Edward Noble in the letter quoted in the Introduction: it seems to indicate that the meaning of an episode is 'not inside like a kernel' in the events themselves but 'outside, enveloping the tale' in the human emotions that the events illustrate.

However, it is important to note that the narrator's impressionistic descriptions take on significance precisely because they are juxtaposed with descriptions that convey a realistic effect. Jacques Berthoud maintains:

> Mythical correspondences (the journey as a quest), literary allusions (the Dantesque grove of death [...]), anthropomorphism and the like, are not solely [...] means of inflating significance; they also express [...] the sense of dream, of phantasmagoria and nightmare [...]. But if such devices help to convey Marlow's feeling of unreality, it is because they work within the context of a much more directly mimetic use of language. (1978: 45)

What the 'directly mimetic use of language' conveys is sober reality as opposed to the emotionally biased reality. In 'Heart of Darkness,' objective reality may often be obscured by the emotional conditions of the observer; however, this does not necessarily mean that objective reality is depicted as something less important than subjective reality. Ian Watt suggests that in an Impressionist painting—such as Monet's 'Impression: the Sunrise'—the focus is on the atmospheric conditions rather than on the sun itself; however, in 'Heart of Darkness,' objective reality is regarded as more important than emotional impression[3]:

> For Conrad, the world of the senses is not a picture but a presence, a presence so intense, unconditional, and unanswerable that it loses the fugitive,

[3] See John G. Peters' *Conrad and Impressionism* (Cambridge University Press, 2001) for further discussion on impressionist painting and literature: 13–22.

42   Y. OKUDA

hypothetical, subjective, and primarily aesthetic qualities which it usually has in the impressionist tradition. (Watt 1980: 179)

The contrast between the world of the senses as a picture and as a presence is indicated, for instance, by the juxtaposition of the threatening impression that the Europeans receive from the wilderness and the neutral impression that the indigenous people receive from the same wilderness. It is only the Europeans, and not the indigenous people, that attribute threatening anthropomorphic qualities to the wilderness and are driven to make ineffectual attacks on it. What this suggests is that the threatening qualities are not inherent in the wilderness itself, but are attributed to it by the Europeans who are conspiring to invade an unknown realm out of their greed for ivory, repressing their feelings of guilt. On the other hand, for the indigenous people the wilderness is their habitat, the place where they can dwell with clear conscience, and therefore part of 'a world of straightforward facts,' as Marlow perceives it to be (61).

The question, however, is, first, to what extent is Marlow aware of the emotional conditions of the Europeans and the indigenous people and second, what ethical values does he hold towards them? The clue to these questions can be found in the story that Marlow tells of the Romans. At the beginning of his narrative, Marlow alludes to the Romans who came to the British Isles nineteen hundred years ago. He tells his audience on the *Nellie* to 'Imagine the *feelings*' (49; emphasis added) of a commander of a trireme going up the Thames facing 'the darkness' (49). He also asks them to 'think of a decent young citizen in a toga [...]. [...] in some inland post *feel* the savagery, the utter savagery had closed round him' and to 'Imagine the growing *regrets*, the *longing* to escape, the powerless *disgust*, the *surrender*, the *hate*' (50; emphasis added). These are all negative feelings felt by the Romans, which suggests that in describing them Marlow is trying to draw the attention of the audience specifically to 'the feelings,' and therefore it may be assumed that he is concerned with the emotional conditions of the Romans.

Next, Marlow goes on to contrast the work carried out by such Roman conquerors to the work carried out by seamen like himself. According to Marlow, seamen are not easily distressed by negative emotions because working with a 'devotion to efficiency' (50) enjoins them to accept such emotions dispassionately. In contrast, conquerors like the Romans are easily distressed by their negative emotions; they work with 'brute force' (50), which impels them to repress their emotions, and ironically by

3 EMOTIONAL REACTIONS, THE IDEA, AND A LIE: 'HEART ... 43

making them inaccessible the Romans subject themselves to the power of their own emotions.

However, what does Marlow mean by 'devotion to efficiency? The ethical value that Marlow attaches to it is indicated in Part 2 by his keen appreciation of a book entitled *An Inquiry into Some Points of Seamanship*, written by a 'simple old sailor' (99):

> Not a very enthralling book; but at the first glance you could see there a singleness of intention, an honest concern for the right way of going to work, which made these humble pages, thought out so many years ago, luminous with another than a professional light. (99)

It suggests that for Marlow 'devotion to efficiency' signifies doing your job with 'a singleness of intention' and 'an honest concern for the right way of going to work.' This entails being neutrally aware of your emotional reality so as to prevent the emotions from taking you unawares and affecting the efficiency of your work; and in such moments fear for the insecurity inherent in the world diminishes: 'when you attend to the mere incidents of the surface, the reality—the reality I tell you—fades. The inner truth is hidden—luckily, luckily. But I felt it all the same' (93). W. L. Courtney suggests that for Conrad '[t]he best and wisest man is he who does the work immediately before his eyes, with the greatest amount of calm efficiency' (*CR2*: 452). For Marlow, the book is 'something unmistakably real' (99); he recognizes it as real because he shares the values of the writer of the book in doing his work. For instance, when Marlow is navigating the company's steamboat up the river, he has to keep on guessing at the channel, discerning the hidden banks, and watching the sunken stones and snags (93); in other words, he has to attend to the incidents of the surface, working with 'a singleness of intention' and 'an honest concern.' He has to, because otherwise he would wreck the steamboat and drown everyone on board.

Conrad's work ethic may have been partially influenced by the Victorian work ethic, such as that of Thomas Carlyle. In *Past and Present* (1843), Carlyle says that contemporary ideas hold that 'an endless significance lies in Work':

> [...] a man perfects himself by working. [...]. Consider how, even in the meanest sorts of Labour, the whole soul of a man is composed into a kind of real harmony, the instant he sets himself to work! Doubt, Desire,

> Sorrow, Remorse, Indignation, Despair itself, all these like helldogs lie
> beleaguering the soul of the poor day-worker, as of every man: but he
> bends himself with free valour against his task, and all these are stilled, all
> these shrink murmuring far off into their caves. The man is now a man.
> (*Past and Present* 189)[4]

'Doubt,' 'Desire,' 'Sorrow,' 'Remorse,' 'Indignation,' and 'Despair,' all these 'helldogs' are in fact emotions, and Carlyle, like Conrad, seems to be saying that working earnestly can help you prevent your emotions from affecting your efficiency.[5]

However, the work ethic which Marlow embraces is more positive. Work holds a positive value for Marlow, because it offers him the chance to familiarize himself with his own emotional propensities; it enables him to keep his latent emotional reality at a safe distance while he worked, so the effects of the emotions are neutralized.

> I don't like work. I had rather laze about and think of all the fine things
> that can be done. I don't like work – no man does – but I like what is in
> the work – the chance to find yourself – your own reality – for yourself –
> not for others – what no other man can ever know. They can only see the
> mere show and can never tell what it really means. (85)

Marlow feels tempted to indulge himself in spinning out fine ideas, but he does not give in to those temptations and persists in doing his work. In contrast, conquerors give in to the temptation of pursuing their ideas and 'think of all the fine things that can be done,' as it is such ideas that enable them to camouflage their stressful emotions most effectively. They pursue these ideas in earnest to escape the stress they feel; however, ironically, by doing so they are enhancing the power of the ideas over them. Sometimes they even commit themselves to the dubious and destructive power of ideas to the extent of believing in them as if they were gods: '[…] an unselfish belief in the idea—something you can set up, and bow down before,' and even 'offer a sacrifice to' (51). This suggests that they regard the ideas in their mind as being able to exercise absolute godlike power over them, holding them responsible for whatever they do. It is Marlow's

---

[4] Book III The Modern Worker, Chapter XI Labour.

[5] In opposition to Marlow, who asserts that there is 'the chance to find yourself' in work (85), Carlyle maintains 'Think it not thy business; this of knowing thyself; thou art an unknowable individual' (*Past and Present* 129).

3 EMOTIONAL REACTIONS, THE IDEA, AND A LIE: 'HEART ...   45

insight into such emotional self-deception that enables him to penetrate the emotional reality of the Roman conquerors and later that of Kurtz's; he realizes that their 'ideas' are in fact their greed in intellectual disguise.

In the course of his journey to the Inner Station, Marlow observes the emotional reactions of the various people he comes across in the trading stations and on the river, and again he assesses their emotional reality in terms of his work ethic.[6] For example, Marlow witnesses two sights from the French steamer which leave strong but contrasting impressions on him: one is the sight of the indigenous men rowing a boat near the shore, and another is a French man-of-war firing at the shore. When Marlow sees the sight of the boat, he is struck by the sense of reality it carries:

> Now and then a boat from the shore gave one a momentary contact with reality. It was paddled by black fellows. You could see from afar the white of their eyeballs glistening. They shouted, and sang; their bodies streamed with perspiration [...]. (61)

Paddling demands strenuous physical exertion, so the boatmen shout and sing to release their emotional stresses which arise from such physical exertion. On witnessing the sight, Marlow feels that he is in 'a momentary contact with reality' (61).

This sight of the paddlers foreshadows another sight which Marlow witnesses later on from the company's steamboat on his way to the Inner Station:

> [. . .] suddenly, as we struggled round a bend there would be a glimpse of rush walls, of peaked grass-roofs, a burst of yells, a whirl of black limbs, a mass of hands clapping, of feet stamping, of bodies swaying, of eyes rolling [...]. (96)

On seeing these natives on the shore, Marlow detects in himself 'the faintest trace of a response to the terrible frankness of that noise, a dim suspicion of there being a meaning in it which you—you so remote from the night of the first ages—could comprehend' (96). These people are under emotional stress, brought on by the sudden appearance of a river

---

[6] Kenneth Asher says, 'if literature is to make a more extensive claim on our ethical attention, a stronger case for the role of emotion will have to be put forward' (25).

46   Y. OKUDA

boat which, to them, may seem like a 'splashing, thumping, fiery river-demon' (145), as it later seems to the indigenous people at the Inner Station. However, instead of considering the steamboat an enemy or a sham hindrance to their emotions, they try to allay their fear by working upon their emotions through their own bodies. In fact, what they are doing here is reminiscent of the origins of the dance, which is:

> Physical expressive movement accompanied by songs (including rhythmic yells) and musical instruments (including beating time with one's hands or feet); the dance is the origin of all art expressed with one's body. It is a universal and instinctive way of releasing suppressed emotions, which is shared by all mankind [...]. (*The Encyclopedia of Cultural Anthropology* [*Bunka-Jinruigaku-Jiten*]: 122, in Japanese; my translation)

According to Curt Sachs, '[t]he dance as "rhythmic motion" does not exclude other rhythmic movements, such as running, rowing, turning a handle, working a treadle' (1937, 1965: 5), which suggests that what the indigenous people are doing in both these scenes—the shouting and singing while rowing the boat in the first scene and the clapping and stamping on the shore in the second scene—can be regarded as reflecting the origins of primitive dances, such as harvesting and sowing songs and hunting or war dances which probably all our ancestors—including Marlow's—must have participated in before setting out to work. Anya Peterson Royce states: 'Dance is one of the most effective vehicles for psychological release because its instrument is the human body. Feedback is instantaneous and catharsis immediate for both the dancer and the observer' (1977: 81). It is natural, therefore, that Marlow, as an observer, should respond spontaneously to the people on the shore. More importantly, this way of relieving emotional stresses, in spite of its primitive appearance, does not involve abusing or sacrificing others. As Marlow rightly discerns, these people on the shore are trying to deal with the stresses of their emotional reality with their own inner strength:

> What was there after all? Joy, fear, sorrow, devotion, valour, rage – who can tell? – but truth – truth stripped of its cloak of time. Let the fool gape and shudder – the man knows, and can look on without a wink. But he must at least be as much of a man as these on the shore. He must meet that truth with his own true stuff – with his own inborn strength. (97)

The sight of the paddlers which Marlow witnesses from the French steamboat is juxtaposed with another sight that Marlow witnesses from the same boat, which is the sight of a French man-of-war firing at the shore at a camp of indigenous people that they consider to be their 'enemies' (62). In contrast to the sight of the paddling men, Marlow says that he felt that 'there was a touch of insanity in the proceeding' (62), that is to say, those aboard the French man-of-war seemed to lack a sound sense of reality. Later on, he is reminded of this sight of the man-of-war when he witnesses the depraved proceedings at the construction site of the railway at the Outer Station, where the indigenous men are considered to be 'criminals' (64), and are left to die in the grove of death when they become too emaciated to work.

What the sights of the man-of-war and the railway site have in common is that, although people are supposed to be engaged in a civilizing endeavour, there is neither a grain of what Marlow calls 'singleness of intention' nor 'an honest concern for the right way of going to work.' These two sights suggest that the white men involved in these proceedings are feeling their own alienation in the wilderness and are trying to deal with their latent primitive and impulsive emotions, such as unreasonable fear and anger, by setting up the natives as 'enemies' or 'criminals' and attacking them as sham hindrances to their emotions. Their way of dealing with their stressful emotions, in spite of their apparently civilized appearance, equipped with 'long eight-inch guns' and dynamite, is in fact aggressive and barbaric, and it entails sacrifices being made by innocent people. The first pair of sights suggest that the natives are like seamen dealing with their emotions with their own 'inborn strength,' whereas the second pair of sights are reminiscent of the Roman conquerors who try to cope with their emotional stresses by exploiting ideas of hostility that would justify their use of brute force.

A similar contrast of emotional reactions is suggested by Marlow's parallel narrations of the white agents he meets at the Central Station and the supposedly cannibalistic tribesmen who are enlisted as members of the crew to work on the steamboat. The agents who do not work but stroll aimlessly about in the yard, obsessed by the illusion of ivory, strike Marlow as 'unreal' (76). Some of them accompany the manager on his upriver journey to the Inner Station, not as members of the crew, but as passengers. On the other hand, the few dozen tribesmen 'enlisted [...] on the way for a crew' (94), not only cut wood for fuel, push the steamboat through the shallows, and test the depth of the water with a

48   Y. OKUDA

pole, but they also impress Marlow by the ability to restrain hunger that they exhibit while they work: 'something restraining, one of those human secrets that baffle probability, had come into play' (104):

> Yes – I looked at them as you would on any human being, with a curiosity of their impulses, motives, capacities, weaknesses, when brought to the test of an inexorable physical necessity. (105)

These men may be tribesmen who practice cannibalism, but at their home villages eight hundred miles away they must have hunted hippos and harvested roots to make the 'stuff like half-cooked cold dough, of a dirty lavender colour' (104),[7] and therefore have habitually learnt how to restrain themselves while they worked. Marlow's appreciation of their restraint manifests his unprejudiced and empathetic insight into human emotions: 'It takes a man all his inborn strength to fight hunger properly. It's really easier to face bereavement, dishonour and the perdition of one's soul—than this kind of prolonged hunger' (105). As Marlow suggests, with about thirty of them on board, they could have easily attacked the Europeans to assuage their hunger, but they possess 'an inborn strength' to restrain their desire and keep the emotional sway to the minimum; in this scene also Marlow applies the phrase 'inborn strength' to the indigenous men, as he did to those on the shore.

The difference of emotional reactions between the native crew and the white agents becomes most apparent when the steamboat is attacked by Kurtz's followers:

> It was very curious to see the contrast of expressions of the white men and of the black fellows of our crew [...]. The whites, of course greatly discomposed, had besides a curious look of being painfully shocked by such an outrageous row. The others had an alert, naturally interested expression but their faces were essentially quiet [...]. (102–03)

The agents are agitated, and seem resentful that such an unexpected incident should happen, but the indigenous crew remain composed and responsive. Here again Conrad enables Marlow to discern that the

---

[7] In the 'Notes' to the Penguin edition of 'Heart of Darkness,' Robert Hampson says that this stuff 'like half-cooked dough' is 'cassava steeped and boiled to form a stiff dough [...] known as *kwanga*' (127–8).

indigenous men manifest a more emotionally mature attitude than the Europeans. This clearly contradicts Achebe's accusation that Conrad manifests an antipathy to black people peculiar to his psychology. Achebe contends that Marlow in 'Heart of Darkness' is prejudiced against indigenous people, and charges Conrad with failing to offer a framework which suggests that Conrad as the author disapproves of what, according to Achebe's interpretation, is Marlow's white racist attitude; he maintains that Conrad 'neglects to hint, clearly and adequately, at an alternative frame of reference by which we may judge the actions and opinions of his characters' (Achebe 10). However, the textual-based analysis from the perspective of emotions demonstrates that, far from neglecting to hint at a frame of reference by which we may judge the actions and opinion of his characters, Conrad 'clearly and adequately' indicates that Marlow attends closely and evenhandedly to the emotions expressed by other characters.

THE IDEA

In Part 1, Marlow narrates and assesses the emotional reactions of the Europeans and the indigenous people on the basis of his insight into human emotions derived from his own experience. However, in Parts 2 and 3, Marlow is faced with Kurtz's emotional reality which, in its extremity, lies beyond anything that Marlow himself has experienced. It is important to note that in the case of Kurtz, Marlow is interested not only in his emotional reactions but also in the idea he pursues. Conrad's attitude towards ideas is generally deprecatory. The word 'idea' is often used in a negative sense, as 'a conception to which no reality corresponds' (*OED*).[8] In his letter to Cunningham Graham, dated 20 December 1897, Conrad writes: 'You are a most hopeless idealist—your aspirations are irrealizable. You want from men faith, honour, fidelity to truth in themselves and others [...]. What makes you dangerous is your unwarrantable belief that your desire may be realized' (*CL1*: 424–25). Conrad accuses him of holding 'aspirations' and 'beliefs' to which no reality corresponds, and which are no more than reflections of his 'desire,' and therefore Conrad says that he is dangerous. For the omniscient narrator of *Nostromo*, 'a man haunted by a fixed idea,' like Charles Gould, is 'insane':

---

[8] The definition III.c. of the entry 'idea' in *OED* says: 'A conception to which no reality corresponds; something merely imagined or fancied.'

50   Y. OKUDA

> Charles Gould's fits of abstraction depicted the energetic concentration of a will haunted by a fixed idea. A man haunted by a fixed idea is insane. He is dangerous even if that idea is an idea of justice; for may he not bring the heaven down pitilessly upon a loved head? (379)

The notion that these quotations convey is that unrestrained emotional attachment to an unrealizable idea, which is a camouflage for one's emotional desires, can be a serious danger to oneself and others.

Marlow's curiosity about Kurtz is awakened for the first time when the chief accountant mentions his name to him and says that Kurtz 'will go far, very far' (70). It is strengthened when the brick maker tells him that Kurtz is 'an emissary of pity, and science, and progress' and 'a special being' (79). However, at the end of Part 1 Marlow says: 'I wasn't very interested in him. No. Still, I was curious to see whether this man who had come out equipped with moral ideas of some sort would climb to the top after all and how he would set about his work when there' (88). At this stage Marlow has not yet had any distinct impression of Kurtz, and therefore he harbours only a mild curiosity about him. However, this mild curiosity turns into an abiding interest when he hears the manager tell his uncle that Kurtz had succeeded in persuading the Administration in Europe to send him to the most profitable station, and relate to him a striking episode:

> [...] Kurtz had apparently intended to return himself, the station being by that time bare of goods and stores, but after coming three hundred miles had suddenly decided to go back [...]. It was a distinct glimpse. The dug-out, four paddling savages and the lone white man turning his back suddenly on the headquarters, on relief, on thoughts of home perhaps, setting his face towards the depth of wilderness, towards his empty and desolate station. (90)

What arouses Marlow's interest is the persuasive power of Kurtz's eloquence and the strength of the irrepressible urge which impels him to turn back to the inner station after coming three hundred miles. Kurtz has become so tenaciously attached to his own ideas that he returns to the Inner Station to carry out these ideas.

3 EMOTIONAL REACTIONS, THE IDEA, AND A LIE: 'HEART ... 51

This glimpse of Kurtz, equipped with persuasive eloquence and inexplicable impulse[9], fascinates Marlow and he very quickly becomes obsessed with the idea of actually hearing Kurtz speak in a forceful and determining voice. Marlow says that, for him, '[the steamboat] crawled towards Kurtz—exclusively' (95); and he even experiences a 'startling extravagance of emotion' (114) verging on 'desolation' (114), when it occurs to him, after the steamboat is attacked, that Kurtz may have died, and so he may never have a chance to hear him talk. (114) Marlow's obsession with the idea of hearing Kurtz talk is not so much the result of his appreciation of Kurtz's moral ideas as a surrender to the fascination of his gift of expression: 'The point was in his being a gifted creature and that of all his gifts the one that stood out pre-eminently, that carried with it a sense of real presence, was his ability to talk, his words—the gift of expression [...]' (114).

When Marlow sees Kurtz for the first time from close quarters on the riverboat at the Inner Station, he has already been informed by the Russian youth that Kurtz has raided the country with his followers and has incited them to offer human sacrifices to himself. Marlow is 'struck by the fire of his eyes and the composed languor of his expression' (134): 'This shadow [Kurtz] looked satiated and calm, as though for the moment it had had its fill of all the emotions' (134–35). However, there is something very curious about Kurtz in this scene. He is 'satiated and calm' because he has been raiding the country and presiding over sacrificial rites, gratifying his lust; and yet, far from manifesting any remorse or guilt for what he has been doing, he nonchalantly approves of the letter which carries 'special recommendations' (135) for Marlow, presumably, to assist him with his supposedly philanthropic work. Moreover, he declares to the manager that: 'I'll carry my ideas out yet—I will return. I'll show you what can be done [...],' and complains, '[...] you are interfering with me' (137), again as if he believes himself to have already begun to carry out his supposedly philanthropic idea.

What this apparently contradictory attitude indicates is that Kurtz has convinced himself that the gratification of his primitive impulses is a justifiable measure in carrying out his ideas: he has 'bowed down' and offered sacrifices to his own idea of 'Benevolence' (118). In Kurtz's diseased mind, raiding the country with his guns is indistinguishable from

---

[9] In *The Shadow-Line*, the narrator defines the word 'impulse' as 'an effect of that force somewhere within our lives which shapes them this way or that' (25).

52   Y. OKUDA

'[appearing] to them [savages] in the nature of supernatural beings,' and urging them to offer human sacrifice is virtually the same as '[exerting] a power for good practically unbounded' (118). This, in fact, is not as contradictory as it seems when seen from the point of view of Kurtz's ingrained habit of justifying his desires with his own ideas, so that he can act with a 'clear' conscience: first, he conceives of a philanthropic idea to justify his desire to gain wealth by plundering ivory and even confides it to his Intended; second, he develops this idea to persuade the Administration in Europe to send him to a trading-post where ivory is to be had so that he can earn percentages; thirdly, he exploits the same idea in rationalizing his desire to raid the country for ivory by writing a report for the International Society for the Suppression of Savage Customs; and finally, he ingeniously adapts this idea to convince himself irrationally that raiding the villages and demanding human sacrifice is a necessary step for achieving his unjustifiable goal, when in fact he is doing no more than gratifying his lust. In a letter addressed to Cunningham Graham, Conrad warns him:

> [...] why do you preach to the converted? [...]. There are no converts to ideas, of honour, justice, pity, freedom. There are only people who, without knowledge, understanding or feeling, drive themselves into a frenzy with words, repeat them, shout them out, imagine they believe in them – without believing in anything but profit, personal advantage, satisfied vanity. (15 June 1898, *CL2*: 70; the original text is in French)

Such egocentric bias is by no means a characteristic peculiar to people of Conrad's age. Three-quarters of a century later, Thomas Merton, a Trappist theologian, observes:

> I think that if there is one truth that people need to learn, in the world, especially today, it is this: the intellect is only theoretically independent of desire and appetite in ordinary, actual practice. It is constantly being blinded and perverted by the ends and aims of passions and the evidence it presents to us with such a show of impartiality and objectivity is fraught with interest and propaganda. We have become marvellous at self-delusion; all the more so because we have gone to such trouble to convince ourselves of our own absolute infallibility. (1975: 7)

As a journalist who professes to have been Kurtz's colleague tells Marlow, Kurtz could 'get himself to believe in anything—anything' (154); it is because Kurtz has 'become marvellous at self-delusion,' and convinced himself of his 'own absolute infallibility' that he sinks to such a state of depravity.

If Kurtz could get himself to believe in anything, he could get himself to believe that he was justified in doing anything. What makes him so bizarrely conceited as to demand such justice is his gift of eloquence. Kurtz sways the native followers, the Russian youth, and the Intended with his eloquence; and he makes even Marlow 'tingle with enthusiasm' (118) by 'the unbounded power of eloquence—of words—of burning noble words' (118). However, the crucial point is not that he sways others, but that he sways and deludes himself with his own eloquence, and, suffers from it as a result. The Russian youth tells Marlow, 'This man suffered too much. He hated all this, and somehow he couldn't get away' (129): 'You don't know how such a life tries a man like Kurtz' (132). Kurtz's desire to 'exterminate all the brutes' (118) does not reflect his desire to annihilate those 'who may not be cooperative or may entertain ideas about resistance,' as Edward Said maintains (201), but his desire to escape from this suffering that he has created for himself.

It is Marlow's imaginative insight into the state of Kurtz's demented intellectual capacity and the befuddled and anguished state of his soul— the seat of the emotions—which enables him to bring him back safely to the boat when Kurtz escapes from it at night and tries to rejoin his indigenous followers:

> Soul! If anybody had ever struggled with a soul, I am the man. And I wasn't arguing with a lunatic either. Believe me or not, his intelligence was perfectly clear – concentrated, it is true, upon himself with horrible intensity, yet clear [...]. But his soul was mad. Being alone in the wilderness, it had looked within itself, and, by heavens! [...] it had gone mad. [...]. He struggled with himself, too. I saw it, -- I heard it. I saw the inconceivable mystery of a soul that knew no restraint, no faith, and no fear, yet struggling blindly with itself. (144–45)

Kurtz's suffering ends with the cry, 'The horror! The horror!' when, as his physical strength weakens, the cloud of his delusory idea thins out and, as if 'a veil had been rent,' the light of reality breaks through the layers of his spurious and preposterous assumptions. He perceives, for the first time, the falseness of his own words, 'the deceitful flow from the heart of an impenetrable darkness' (113–14), and becomes aware of the ignorance of his own emotionality, his blindness to the inner forces of darkness: 'Mr Kurtz lacked restraint in the gratification of his various lusts [...]. Whether he knew of this deficiency himself I can't say. I think the knowledge came to him at last, only at the very last' (131).

Marlow's attachment to the idea of hearing Kurtz talk is such as all of us might succumb to, as we all get attached to certain ideas sometimes; however, Kurtz's attachment to his idea is tenacious, demented, and dangerous; his civilizing, high minded ideas are really a dangerous emotional condition parading as an idea. This emotional condition is, in fact, an exaggerated version of the emotional condition of the whole European trading and colonizing impulse.[10]

A Lie

In the course of the narrative, Marlow has been gradually developing a sensitivity to the emotional expression of others, which is what enables him to arrive at the imaginative understanding of Kurtz's emotional surrender. This understanding in its turn enables him to surmise the circumstances that Kurtz is in at his deathbed, and also to infer the meaning of his last words: 'Did he live his life again in every detail of desire, temptation, and surrender during that supreme moment of complete knowledge?' (149). To understand the whole process of Kurtz's delusion, Marlow, who does not share such an emotional condition, has had to use his imagination to the limits of his ability; that is why, after he returns to Europe, he says: 'It was not my strength that wanted nursing, it was my imagination that wanted soothing' (152).

A year after Kurtz's death, Marlow visits Kurtz's intended in Brussels. It seems that his imagination has not been sufficiently soothed by then, because as soon as he stands at the door of her house, Marlow begins to have visionary and auditory hallucinations: he sees Kurtz and hears his voice, and is reminded of 'the tempestuous anguish of his soul' and the complacent demand for justice:

---

[10] According to Antonio Damasio, '[...] there is something quite distinctive about the way in which emotions have become connected to the complex ideas, values, principles, and judgments that only humans can have, and in that connection lies our legitimate sense that human emotion is special' (1999: 35).

I remembered his abject pleading, his abject threats, the colossal scale of his vile desires, the meanness, the torment, the tempestuous anguish of his soul. And later on I seemed to see his collected languid manner, when he said one day, 'This lot of ivory now is really mine. The Company did not pay for it. [...] I am afraid they will try to claim it as theirs though. H'm. It is a difficult case. What do you think I ought to do – resist? Eh? I want no more than justice.' (156)

The impression that Marlow has derived from the photograph of the Intended before he visits her is that she wore a 'delicate shade of truthfulness' upon her features, and that 'she seemed ready to listen without mental reservation, without suspicion, without a thought for herself' (154–55). However, when he actually meets her, he finds her not only forlorn, but rather overbearing. She says to Marlow in an obtrusive way, 'You knew him well,' and then, 'you admired him [...]. It was impossible to know him and not to admire him' (158); and when Marlow seems perplexed by her use of the word 'admire,' and tries to rephrase it by muttering, 'It was impossible not to –,' she cuts him short by saying 'Love him,' silencing him into 'an appalled dumbness' (158). She may have listened to Kurtz's plans and ideas 'without mental reservation, without suspicion, and without a thought for herself,' swayed by his eloquence, but she certainly does not do so with Marlow.

Kurtz's Intended is possessed by her idea of Kurtz almost as much as Kurtz was possessed by his own ideas. Marlow listens to her with patience for a while, but when she finally says 'He died as he lived' (161), he cannot help feeling 'a dull anger' (161) at the falsehood of the implied irony suggested by her words. Yet this anger is soon dispelled by what she says next, the only words of truth that she utters: 'And I was not with him' (161). On hearing these words, his 'dull anger' is overtaken by 'a feeling of infinite pity' (161). She says, 'I would have treasured every sigh, every word, every sign, every glance. [...] I think of his loneliness. Nobody near to understand him as I would have understood' (161), and he is touched by this expression of mortification at being absent from Kurtz's deathbed.

Marlow's emotional attitude towards the Intended is different from his attitude towards Kurtz. Towards Kurtz he says, 'I wasn't touched, I was fascinated' (149). Fascination is a strong feeling of interest, whereas 'a feeling of infinite pity' involves tender concern for the distress of another, prompting a desire for its relief, and therefore 'pity' is synonymous with such words as 'sympathy' or 'compassion.'[11] This feeling of pity, however, puts Marlow in a difficult position when subsequently she demands that Marlow repeat Kurtz's last words to her so that she can have something to live with. At first, Marlow is nearly swayed by the hallucinatory voice of Kurtz, which irrationally claims the justice of his supposedly philanthropic deed that ended with his cries of horror as its reward. However, at the very last moment Marlow manages to repulse the influence of Kurtz's hallucinatory voice and regains emotional independence; he says, '*I pulled myself together* and spoke slowly' (161; emphasis added); 'To pull oneself together' in this context means 'to recover control of oneself or one's emotions' (*OED*). It implies that at this crucial moment Marlow repulses the sway that Kurtz's eloquence holds on him emotionally and regains his self-possession. This is borne out by the fact that as soon as Marlow manages to pull himself together, Kurtz's illusory voice stops.[12] He has finally 'laid the ghost of his gifts with a lie' (115); that is to say, he puts an end to the detrimental power of Kurtz' eloquence. It is only then that Marlow tells the Intended, of his own free will, that Kurtz's last word was her name. The consequence, ironically, is that Kurtz's illusory voice is replaced by the echo of his 'magnificent eloquence' (131), the cry of the Intended herself, 'I knew it—I was sure' (162), which confirms the depth of her self-deceit.

In telling her the circumstantial lie, Marlow refuses to succumb to Kurtz's demand to convey his version of justice, together with his last words, 'The horror! The horror!' (150). Instead, he acts in fidelity to the passing emotion of pity, which prompts him to spare the distress of the Intended. He may have realized that if he surrendered to Kurtz's demand and told her the truth, she would experience a disillusionment almost as powerful as Kurtz's at his deathbed, and such an experience might inflict a lifelong trauma on her. Marlow tells the Intended a lie which involves deception, but he does not tell it for his own sake; he does so to spare another pain of futile suffering: 'Hadn't he said he wanted only justice?

---

[11] 'Literally, compassion means feeling or suffering *with* another person (Latin: *com-*, together + *pati*, to suffer)' (Sander & Scherer 91).

[12] The phrase 'to pull oneself together' seems to have carried a significance for Conrad, as can be inferred from his use of the phrase in *A Personal Record*, when he confesses that an 'unforgettable Englishman' 'helped me *to pull myself together*' and consequently '[turned] the scale at a critical moment' (41) in his life.

But I couldn't. I could not tell her. It would have been too dark—too dark altogether [...]' (162).

In this scene, Marlow's expression of pity is closely connected to the allusions to the pose of a Buddha in 'Heart of Darkness' (50, 162). In reference to these allusions William Bysshe Stein says: '[...] whatever its significance, to overlook the frame of the Buddha Postures in which Conrad's first-person narrator views its development is to lose sight of an important aspect of its meaning' (281). In Buddhism the figure of the Buddha carries a special emphasis on *karunā*:

> The outstanding quality of all bodhisattvas and buddhas [...]. *Karunā* is often translated as "pity" or "sympathy"; since these notions tend to suggest passive attitudes that do not contain the quality of active help that is an essential part of *karunā*, the concept of "compassion" is more suitable. (*The Shambhala Dictionary of Buddhism and Zen* 1991: 113)

'Compassion' is a non-egoistic emotion, which prompts one to relieve or prevent the sufferings of other; and in his essay 'The Life Beyond' Conrad says: 'What humanity needs is not the promise of scientific immortality, but compassionate pity in this life and infinite mercy on the Day of Judgment' (*Notes on Life and Letters* 69).

Part I discussed two works in which Conrad focuses his attention on the emotional characteristics of individual characters, Jim and Kurtz. Part II takes up two novels in which he directs his attention to emotional elements in terms of groups of characters as well as individuals, and explores the emotional tendencies shared by the characters, which, if they are recognized, may strengthen our solidarity with others.

PART II

Common Subjective Tendencies

CHAPTER 4

Nature, Identity, and Emotions: *Nostromo*

> The hollow clatter they [the sculls] made in falling was the loudest noise he had ever heard in his life. It was a revelation. It seemed to recall him from far away. Actually the thought, 'Perhaps I may sleep to-night,' passed through his mind. But he did not believe it. (*Nostromo*)

Part II takes up two novels, *Nostromo* (1904) and *The Secret Agent* (1907); it examines the emotional propensities of a group of characters and identifies a common pattern in the same overarching framework of the Conradian world view. Chapter 4 links Nature in *Nostromo* to the characters' identities, and addresses the problem of reconciling one's attachment to self-image with the awareness of being part of Nature; in doing so it demonstrates the two aspects of the way the characters forge their identity: emotional reaction and practical action. On the other hand, Chapter 5 compares and contrasts a group of characters in pairs and reveals the emotional sequence that they all follow.

Nostromo was first serialized in *T.P.'s Weekly* from 29 January to 7 October 1904, and after considerable revision, published by Harper in Britain on 14 October and in America on 23 November 1904. One major theme of the novel is Nature. In *Nostromo* Nature is depicted as 'the whole scheme of things of which we form a helpless part' (497), a topic which has attracted the attention of reviewers and critics since the time of its publication. As mentioned earlier, in 'Mr. Conrad's Art' (1904),

© The Author(s), under exclusive license to Springer Nature
Switzerland AG 2024
Y. Okuda, *Emotions and Contingencies in Conrad's Fiction*,
https://doi.org/10.1007/978-3-031-66723-7_4

62   Y. OKUDA

Edward Garnett notes that in *Nostromo* Nature is regarded as a changeable and controlling force and the characters are closely involved with it:

> In Mr. Conrad's vision we may image Nature as a ceaselessly-flowing river of life [...]. The author's pre-eminence does not lie specifically in his psychological analysis of character, but in the delicate relation of his characters to the whole environment – to the whole mirage of life in which their figures are seen to move. (*CR*1: 204)

For Ian Watt, Conrad's characters are only a part of the overall plan of the narrative: 'There is [...], and particularly in the case of *Nostromo*, a sense that Conrad's novel does not exist just to provide characters, but, rather, that it is a literary entity of which characters are only part; and that part must be related to the total design' (1988: 49). Although in *Nostromo* the natural features, such as the Golfo Plácido and Higuerota, are brought to the fore,[1] the view of Nature as the whole of physical world, including humans, corresponds with the world of *Lord Jim* in that it is also characterized by impermanence.

In *Nostromo*, the characters' identities are closely linked to Nature; and to ascertain how they are linked to Nature it is necessary to consider the characters both collectively and independently. Robert Penn Warren maintains that Conrad 'had little concern for character independently considered' (Warren in Carabine 577). Similarly, Peter K. Garret claims that the suggestions that the novel conveys are 'not primarily about the nature of individual characters or society but about the nature of the universe' (163). In contrast, Bruce E. Johnson claims that '*Nostromo* is a study of identity' in which 'various conceptions of self are brought into elegant parallels and contrasts' (Johnson in Cox 112).

If *Nostromo* is a study of identity, how is personal identity generally forged in the novel, and how is it conceived by the respective characters? The chapter suggests that in this novel identity is closely bound up with the conception of Nature, a relationship that has not often been explored previously.[2] It discusses this issue through a close reading of the text, first,

---

[1] Royal Roussel points out that the landscape in *Nostromo* is 'a constant, detached presence of which the reader is always aware' (111).

[2] Hugh Epstein maintains that in *Nostromo* '[t]he senses, which confirm our singularity as organisms that harbour impressions by which the world is uniquely and separately

by examining the characteristics of Nature through the Golfo Plácido, and then indicating the two bases of personal identity in the novel and analysing how each of the main characters conceives his or her identity in the framework of a contingent world.

NATURE AND ITS POWER OVER HUMANS

Nature in *Nostromo* is introduced early in the opening chapter of the novel, and impressed deeply on the reader's mind 'before the characters take their places in the foreground' (Garnett; *CR*1: 160). It is depicted as constantly changing, and this sense of change is manifested in the opening chapter by the clouds over the Golfo Plácido. The gulf is like 'an enormous semi-circular and unroofed temple open to the ocean with its walls of lofty mountains hung with the mourning draperies of cloud' (8). The clouds over the gulf are at once moving, beautiful, and threatening; they hint at the impermanence of the world of the novel: 'The head of the calm gulf is filled on most days of the year by a great body of motionless and opaque clouds' (5). When the dawn breaks behind the mountains, overtopped by Higuerota, their shadow is cast on the gulf, but 'as the midday sun withdraws from the gulf the shadow of the mountains, the clouds begin to roll out of the lower valleys' (6). Then the clouds 'travel out slowly to seaward and vanish into thin air as if it had dissolved itself into great piles of grey and black vapours' (6). Finally, 'at night the body of clouds advancing higher up the sky smothers the whole quiet gulf' (6).[3]

Higuerota, too, is depicted as subject to change in Chapter 5. The chairman of the railway board arrives too late to see what the engineer-in-chief has been contemplating as he sits at the door of a hut: 'the changing hues on the enormous side of the mountain' (40). Like the clouds over the gulf, the sunset brings incessant changes to Higuerota. Leonard Orr notes that Higuerota is featured 'actively and changeably' as 'the movement of clouds, shadows, sun, smoke, vapours, and so on lend movements to the mountain' (119).

---

known, also immerse us in a physics in which we are merely minute participants, caught up in the impersonal unfolding of a cosmic event' (2020: 237).

[3] In *The Mirror of the Sea*, Conrad says: 'Love and regret go hand in hand in this world of changes swifter than the shifting of the clouds reflected in the mirror of the sea' (25).

The dynamic and changeable Nature in the novel holds a controlling power over the characters. In the first paragraph of Chapter 1, the omniscient narrator tells us that, as soon as they enter the gulf, 'the ships from Europe bound to Sulaco lose at once the strong breezes of the ocean' and 'become the prey of capricious airs that play with them' (5). The helplessness of the ships in the face of the winds of the gulf highlights the pervasive power of Nature's changeability over man and foreshadows the scene in which Nostromo and Decoud drift in the Golfo Plácido on the lighter carrying the silver ingots in Part 2, a topic to which I will return later.

THE TWO BASES OF PERSONAL IDENTITY

In *Nostromo*, not only the natural world but also the characters are subject to change as 'a helpless part' of Nature. However, as Conrad argues in *A Personal Record*, human beings are 'averse from change and timid before the unknown' (114), and therefore they try to defy their place in the world. John Galsworthy phrases this paradox very quaintly: 'The Universe is always saying: The little part called man is smaller than the whole! Man cannot grasp that statement. He ducks his head resentfully beneath his wing, and hides from contemplation of this truth. It is he who thus creates the irony of things' (Galsworthy in Watt 1973: 90). In the novel, the characters create the irony of things by forming an illusory and static identity in defiance of the fact that they themselves are part of Nature and therefore are also subject to change. For Conrad, 'identity' is the positive concept we have of our own characteristics, feelings, or beliefs that has a benefit in distinguishing us from others and, therefore, it coincides with Decoud's definition of 'conviction': 'What is a conviction? A particular view of our personal advantage either practical or emotional' (189). The particular view of personal advantage that the characters hold of themselves is based primarily on their emotional reaction and subordinately on their practical action.

In this novel, personal identity is referred to repeatedly as 'a view of personal advantage,' not only by Decoud but also by the omniscient narrator; the word 'advantage' here means anything that is a benefit

4 NATURE, IDENTITY, AND EMOTIONS: *NOSTROMO* 65

to one's self-image.[4] Moreover, both use the phrase 'personal advantage' in conjunction with the word 'conviction.' The narrator uses these expressions for the first time in reference to Giorgio Viola, the republican hotel keeper: 'The spirit of self-forgetfulness, the simple devotion to a vast humanitarian idea [...] left its mark upon Giorgio in a sort of austere contempt for all *personal advantage* [...]. There was in old Giorgio an energy of feeling, a personal quality of *conviction*' (31–32; emphasis added). Giorgio may disdain personal advantage, but it can be felt in his attitude. The narrator uses the words again in reference to Sotillo, the Commandant of Esmeralda, when he says that Sotillo 'had no *convictions* of any sort upon anything except as to the irresistible power of his *personal advantages*' (285; emphasis added). The fact that the same expressions are used by both the omniscient narrator and one of the major characters gives these expressions considerable significance in the novel.

Each of the five main characters in *Nostromo*—Charles and Emilia Gould, Dr Monygham, Martin Decoud, and Nostromo—holds a particular view of his or her own personal advantage, grounded in specific emotional reactions and sustained by practical action. The emotional reactions set in against events brought about accidentally, which threatens to break the illusion of stable identity, and is followed by a practical action which helps to intensify the illusion: 'Action is consolatory. It is the enemy of thought and the friend of flattering illusions. Only in the conduct of our action can we find the sense of mastery over the Fates' (66).[5] The degree to which a particular view of personal identity is estranged from or set at odds with their original identity as 'a helpless part' in the scheme of Nature depends on the view of the character.

IDENTITY FOUNDED ON A FIXED IDEA: CHARLES GOULD

Charles Gould's particular view of his personal advantage is based on his resentment against his father's premature death, which prevented him from demonstrating to his father his potential, and also on his successful

---

[4] An 'advantage' is 'anything that is to the good or is a benefit; any condition, circumstance, opportunity, or means that helps in getting something desired' (*Thorndike English Dictionary*).

[5] In 'Autocracy and War,' Conrad maintains that 'Action, in which is to be found the illusion of a mastered destiny, can alone satisfy our uneasy vanity, and lay to rest the haunting fear of the future [...]' (*Notes on Life and Letters* 109).

66   Y. OKUDA

working of the mine to maintain its value. Charles Gould's father died prematurely because his sense of identity was affected by a threatening sense of change caused by the unexpected imposition of the concession:

> He exaggerated to himself the disadvantages of his new position, because he viewed it emotionally. His position in Costaguana was no worse than before. But a man is a desperately conservative creature, and the extravagant novelty of this outrage upon his purse distressed his sensibilities [...]. (56)

His father overreacted to the change of circumstances brought about by the imposition of the concession, because he reacted to it 'emotionally,' and so it affected the emotional basis of his view of personal advantage. He fails to renew the illusion of his identity by taking some kind of action, and as a result becomes obsessed with persecuting hallucinations. He also fails to appreciate both the value of the mine and the potential of his son, which is why Gould feels attracted by Holroyd's readiness to take up both '[h]is personality and his mine' (78).

Charles Gould's conception of the San Tomé Mine is different from that of either his father or Mrs. Gould. He becomes acquainted with the mine for the first time as an abstract concept mentioned in one of his father's letters when he is fourteen, and manages to form 'a definite conviction that there was a silver mine in Sulaco [...] connected closely with the "iniquitous Gould concession"' (57) a year later. By the time he is twenty he has 'fallen under the spell of the San Tomé mine' (59); that is to say, he surrenders to its influence prior to his father's death. Then when his father dies unexpectedly, his impression of the transience of life affects his own identity and propels him to return immediately to Sulaco so that he can renew the illusion of his identity vicariously through the action of redeeming the mine. Ian Watt observes that 'what he [Charles Gould] does, or chooses to do, was, in the last analysis, only done so that he could prove his father had been wrong' (1988: 61). His father's premature death makes it necessary for his son to work the mine successfully in order to preserve his renewed sense of personal identity: 'His breathing image was no longer in his power. This consideration, closely affecting his own identity, filled his breast with a mournful and angry desire for action' (59). Paul Kirschner maintains that '[p]recisely because the father is dead, the son's commitment to the mine is perpetual; you cannot finally prove your point to a ghost; you must go on proving it' (71). Moreover, Charles

Gould, 'with the roundabout logic of emotions' (85), persuades himself that the action would be taken for the sake of his father, not himself; it was meant to rectify, in his eyes, the injustice suffered by his father: 'The mine had been the cause of an absurd moral disaster; its working must be made a serious and moral success. He owed it to the dead man's memory. Such were the [...] emotions of Charles Gould' (66).

It should be noted, however, that even at this point Gould has not yet come into direct contact with the San Tomé mine. For Charles Gould, the San Tomé mine is, first and foremost an abstract, not a real entity, and that is why when he is qualifying to become a mining engineer, he finds studying the scientific aspect of mines 'vague and imperfect in his mind' (59). Like his father, Gould fails to perceive the real identity of the mine under the mistaken assumption that 'the mine preserved its identity, with which he had endowed it as a boy; and it remained dependent on him alone' (82). In reality, the mine has an identity independent of its owner. The San Tomé mine is located in the San Tomé Gorge, which is part of the San Tomé Mountain; that is to say, it belongs to the same natural world as the sierra and the gulf, characterized by impermanence. Historically, it was worked by the Spanish, using slaves in the early days, but was abandoned, so, as John G. Peters suggests, it returned to a 'co-existent state with humanity' (2018:10). Then it was worked by an English company after the War of Independence, but again it had to be abandoned and it reverted to Nature. By the time Charles Gould arrives in Sulaco with his new wife and begins to work it, '[i]t was no longer an abandoned mine; it was a wild, inaccessible, and rocky gorge of the Sierra' (54). As such, the mine retains its original identity as part of the impermanent natural world irrelevant to Gould's conception of the mine as a working concern.

Gould's failure to perceive the mine as an actual excavation space constituting a part of the natural world is bound to create an ironic situation. He becomes fixated on his idea of the mine as tenaciously as the legendary gringo ghosts on the peninsula of Azuera are said to be attached to the treasure: 'Charles Gould's fits of abstraction depicted the energetic concentration of a will haunted by a fixed idea. A man haunted by a fixed idea is insane. He is dangerous even if that idea is an idea of justice; for may he not bring the heaven down pitilessly upon a loved head?' (379). As the emotional basis of his view of his personal advantage is not love for his wife but attachment to the abstract idea of the mine, he becomes more and more estranged from Mrs. Gould in the flesh.

A Reflection of Nature: Emilia Gould

In contrast to Charles Gould, whose perception of the mine is abstract and antipathetic to Nature, Emilia Gould's perception of the mine is concrete and sympathetic to Nature. The water-colour painting she draws is referred to not as a depiction of the San Tomé mine but of the 'San Tomé mountain' (70) or the 'San Tomé gorge' (211) which is located in 'the Higuerota range' (101).

The basis of Mrs. Gould's emotional reaction, unlike her husband's, changes according to the circumstances she is in. Mrs. Gould was inspired by her husband's 'vague idea of rehabilitation' (74) affected by 'the great pitifulness of that lonely and tormented death in Constaguana' (62); she was propelled by her 'woman's instinct of devotion' (74) to surrender to Charles Gould's idea. However, this took place when she was still in Italy, before she emigrated to Sulaco. Once in Sulaco, her devotion is bestowed less on the dead father-in-law, who '[remains] too shadowy a figure for her to be credited with knowledge […]' (74) and more on the life of the people she witnesses in Sulaco. Mrs. Gould is a dynamic character who changes as she becomes more and more involved with the life in Sulaco.

The change that comes over her can be discerned, for instance, in the difference of attitude she manifests in the two conversations she holds with her husband in his room, once in Part 1 and again in Part 2. The first conversation takes place a year after their marriage when she visits her husband's room just after Holroyd and his party have left the house, in Part 1, Chapter 6. In this scene, she merely confesses to her husband that she has been made to feel 'impatient and uneasy' (70) by their guests' materialistic attitude; she criticizes Holroyd's patronizing religious posture, boasting that he 'endowed churches every year' (71), contrasting his arrogant attitude with the humble religious attitude expressed by the common people of Sulaco. However, in a similar scene that takes place about 6 years later, in Part 2, Chapter 6, she has become acutely distressed and even repentant. She protests to her husband, 'it is impossible for me to close my eyes to our position' (207), and speaks regretfully of the running of the mine, saying, 'Ah, if we had left it alone […]' (209).

Emilia Gould changes because her identity is closely involved with the changing circumstances that surround her. Her identity, if she is aware of it at all, is emotionally based on her innate 'unselfishness and sympathy' (67) and practically based on her gift 'in the art of human intercourse which consists in delicate shades of self-forgetfulness and in the suggestion of universal comprehension' (46). Mrs. Gould holds no cherished ideas or convictions of her own and so she has 'no concern with the erection or demolition of theories any more than with the defence of prejudices' (67); that is to say, her attention is not occupied by the need to justify her ideas and her personal feelings, and therefore she can afford to bestow affectionate attention on whoever and whatever happens to be there before her. For instance, she watches with affectionate interest what goes on every day in the patio of her Spanish house: 'Subdued voices ascended in the early mornings from the paved well of the quadrangle [...]. Barefooted servants passed to and fro, issuing from dark, low doorways below; two laundry girls with baskets of washed linen; the baker with the tray of bread made for the day [...]' (68). She accompanies her husband all over the province in their search for labour, giving her thoughts to the ancestors of the Indians she sees on the way, and turning her mind to their future:

> [...] the trudging files of burdened Indians taking off their hats, would lift sad, mute eyes to the cavalcade raising the dust of the crumbling *camino real* made by the hands of their enslaved forefather. And Mrs. Gould, with each day's journey, seemed to come nearer to the soul of the land in the tremendous disclosure of this interior unaffected by the slight European veneer of the coast town, a great land of plain and mountain and people, suffering and mute, waiting for the future in a pathetic immobility of patience. (87–88)

She appreciates the untold suffering and extreme patience of the people, ready to give compassionate attention to the 'silent sad eyes' of the men passing before her eyes, carrying loads on the road, perceiving in their expression 'the disregard of human labour' behind the stonework of bridges and churches. (89) Emilia Gould can view the land 'with a deeper glance than a true born Costaguanero could have done' (86), because she is 'intelligently sympathetic' (86) and has 'an alert perception of values' (46).

Not only does she contemplate sympathetically the peopled scenes that unfold before her eyes, but she also responds alertly and sympathetically to the individuals that she encounters. For example, when she enters her husband's study after Holroyd's party has left her house, she first 'looks about the room,' then 'surveys him from head to foot,' and noticing how thin he is, thinks 'He overworks himself' (72); when Monygham says

70   Y. OKUDA

that it is unreasonable to demand that a man should think of others so much better than he can of himself, she 'hastens to drop the subject' (45); and when she visits Nostromo on his deathbed, she perceives '[a] pained, involuntary reluctance [lingering] in his tone, in his eyes' (560), and refuses to hear where the treasure is. She gives her sympathetic attention generously and indiscriminately, with perspicacity.

The emotional basis of Mrs. Gould's view of her personal advantage is hard to identify precisely because she is self-forgetful, that is to say, she is not ordinarily attached to her own needs or feelings. This, however, does not mean that she is incapable of feeling strong emotions. Unlike her husband who fails to '[pay] much attention to the state of his feelings' (72), Mrs. Gould is aware of her own feelings: for instance, she recognizes 'her own appalled indignation' at the political atrocities perpetrated in the country (49), but hardly ever remains obsessively attached to her feelings or tries to assert them, even to her husband. The only exception, however, occurs in the second scene that we looked at earlier. In this scene, Mrs. Gould sits in her husband's room looking 'thoughtful' and she says to him 'with feeling': 'There is an awful sense of unreality about all this' (207). After telling him that it is impossible for her to close her eyes to their position, she asks him how far he means to go. His answer is, 'Any distance, any length, of course,' and on hearing this she represses a shudder (208), as if she had heard what Gould had said to the engineer-in-chief in the great sala after she withdrew into the drawing-room: 'The Gould Concession has struck such deep roots in this country, in this province, in that gorge of the mountains, that nothing but dynamite shall be allowed to dislodge it from here' (205–206). It suggests that he does not care at all about his wife's 'hospitals,' 'schools,' or 'ailing mothers and feeble old men' (217); what has 'struck deep roots in this country, in this province, in that gorge of the mountains' is the illusion of his identity. The only thing he cares about is the preservation of the mine for the sake of his own identity. Then, expressing her regret at the running of the mine, Mrs. Gould gazes at her water-colour sketch of the San Tomé gorge when it was just a part of the mountain, which seems to suggest that she is aware of the essential identity of the mine as part of Nature; and on this occasion, Mrs. Gould, for once, asserts her own feelings about the mine in opposition to the feelings of her husband: 'He confronted his wife with a firm concentrated gaze, which Mrs. Gould returned with a brave assumption of fearlessness before she went out, closing the door

4 NATURE, IDENTITY, AND EMOTIONS: *NOSTROMO* 71

gently after her' (209).[6] The scene foreshadows her assent in the subsequent scene to Decoud's appeal not to inform her husband and let the silver come down from the mine. Her dialogue with her husband in the previous scene furnishes her with a tacit answer to Decoud's question: 'Mrs. Gould, are you aware to what point he has idealized the existence, the worth, the meaning of the San Tomé mine?' (214), and she has to accept that it has deprived her of her conjugal happiness.

The confrontation between Charles Gould and his wife signifies also the conflict between artificiality and nature, which is underlined in the next paragraph by the juxtaposition of the corridor she exits into and the room Charles Gould remains in: 'In contrast with the white glaring room the dimly lit corridor had a restful mysteriousness of a forest glade, suggested by the stems and the leaves of the plants ranged along the balustrade of the open side [...] and Mrs. Gould, passing on, had the vividness of a figure seen in the clear patches of sun that chequer the gloom of open glades in the woods.' (209–10) In this passage, Charles Gould is shown entrapped in 'the white glaring room' unable to free himself from his 'fixed idea' (379), whereas Mrs. Gould is shown 'passing on' freely through 'the dimly lit corridor' reminiscent of 'the gloom of open glades in the woods,' unimpeded by any fixed idea of her own. This, as a matter of fact, is the second time she is depicted in relation with plants; in Part 1, Chapter 6, she lingers in the corridor on her way to her husband's room 'approaching her face to the clusters of flowers here and there' (9). Mrs. Gould, unattached to any idea, is able to take things as they come, one after another, moving on as naturally as the clouds that travel out over the Golfo Plácido.

Apart from the second scene that takes place in Gould's room, Mrs. Gould never directly or indirectly confronts others. Ordinarily, she fascinates people by something 'subtly devoted, finely self-forgetful in its lively readiness of attention' (157). The words 'self-forgetfulness' or 'self-forgetful' are used repeatedly to describe Mrs. Gould. According to Conrad, 'to forget one's self' means 'to surrender all personal feeling' (*The Mirror of the Sea* 30), also echoed in *A Personal Record*: 'The unwearied self-forgetful attention to every phase of the living universe reflected in

---

[6] John G. Peters notes that 'Conrad presents two contrasting views of the natural world in the novel: Charles Gould's that sees the natural landscape as a means toward economic development and Emilia Gould's that validates that landscape as it exists, prior to mining the silver' (2019: 604).

our consciousness may be our appointed task on this earth' (92). This, in turn, is reminiscent of the significant vision Mrs. Gould has in the garden of the Casa Gould: 'It had come into her mind that for life to be large and full, it must contain the care of the past and of the future *in every passing moment of the present*' (521; emphasis added). Watt maintains that the 'moral closeness and realism' of the portrait of Mrs. Gould is 'not wholly pessimistic in the values they imply' (1988: 84). Her attention to the inexorable passage of time suggests that her identity is based firmly on the impermanence of Nature.

HUMILITY BEFORE NATURE, AUDACITY BEFORE MEN: DR. MONYGHAM

Dr. Monygham's renewed view of his personal advantage is firmly based on his devotion to Mrs. Gould and sustained by his resolution to play the dangerous role of a betrayer to secure her safety. Dr. Monygham's sense of identity has undergone a considerable change. The view he previously held was founded emotionally on his fear of Father Béron, the army chaplain who is said to have presided over his torture and compelled him to betray his friends. The experience convinced him not so much of his advantage but of his personal disadvantage, and made it impossible for him to entertain the self-flattery, or self-conviction, that could furnish him with sufficient impetus to take action. However, by the time Dr. Monygham meets Nostromo in the Custom House this view of personal disadvantage has given way to a renewed view of his personal advantage. The emotional basis of the previous cynical personal identity, his fear of Father Béron, has been replaced by respectful devotion to Mrs. Gould. Consequently, he too has grown susceptible to the kind of self-flattery that drives a person to action. In his case, this action is to betray Sotillo in order to protect Mrs. Gould by securing the safety of the mine:

> The doctor was loyal to the mine. It presented itself to his fifty-years' old eyes in the shape of a little woman [...] with [...] the delicate preciousness of the inner worth [...] revealed in every attitude of her person. As the dangers thickened round the San Tomé mine this illusion acquired force, permanency, and authority. It claimed him at last! This claim, exalted by a spiritual detachment from the usual sanctions of hope and reward, made Dr. Monygham's thinking, acting, individuality, extremely dangerous to himself and others [...]. (431)

Dr. Monygham becomes convinced that he is the only person who can secure Mrs. Gould's future safety, because his emotional well-being is bound up with her personal well-being.

Before Montero started the revolution, Dr. Monygham was able to observe the existing state of circumstances objectively. The engineer-in-chief even considers him to be 'a wise man' (310), but it is not clear where Monygham gained his wisdom. One clue, however, is given by the omniscient narrator when he relates Dr. Monygham's humiliating experiences during the reign of Guzmán Bento and the ensuing life he spent in the wilderness of Costaguana: 'he had lived for years in the wildest part of the Republic, wandering with almost unknown Indian tribes in the great forests of the far interior where the great rivers have their sources. But it was mere aimless wandering; he had written nothing, collected nothing, brought nothing for science out of the twilight of the forests, which seemed to cling to his battered personality' (311). He may not have written or collected anything, nor brought anything for science, but he has gained an insight into the insignificance of human beings in the face of Nature:

> Having had to encounter single-handed during his period of eclipse many physical dangers, he was well aware of the most dangerous element common to them all: of the crushing, paralyzing sense of human littleness, which is what really defeats a man struggling with natural forces, alone, far from the eyes of his fellows. (433)

Dr. Monygham, therefore, is aware of human littleness when faced with natural forces. However, this awareness regards Nature as something that confronts, rather than embraces, human beings, and therefore he has failed to learn to live in harmony with it like Mrs. Gould. He may be 'eminently fit to appreciate' (433) what Nostromo must have gone through in the darkness of the gulf but, ironically, he lacks the very thing that he admires in Mrs. Gould: the 'humanizing influence' (45) that derives from her sympathetic alertness to values. As a result, when he encounters Nostromo at the Custom House, he fails to respond to Nostromo's feelings, blinded by his conviction that he is the only person who can secure Mrs. Gould's safety.

Not only does he fail to appreciate Nostromo's courage in overcoming the sense of littleness in the gulf, but he crushes his self-esteem by telling him that he wished that Nostromo had surrendered the silver to Sotillo.

74   Y. OKUDA

Dr. Monygham believes that if Sotillo had been offered the silver, he would have absconded with the booty, which would have diminished the danger that the mine and, accordingly, Mrs. Gould was exposed to. Dr. Monygham commits himself to the safety of the mine, oblivious to his own insight into man's place in Nature, and shatters Nostromo's self-confidence so that Nostromo loses his power of decision and is easily persuaded by Dr. Monygham and Giorgio to ride to Barrios in Cayta to save the Europeans in Sulaco. The ride, though successful, takes 6 days which makes it impossible for him to return to Decoud on the Great Isabel 'in a night or two' (302) as he said he would, and consequently, after waiting for him another week, Decoud commits suicide. Jacque Berthoud maintains that '[t]his unexpected confrontation [between Dr. Monygham and Nostromo], developed over two chapters, can be regarded as the climax of the novel, for on it hangs the outcome of the Sulaco crisis and the fate of all the major characters' (122).

A Sign from Nature: Decoud

Forsaken by Nostromo, Decoud also experiences the 'crushing, paralysing sense of human littleness' on the Great Isabel, in the solitude surrounded by the gulf. The emotional basis of Decoud's view of his personal advantage lies in an incident which took place when he was a young man of twenty; it took the form of an emotional reaction against a threat posed by the young Antonia Avellanos to his view of his personal advantage, which was founded on the superiority of his intellect: 'On one occasion, as though she had lost all patience, she flew out at him about the aimlessness of his life, and the levity of his opinion [...]. This attack disconcerted him so greatly that he had faltered in his affection of amused superiority before that insignificant chit of a school-girl' (155). Antonia's attack disconcerts Decoud because he is intelligent enough to be vaguely aware that his own view of his personal advantage is based on an unwarranted sense of his intellectual superiority. He cannot help admiring her for shrewdly pointing out his defect, which also makes him feel that he cannot merit her admiration.

By the time he is thirty, this complex sense of admiration, mingled with a sense of inferiority, has developed into an illusory love for Antonia. During those 10 years, Decoud has studied law but otherwise he has only 'dabbled in literature,' vaguely hoping to become a poet (151), without entering any profession; and never having committed himself to a

4 NATURE, IDENTITY, AND EMOTIONS: *NOSTROMO* 75

profession, he never experiences a sustained emotional involvement which compels him to face up to the reality of his own emotions, and therefore remains emotionally immature. However, when he receives a letter from Don José Avellanos, written in Antonia's handwriting, appealing to him to accept the position of an executive member of the patriotic small-arms committee of Sulaco, he not only accepts it and manages to purchase a consignment, but decides to see the consignment delivered safely to Sulaco. His real motive is to see Antonia, as his sister acutely perceives (155), and to marry her so that he can get even with her over the threat that she posed to his identity 10 years earlier. In taking this action, however, Decoud unwittingly commits himself to a different cause from that which he had intended. It awakens in him 'the genuine impulses of his nature' (153), his love for his country, which gradually strengthens and becomes the emotional basis of his renewed view of personal advantage, replacing his love for Antonia. Actually, even before he leaves Europe, he surprises his sister by 'the earnestness and ability he displayed in carrying out his mission' (154), and when he arrives in Sulaco, never having contemplated his country with such commitment and knowledge before, he is 'moved in spite of himself by the note of passion and sorrow unknown on the more refined stage of European politics' (156). Nevertheless, in the course of his conversation with Antonia during the reception at the Casa Gould, he keeps on asserting that he is not a patriot, and even blames Antonia for keeping him in Sulaco and making him act like a patriot. It is on this occasion that Decoud defines the word 'conviction' to declare to Antonia that the emotive cause of his action is his love for her and not his love for his country. However, as Albert Guerard maintains, 'So far from believing in or caring about nothing, he has an ideal of lucidity and of intellectual honesty, he is very much in love, and he is [...] a patriot' (200). Decoud seems to have convinced himself that the only way that he can get even with Antonia over the humiliation that he experienced in his youth is by marrying her, but the fact is that he has already got even with her, because he has, unwittingly, become a true patriot in her eyes (478).

If Decoud had acknowledged his patriotism as the emotional basis of his renewed view of his personal advantage, he might have survived the ordeal on the Great Isabel. Decoud is acute enough intellectually to perceive how a person forms the view of his or her personal advantage; however, it is an intellectual, not an emotional understanding, and he is not strong enough to face up to his own feelings and recognize the true emotional basis of his view, which alone can spur him to practical action. Significantly, the last chance to take practical action that will enable him to survive presents itself to him not before but after he leaves the shore of the Great Isabel on a boat with the intention of committing suicide. For a whole week Decoud has been dreading the sleepless nights in which the silence seems to remain 'unbroken in the shape of a cord to which he hung with both hands' (499). The mental image suggests the precariousness of his life, as he is thought-bound, aware only of the melancholy thoughts in his mind, whereas action can only be taken with the body: 'In our activity alone do we find the sustaining illusion of an independent existence as against the whole scheme of things of which we form a helpless part. Decoud lost all belief in the reality of his action past and to come' (497). The last two words, 'to come,' suggest that at this juncture there is still a chance for him to survive by rowing back to the Great Isabel, but he forfeits the opportunity:

> When the gulf had grown dark, he ceased rowing and flung the sculls in. The hollow clatter they made in falling was the loudest noise he had ever heard in his life. It was a revelation. It seemed to recall him from far away. Actually the thought, 'Perhaps I may sleep to-night,' passed through his mind. But he did not believe it. (500)

Some critics have indicated that the cause of Decoud's death is his confirmed scepticism, and others have suggested that it is the oppressive solitude. He may well have been practically paralysed by his own disposition to analyse everything intellectually and regard any conviction as 'wrong-headedness' (200),[7] or he may have been deprived of the sense of living by the lack of any sign of life on the Great Isabel, shunned even by the sea-birds of the gulf (496). However, there was a sign from Nature, for the sound made by the sculls does not come from his mind but belongs to the natural world. No matter how mundane it may seem, what finally determines his fate is his failure to take action at the crucial moment in response to the sound of the sculls which awakens in him the vague hope and sets off the thought, 'Perhaps I may sleep to-night.' The thought, in contrast to his melancholy thoughts, was triggered by the real sound made by the falling sculls, and, as such, it suggests that in reality

---

[7] Paul B. Armstrong maintains that 'The despair of ideology [...] is for Conrad the ultimate inability of any conviction to withstand demystification' (156).

sleeplessness is also subject to changes, but he fails to embrace its significance.[8] Decoud creates an ironic situation for himself by failing to accept the impermanence of the world.

THE POWER OF NATURE: NOSTROMO

Nostromo's identity was once in harmony with the impermanence of Nature. Before the failure of the mission, his identity was based emotionally on his vanity or self-love sustained by 'the adulation of the common people and the confidence of his superiors' (193), and the practical basis was his innate ability to respond to the immediate circumstance from moment to moment, resourcefully and effectively, with his good eyes, steady hands, and judgement (276). In contrast to Decoud whose grasp of reality was essentially mental and intellectual, Nostomo's was physical and emotional. He declares, 'It concerns me to keep on being what I am: every day alike' (253), but his egoism is kept within bounds for, apart from the feelings of pleasure and satisfaction that he derives from people's adulation, he is forgetful of his own needs and feelings, and therefore he too can afford to be alert, attentive, and observant, like Emilia Gould. For instance, on one occasion he spots Ribiera in difficulties from the window of the office of the *Porvenir* and succeeds in rescuing him; and on another occasion when a 'ragged mozo' begs him for employment on the wharf, after 'looking down critically' at him, he '[shakes] his head without a word' (127). Before the failure of the mission of removing the silver, the view of his personal advantage was firmly and solely based on his vanity, stemming from the self-regard he had for his natural abilities, and therefore as long as his vanity was satisfied, he could act in harmony with Nature.

However, this view of his personal advantage alters as a result of the partial failure of his mission to remove the silver. When Nostromo becomes aware that the success or the failure of the mission does not depend on his innate ability—on his good eyes, steady hands, and judgement—, as it has on previous occasions, the emotional basis of his identity

---

[8] The episode is curiously reminiscent of a Zen story in which a monk called Shikan Kyogen, who was once proud of his book learning, attains enlightenment, not through intellectual learning, but by responding to the sound of a stone accidently hitting a bamboo shoot while he is sweeping the grounds. In contrast to Decoud, Kyogen responds positively to the manifestation of Nature.

is affected, and he loses the self-conviction that had given him the impetus to act spontaneously. Decoud is surprised when he notices on the lighter that Nostromo is growing 'nervously resentful,' and eventually he becomes convinced that Nostromo has changed: 'the usual characteristic quietness of the man was gone. It was not equal to the situation as he conceived it' (282). Having lost the self-conviction that he can judge a situation well and act accordingly, Nostromo is easily persuaded by Dr. Monygham after he leaves the Custom House. Nostromo forfeits the only chance of escaping from Dr. Monygham when, overcome with 'the weariness of irresolution,' he allows Dr. Monygham to overtake him by slowing down his pace (461). What, above all, demonstrates Nostromo's loss of good judgement is his infatuation for Giselle. He attaches himself to Giselle well aware that she is 'incapable of sustained emotion' (547). Giselle, on the other hand, attaches herself to Nostromo because she believes that he can take her away from the Great Isabel and thus deliver her from her sister's tyranny. She appeals to him out of her fear for her sister more often than out of her love for him: 'Giovanni, carry me off to-night, from my fear of Linda's eyes' (539). Such a love cannot possibly provide Nostromo with a firm emotional basis for a renewed view of his personal advantage.

The problem is that Nostromo has not only lost his former sense of identity but is unable to gain a new sense of identity because, like Decoud, he is not able to identify the real emotional basis of his renewed view of personal advantage—his resentment towards something or someone that has prevented him from displaying his innate abilities and achieving complete success in the mission. Even on his deathbed, he cannot identify what or who has betrayed him; he mutters, 'I die betrayed—betrayed by—' (559) but fails to finish the sentence. What or who could have betrayed him? Teresa Viola could not have betrayed him by her curse, because the curse makes him more resolute than irresolute: 'She died thinking I deprived her of Paradise, I suppose. It shall be the most desperate affair of my life' (268). Neither could the Europeans who gave him the mission have betrayed him, because they also stiffen his resolution: 'I am sent out with it into this darkness [...] as if it were the last lot of silver on earth to get bread for the hungry with. Ha! Ha! Well, I am going to make it the most famous and desperate affair of my life' (265). The answer, therefore, must be sought elsewhere. Because he cannot identify what or who has betrayed him, Nostromo clings to the treasure, mistaking the effect for the cause.

4 NATURE, IDENTITY, AND EMOTIONS: *NOSTROMO* 79

At this point I would like to return to the opening discussion on Nature. The emotional basis of Nostromo's renewed view of his personal advantage, the cause of his resentment, is not easy to identify; yet, it is foreshadowed in the opening chapter of the novel in the description of the characteristics of the Golfo Plácido. In Part 1, Chapter 1, I noted the peculiar characteristics of the gulf: the lack and caprice of its breeze. Part 2, Chapters 8 and 9 reintroduce this theme by the repeated references to the atmospheric conditions of the gulf. Nostromo was once a boatswain on a Genoese ship where he would have acquired a keen sensibility to atmospheric conditions. Even before he embarks on the lighter with Decoud, when he is talking to Dr. Monygham at Viola's house, Nostromo expresses his concern about the wind: 'Nostromo, glancing contemptuously at the doctor, lingered in the doorway rolling a cigarette, then struck a match and, after lighting it, held the burning piece of wood above his head till the flame nearly touched his fingers. "No wind!" he muttered to himself' (258–9). Once they are in the gulf, the wind keeps on failing and fanning up again until it completely dies out so that Nostromo is 'not even certain which way the lighter [is heading]' (263). The omniscient narrator says that 'the denser the darkness generally, the smarter were the puffs of wind [...]; but to-night the gulf [...] remained breathless' (265).

Ironically, the only character who is concerned about the atmospheric conditions of the gulf is the supposedly obtuse Captain Mitchell, a former seaman of long standing. Captain Mitchell recommended Nostromo in the first place as the only man for the task as 'a sailor' (320), indicating that he knew that the success of the task of removing the silver on the lighter would require the experience of a seaman. The chief engineer informs Monygham at Viola's house: 'By Captain Mitchell's reckoning— and he ought to know—it [the lighter] has been gone long enough now to be some three or four miles outside the harbour' (315–6). Captain Mitchell had reckoned that the lighter must be several miles outside the harbour because the night was so dark; he reminisces later that '[t]he night was excessively dark—the darkest I remember in my life' (271); and as generally in the gulf there was more wind when the darkness was thicker, he supposed that the lighter must have sailed a safe distance, a fact later confirmed by the omniscient narrator:

In this last conclusion Captain Mitchell was misled by the assumption drawn from his observation of the weather during his long vigil on the

> wharf. He thought that there had been much more wind than usual that night in the gulf; whereas, as a matter of fact, the reverse was the case. (339)

This unexpected atmospheric condition, the lack of breeze on the gulf despite its darkness, is the real cause of the failure of Nostromo's mission. Nostromo has been, so to speak, 'betrayed' by the Golfo Plácido but, unable to recognize this fact, he fails to grasp the true nature of his emotional crisis. The last scene of the gulf takes the reader back full circle to the opening scene of the novel suggestive of impermanence, yet 'overhung by a big white cloud shining like a mass of solid silver' (566); the simile 'like a mass of solid silver' evokes the illusionary sense of silver as incorruptible metal, but in fact it is made of 'big white cloud' (566) subject to change, thus adding an ironic effect to the illusion of Nostromo's genius dominating over the gulf, created by Linda's passionate cry: 'I shall never forget thee. Never!' (566). It may be said that of all the five main characters, Nostromo is depicted as the character most directly affected by Nature.

In *Nostromo*, the characters conceive their identity either in defiance of or in conformity with Nature, unaware of the fact that they themselves embody Nature. The essential feature of their emotional reaction and their choice of practical action may differ, but the fundamental basis of personal identity is the emotional reaction to the constant changes inherent in Nature, and therefore the principal factor that shapes the lives of the characters is the compulsive power of emotion. Bruce E. Johnson notes that 'it is easy to see how a great many of Conrad's characters are placed by their relation to nature, by the degree to which they accept, deny, distort, or are simply unaware of Nature' (124). Similarly, the readers are also placed in a position to reflect on their relation to Nature.[9] Some readers express strong pessimism towards Nature as it is presented in *Nostromo*: 'the fabric of life is manufactured by some devilish process the purpose and logic of which is profoundly anti-human' (Said 107). They apparently assume Nature to be something that exists in opposition to humans, ascribing human feelings to Nature and accusing it

---

[9] In an article entitled 'A Choice of Nightmares: The Ecology of *Heart of Darkness*', Jeffrey Mathes McCarthy explores 'Heart of Darkness' from the perspective of ecology and maintains that '*Heart of Darkness* is about repositioning human beings within a new understanding of nature' (620).

of hostility and cruelty. In contrast, there are readers who find consolation in regarding the impermanence of Nature as an inevitable aspect of ourselves. Galsworthy, for instance, appreciates Conrad's works in this sense and observes: 'He has the power of making his reader feel the inevitable oneness of all things that be, of breathing into him a sense of solace that he himself is part of a great unknown Unity' (Galsworthy in Watt: 1973: 89). In either case, *Nostromo* challenges both the characters and the readers to find their places in relation to Nature.

Nostromo explores how emotion is involved in forging personal identity through a group of characters in a setting of a city in a republic. In contrast, the setting of *The Secret Agent* is confined to just a section of a metropolis, so at first glance it may be difficult to make out that both novels address the theme of emotion and identity. While *Nostromo* foregrounds the problems that accompany the renewal of identity, *The Secret Agent* foregrounds those that accompany the preservation of identity.

CHAPTER 5

Surprise, Anger, and Obsessive Thought: *The Secret Agent*

[…] a cortège of dismal thoughts […] crowded urgently round him like a pack of hungry black hounds. (*The Secret Agent*)

The Secret Agent explores the emotional and mental lives of the characters in the framework of what the omniscient narrator calls 'this world of contradictions' (84). Begun as a short story provisionally entitled 'Verloc,' *The Secret Agent* first appeared in a serialized version in *Ridgway's: A Militant Weekly for God and Country* from 6 October to 15 December 1906. After considerable revision, it was published in book form by Methuen in London on 12 September 1907 and Harper's in New York a few days later. Conrad maintained that the intention of the novel had not been to consider anarchism, either politically or philosophically (*CL3*: 354),[1] but to tell the story of Winnie Verloc 'to its anarchistic end of utter desolation, madness and despair' ('Author's Note' xv). However, notwithstanding his claim, the criticism of *The Secret Agent*, which ranges widely from the analysis of social background to narrative irony, has tended to focus more on political rather than psychological issues, with a few exceptions,

---

[1] In a letter to John Galsworthy, 12 September 1906.

© The Author(s), under exclusive license to Springer Nature Switzerland AG 2024
Y. Okuda, *Emotions and Contingencies in Conrad's Fiction*, https://doi.org/10.1007/978-3-031-66723-7_5

83

84   Y. OKUDA

such as psychological analysis of the author or contemporary theories of degeneracy.[2]

In contrast to the more recent criticism, a significant number of contemporary reviews of the novel refers to the issue of the psychological analysis of the characters. For example, a reviewer for *The New York Times Saturday Review of Books*, 21 September 1907, praises Conrad for his analysis of 'the human creature, composite of conscious and unconscious impulses, obscurely motived in the roots of being and the tangle of desires and associations […]' (*CR2*: 407), whereas a reviewer for *The Nation*, 26 September 1907, complains that 'the events are so overlaid with description, analysis, and the study of the psychological side of the characters that the book is hard to read' (*CR2*: 412).

Besides the issue of the psychological analysis of the characters, contemporary reviewers pay attention to the issue of events or action in *The Secret Agent*. A reviewer for *The Dial*, 16 October 1907, after calling it 'a good story completely smothered by analysis,' expresses dissatisfaction by saying that 'a novel upon such a theme as this calls for action, and again action, and of this we get next to nothing' (*CR2*: 422–23),[3] whereas a reviewer for *Outlook* (London), 16 November 1907, maintains: 'The events he relates are not suggestive of pre-ordained destiny […]: they are just the logical results of given circumstances acting upon certain temperaments' (*CR2*: 398). He then concludes that '[t]he book is a masterpiece of elemental emotions' (*CR2*: 398). This comment on events being subject to emotions reminds us of Conrad's instruction to Edward Noble, quoted in the Introduction: 'you must treat events only as illustrative of human sensation—as the outward sign of inward feelings' (*CL1*: 252). The letter suggests that Conrad regarded events as things that happen by chance, which are created by the author with the intention of drawing out the characters' emotional reactions to them.[4]

---

[2] See Norman N. Holland's 'Style as Character: *The Secret Agent*' and Robert G. Jacob's 'Comrade Ossipon's Favorite Saint: Lombroso and Conrad.'

[3] In his letter to William Blackwood, dated 31 May 1902, Conrad maintains that his work is, 'in its essence […] nothing but action—action observed, felt and interpreted with an absolute truth to my sensations […]—action of human beings that will bleed to a prick, and are moving in a visible world' (*CL* 2: 418).

[4] In *Anatomy of Criticism*, Northrop Frye maintains: 'As tragedy moves over towards irony, the sense of inevitable event begins to fade out, and the sources of catastrophe come into view. In irony catastrophe is either arbitrary and meaningless, the impact of an

5 SURPRISE, ANGER, AND OBSESSIVE THOUGHT: ... 85

In addition to emotions and events, another issue that contemporary reviewers pay attention to is the thoughts and thought processes of the characters. A reviewer for *Country Life*, 21 September 1907, notes how '[i]n page after page [Conrad] discourses fluently about the ideas that were coursing through the brain' (*CR2*: 355), and a reviewer for *The Boston Evening Transcript*, 9 October 1907, protests that '[w]hen a novelist is thinking continuously of the thoughts of his characters, as Mr Conrad is, he is certain to produce a vague and incomprehensible effect [...]' (*CR2*: 419–20). However, according to Keith Oatley, 'Emotions are based on what we know, and they include thoughts, sometimes obsessive thoughts, about what has happened or what might happen next' (3); a writer can therefore convey an emotional aspect of a character through his thoughts.

IRONY AND THE WORLD OF CONTRADICTIONS

In contrast to the broader background of *Lord Jim*, which ranges from the Arabian Sea to Patusan, or that of *Nostromo*, which covers the whole of Sulaco and beyond, the background of *The Secret Agent* is somewhat narrow, for it is confined to a few square miles of London. In a city like London, it may seem that the characters 'would never be taken unawares, and never be called upon to grapple with fate' (*Lord Jim* 342), yet they are, because London in *The Secret Agent* is characterized by the same insecurity as Patusan and Sulaco. The narrator therefore says that '[t]rue wisdom' is 'not certain of anything in this world of contradictions' (84).[5]

Conrad's view of the universe is reminiscent of the Romantic and Modernist propensity towards ironic scepticism:

> At the heart of irony as conceived by most 19th century thinkers was a Romantic tendency to confront, rather than dismiss, the disorder, contingency and unintelligibility of the world. An ironic vision acknowledges that the world can be viewed from various irreconcilable perspectives, and rejects any foreclosure of the world's absurdity into some spurious unity.

---

unconscious (or, in the pathetic fallacy, malignant) world on conscious man, or the result of more or less definable social and psychological forces' (285).

[5] Booth says that '[t]he wise man will always be the one who knows that there are ironic limitations on every pretension to wisdom, no matter how profound he may become, no matter how careful his formulations' (274).

86   Y. OKUDA

[…]. Modernist irony is usually regarded as a development of Romantic irony, and entails a double posture: both a negation of prevailing values and institutions, and a helpless complicity with them. (Cuddon 2014: 372–73)

The narrator of *The Secret Agent* also seems to acknowledge that 'the world can be viewed from various irreconcilable perspectives' and manifests a denial of and complicity with prevailing values and institutions. Wayne Booth observes that in literature '[…] all truths can be undermined with irony of contrary truths *either* because the universe is essentially absurd and there is no such thing as coherent truth *or* because man's powers of knowing are inherently and incurable limited and partial' (267; emphasis original). This attitude, especially the latter, explains why the narrator of the novel adopts a pervasive ironical tone. Jacob Lothe maintains that:

[…] what we have in *The Secret Agent* is in a way a fictional presentation of a set of existential and ideological contradictions and unresolved problems […].
    As the presentation of textual revelation of these contradictions are intimately related to the novel's narrative method, the contradictions which the authorial narrator presents simultaneously suggest a partial reason for his need for distancing irony and a sceptical stance. (1989: 261)

The narrative method reveals that the authorial narrator of *The Secret Agent* adopts an ironic distance and a sceptical stance in order to cultivate a tolerant attitude in the reader toward 'existential and ideological contradictions and unresolved problems' in the novel. Booth maintains that, as readers, 'we should be able to accept, in novels, plays, and poems, the emotional power and interest of many views which we think untrue' (276).

    How then is the narrator's ironic stance reflected in the depiction of the psychological aspects of the main characters? Interestingly, Conrad not only depicts the dispositional emotionality of each character, but he also hints at the more general, underlying emotional tendencies that the characters share. David Prickett maintains:

Throughout *The Secret Agent* there is an emphasis upon the common subjective tendencies of the characters, however much their beliefs differ […]. They are all implicated within the conditions of the world represented in the novel, and it is futile to attempt to criticize them from an imaginary position outside of or beyond them. (Prickett in Simmons and Stape 2007: 54)

As Prickett points out, there is an interesting emphasis on 'the common subjective tendencies of the characters' in *The Secret Agent*, but the emphasis does not necessarily reflect the influence of the psychoanalytic theories of the period. Paul Kirschner maintains that '[a]ny influence of psycho-analytic theories on Conrad during his major phase (1894–1909) seems unlikely' (277).[6] In *The Secret Agent* Conrad introduces an original psychological pattern which he applies to each of the six main characters— Verloc, the Professor, Chief Inspector Heat, the Assistant Commissioner, Stevie, and Winnie Verloc. Edward Verrall Lucas points out that *The Secret Agent* is 'more of a portrait gallery than a story' (*CR2*: 352–53); the gallery exhibits the portraits of the main characters, each of which is what Conrad, in his letter to Hugh Clifford, 9 October 1899, calls 'a *picture* of a mental state' (*CL2*:201; emphasis original).

This chapter will examine the mental and emotional life that Conrad assigns to these six major characters in order to determine the common emotional sequence that they all follow, and to demonstrate that such a sequence is based on the narrator's view of 'this world of contradictions.' From the point of view of their emotional propensities as well as social position, it is possible to classify the six characters into three groups in the following order: first, Verloc and the Professor, second, Heat and the Assistant Commissioner, and third, Stevie and Winnie Verloc.

Indolence and Intransigence: Verloc and the Professor

The first two characters, Verloc and the Professor, are professed anarchists, no matter how unconventional they may be. Ostensibly the two characters are very different, as Verloc lives in self-indulgent ease and the Professor lives a life of self-imposed severity. However, they are similar in their unconscious defiance of the uncertainty inherent in the world, and

---

[6] Some affinity can be discerned, however, between Conrad's emphasis on the common subjective tendencies in *The Secret Agent* and the emphasis placed by a more recent psychological therapy. According to Keith Oatley, cognitive behavioral therapy, developed in the 1960s by an American psychiatrist Aaron T. Beck (1921–2021), also gives attention to events, emotions, and thoughts (53).

88   Y. OKUDA

in their readiness to go to any length in order to safeguard their self-image against that contingency.

Verloc's psychological temperament is characterized by indolence, a disposition to avoid any trouble and a love of ease. The word 'disposition' signifies 'the more or less enduring features of an organism that interact with current conditions (circumstances and events)' (Hogan 2018a: 179). The narrative begins by indicating Verloc's indolence through such observations as '[he] left his shop nominally in charge of his brother-in-law' (3) and 'his wife was in charge of his brother-in-law' (3). These sentences, together with such phrases as 'Mr. Verloc cared but little' (3) and 'his ostensible business' (3) are indicative of his indolent disposition, and the narrator impresses this fact on the reader throughout Chapter 1 with such graphic descriptions as: 'he had an air of having wallowed, fully dressed, all day on an unmade bed' (6). The overall impression of Verloc is that he is indolent both in temperament and in conduct. However, Verloc himself is totally unaware of his own disposition; his self-deception as to his domestic and professional life, and more importantly as to himself, is such that it verges on the absurd and the comical. He believes himself to be attractive enough as a husband to his wife to be 'loved for himself' (261), and competent enough as an anarchist, a police informer, and an *agent provocateur*.

Ironically, this reluctance to exert oneself and the lack of awareness of it is, far from being a rare phenomenon, something that a reader might recognize in himself, and even feel familiar with. Only, in Verloc's case, he '[embraces] indolence from an impulse' (12) and devotes himself to it with 'inert fanaticism,' in other words, he is unconsciously committed to the preservation of his own sense of security at the expense of everything else. Verloc wishes to preserve his sense of indolent security unchanged, just as Toodles wishes to preserve 'his social beliefs and personal feelings [...] unchanged through all the years allotted to him on this earth' (217). Therefore, as long as he can live in this state of illusory security, Verloc feels no scruples about making use of 'the vices, the follies, or the baser fears of mankind' (13), and is even ready to let others make use of himself, so his fellow anarchists make use of him as an orator, Chief Inspector Heat makes use of him as a police informer, Vladimir makes use of him as an *agent provocateur*, and Winnie makes use of him as the provider of Stevie's livelihood.

However, Vladimir's unexpected threat to dismiss him as an *agent provocateur* unless he initiates action and executes a bomb attack on

5 SURPRISE, ANGER, AND OBSESSIVE THOUGHT: ... 89

the Greenwich Observatory puts Verloc in a difficult position with his fellow anarchists and jeopardizes his status as a police informer. The unexpected proposal arouses an intense surprise in Verloc, which is immediately followed by frustrated anger. The first emotion, 'surprise,' is one of the six basic emotions,[7] and it is defined technically as a 'peculiar state of mind, usually of brief duration, caused by encountering unexpected events of all kinds' (Sander and Scherer 386). Verloc is so 'startled and alarmed' (26) by Vladimir's preposterous proposition that he seems to fall into 'a state of collapsed coma' (34); but this lasts only for a brief duration, and is soon replaced by another emotion, anger.

The word 'anger,' together with its adjectival form 'angry,' appears twenty-three times in *The Secret Agent*. In cognitive psychology, the emotion is defined as:

> [...] negatively valenced[8] emotion characterized by high arousal and is considered to be one of the basic emotions [...]. From a functional perspective, anger is assumed to be elicited by unwanted or harmful circumstances and to serve the purpose of mobilizing energy to remove or attack the cause of such circumstances. (Sander and Sharer 2009: 32)

As far as literature is concerned, Keith Oatley says that, after the love story, '[t]he second most common story worldwide is of anger' (Oatley in Sander and Scherer 242); this indicates that anger is the most common and intense emotion next to love, and it is closely related to the difficulties of living in a world of contradictions. According to Oatley, anger is also a kind of emotion which occurs rather suddenly: 'We feel suddenly happy [...]. Or we may feel anger at a slight. Such an emotion fills our consciousness' (2004: 3). For example, on his way to the Embassy, Verloc surveys the townscape of 'opulence and luxury' (12) with complacency, because, for him, it is a sign of the social security which he has served to maintain, and which, in its turn, guarantees his personal security. However, on his way back from the Embassy to his shop in Soho, he fails to take any notice of the same townscape, because the appearance of the townscape

---

[7] Basic emotions, identified by the American psychologist Paul Eckman, include anger, disgust, fear, enjoyment, sadness, and surprise. (Sander and Scherer 69).

[8] The term 'valence' is used 'to describe the positive or negative character of emotions, of components of the emotional response such as subjective feelings or behavioural responses, and of emotion-eliciting stimuli' (Sander and Scherer 401).

90   Y. OKUDA

as he had assumed it has been pierced by reality on account of Vladimir's threat, and he is now obsessed by 'a dream—an angry dream' (37). By the time he arrives home, the anger has set off an angry train of thought; what impresses Winnie and her mother at dinner that night is Verloc's taciturnity which is 'so obviously thoughtful' (39). The anger aroused by Vladimir has mobilized in Verloc's indolent mind an angry train of thought which lasts nearly to the end of the narrative: in Chapter 3, the sound of the word 'science' provokes anger in Verloc, conjuring up in his mind the mental vision of Vladimir; in Chapter 8, 'a cortege of dismal thoughts' follows him during his walk and '[crowds] urgently round him, like a pack of hungry black hounds' (177) when he returns home; and in Chapter 11, he is suddenly seized by a bizarre desire to cudgel everyone at the Embassy 'for half-an-hour' (244). In Verloc, Conrad is tracing an emotional sequence which proceeds from an unforeseen event that arouses surprise, and then anger, followed by obsessive angry thoughts.

Verloc's fear of the mental vision of Vladimir is a manifestation of his fear of the insecure world which poses a threat to his strong desire for indolent security:

> Mr Verloc felt the latent unfriendliness of all out of doors with a force approaching to positive bodily anguish. [...]. The prospect was as black as the window-pane against which he was leaning his forehead. And suddenly the face of Mr Vladimir, clean-shaved and witty, appeared [...]. (56–57)

The nature of the reactive emotions and thoughts set off by an unforeseen event depends entirely on the surprised person's habitual emotional state and the surrounding circumstances, and Verloc's habitual state of indolence at home has evoked feelings of desolation and fear towards the 'latent unfriendliness of all out of doors.' As the Assistant Commissioner suggests to Sir Ethelred in Chapter 10, another person might have felt and thought very differently from Verloc. (219) Nevertheless, Verloc's dispositional indolence in temperament and conduct is such that he does not even hesitate when it comes to making use of his mentally retarded brother-in-law to execute the bomb attack in place of himself; having 'gauged the depth of Stevie's fanaticism' (229), he contrives to inflame Stevie's anger and fear.

The second character, the Professor, is an independent anarchist whose disposition is marked by tenacious attachment to a fixed idea, the conviction that he was 'a moral agent' entrusted with the mission of destroying

5 SURPRISE, ANGER, AND OBSESSIVE THOUGHT: ...   91

public faith in the current legal institutions by physical destruction of what is. As the son of a self-righteous itinerant preacher, the Professor, in his youth, practiced the cult of worldly success founded on his 'exalted conviction of his merits' (75) and his expectation of rewards for '[h]is struggles, his privations, his hard work to raise himself in the social scale' (75). However, when, to his dismay, he discovered that his 'frenzied puritanism of ambition (81)' was thwarted by the legal system which seemed to neither recognize his merits nor reward his efforts, the rude awakening sets off resentful thoughts that, over the years, develop into a fixed idea. The narrator comments ironically that for the Professor '[t]o see it [the ambition] thwarted opened his eyes to the true nature of the world, whose morality was artificial, corrupt, and blasphemous'; he suggests that it demonstrated that 'the way of even the most justifiable revolutions is prepared by personal impulses disguised into creeds' (81). In fact, the Professor gives in to his impulse, because to his sense of justice 'the price exacted [loomed] up monstrously enormous, odious, oppressive, worrying, humiliating, extortionate, intolerable' (53); that is to say, the Professor 'had genius, but lacked the great social virtue of resignation' (75). On this point, the Professor differs from Verloc, who, according to the narrator's classification of revolutionary reformers, belongs to those who are temperamentally easily 'overcome by his dislike of all kinds of recognized labour' (53). Nevertheless, they both lack the resignation to accept 'this world of contradictions' (84).

The Professor's manner of resisting such a world, however, is more sophisticated than Verloc's; it is manifested in his deceptive appearance and devious arguments. He has a strong tendency to translate specific events into abstract ideas, which is suggestive of his covert desire to avoid facing awkward facts which threaten to break down his conviction. The Professor is ostensibly unemotional, incurious, and self-confident. The words 'self-confident' and 'self-confidence' are used several times to describe his demeanor in such phrases as 'the supremely self-confident bearing of the individual,' (62) 'a look of staring self-confidence' (64), and 'his dispassionate self-confident manner' (72), yet these phrases refer only to his 'bearing,' 'look,' and 'manner' and they do not refer to the marks of his character. He looks unemotional because he has acquired the habit of repressing emotions and awkward thoughts so as to put aside his moral scruples; this is why, when arguing back to Ossipon, he repeatedly uses such strong words as 'never' and 'perfect(ly).' (64, 65, 66, 69)

However, by repressing his emotions and silencing his scruples so that he can remain attached to his fixed idea and stave off any misgivings, the Professor has, in fact, made himself vulnerable to his deep-seated fear of the reality he ignores: 'The resisting power of numbers, the unattackable stolidity of a great multitude, was the haunting fear of his sinister loneliness' (95). Such a fear is, in fact, not based on reality, but on the Professor's groundless assumption that he has been entrusted with the mission to inspire fear in the mass of mankind so as to destroy their faith in the current legal system. The idea is devoid of substance, and exists only in the Professor's mind, which, like the 'extremely large cupboard' with 'a heavy padlock' in his single back room (62), shuts out any reality which may pose a threat to his idea of himself as a moral agent. He therefore remains '[standing] still in a monstrous illusion of final certitude attained in morals, intellect and conscience' ('The Censor of Plays' 76); in other words, he has locked himself up in his own mind. When he goes out, the Professor always holds a rubber ball in his right hand, which is connected by a tube to actuate the detonator he carries inside a flask in his pocket. He says that he carries it so that he can destroy himself and 'everything within sixty yards' (66), if the police attempt to arrest him. However, its real purpose is to safeguard the fixed idea on which his sense of identity is grounded. The detonator therefore possesses the same significance as the dynamite does for Charles Gould in *Nostromo*.

Verloc and the Professor go through the same emotional sequence which proceeds from surprise to anger or resentment, and then to obsessive thought or a fixed idea, even though their thoughts differ in detail. They both fail to accept the fact that personal assumptions may be contradicted by an impersonal and impermanent world, and attempt to preserve their assumed identity out of a self-seeking impulse, not altruistic desire. In this sense, Verloc and the Professor differ from Charles Gould, who acts in the belief that he is rectifying the injustice suffered by his father, and Dr. Monygham, who acts in the belief that he is securing the safety of Mrs. Gould.

Security and Insecurity: Heat and the Assistant Commissioner

Chief Inspector Heat and the Assistant Commissioner are both members of the police force. Chief Inspector Heat is attached to his profession, because he depends heavily on it for his sense of security, whereas the

Assistant Commissioner, who is aware of the illusory nature of security, customarily lives by his sense of insecurity. However, ironically, the Assistant Commissioner as well as Heat are driven to act out of self-interest when they become involved with the bomb affair.

Chief Inspector Heat is content with the professional position he is in, as it enables him to make the most of his talents: he is endowed with the 'trained faculties of an excellent investigator' (88) and is respected for '[h]is bodily vigour, his cool inflexible manner, his courage and his fairness' (92), which makes him 'conscious of being the great expert of his department' (84) and even 'of having an authorized mission on this earth and the moral support of his kind' (96). However, at the same time, it makes him proudly attached to his profession, and to display a tendency to assume that circumstances will always be favourable to him.

'Attachment' is 'an enduring disposition towards attachment bonds, prominently including a fundamental feeling of security or insecurity in such bonds' (Hogan 2018a: 177). Chief Inspector Heat is attached to his professional position, because it suits him temperamentally and therefore it instils a sense of security in him. However, as mentioned in Chapter 2, a sense of security is 'a bad counsellor' (*The Mirror of the Sea* 30), because it encourages holding on to assumptions which may be contradicted in this world. During the interview with the Assistant Commissioner in his private room, Chief Inspector Heat's sense of security is unexpectedly threatened when the Assistant Commissioner asks him point-blank, 'Now what is it you've got up your sleeve?' (115). Heat stares at him, but 'behind that professional and stony fixity there was some surprise too' (115), and then he begins to speak 'in a procrastinating manner, like a man taken unawares by a new and unexpected experience' (116).

In describing Heat's surprise and angry thoughts, the narrator adopts the simile of a tightrope artist betrayed by the manager of the hall who suddenly starts to shake the rope in the middle of a performance, and goes on to say: 'Indignation, the sense of moral insecurity engendered by such a treacherous proceeding joined to the immediate apprehension of a broken neck, would, in the colloquial phrase, put him in a state' (116). Chief Inspector Heat, with his 'consciousness of universal support in his general activity,' must have assumed that the Assistant Commissioner, who is, so to speak, in the position of a 'manager,' would never interrupt his performance by asking such a point-blank question. In the case of Chief Inspector Heat, the surprise evoked by the Assistant Commissioner's unforeseen demand takes the usual course and is soon replaced by indignation, followed by a train of thought:

> The indignation of a betrayed tight-rope performer was strong within him [...]. To have his performance spoiled was more than enough to account for the glow of honest indignation. And as thought is no respecter of person, the thought of Chief Inspector Heat took a threatening and prophetic shape. 'You, my boy,' he said to himself, keeping his round and habitually roving eyes fastened upon the Assistant Commissioner's face – 'you, my boy, you don't know your place, and your place won't know you very long either, I bet.' (124)

This thought testifies to the intensity of his indignation, and yet when the Assistant Commissioner repeats the demand to submit his discovery, Chief Inspector Heat yields to the demand unresistingly. This is because his unexpressed indignant thought addressed to the Assistant Commissioner is 'immediately followed' by the reflection that if he refuses obstinately to submit his discovery, he may also risk losing his job, in which case he will lose the sense of security that he derives from his profession. Chief Inspector Heat may have been 'not very wise—at least not truly so' (84), but just before the interview, he is exposed to the sight of the dismembered body of Stevie, and beset by 'sympathy, which is a form of fear' (88) that even enables him to rise above 'the vulgar conception of time' (88) behind the assumption that if the death was instantaneous, the agony also must have been instantaneous. He also experiences the 'gratuitous and accidental success' of picking up, of all things, the velvet collar with the address of the man sewn on it. (90) On the whole, the complexion of the case 'forced upon him the general idea of the absurdity of things human' (91), and therefore it may well have strengthened his habitually weak sense of insecurity.

The Assistant Commissioner, on the other hand, is not dependent on his profession for his sense of security as, according to the narrator, his nature is 'one that was not easily accessible to illusions (99)': 'His thought seemed to rest poised on a word, as though words had been the stepping-stones for his intellect picking its way across the waters of error' (98). The simile of picking one's way across the waters of error refers to the characteristics of a thought process and not to an attitude towards life. Nevertheless, it is reminiscent of the following passage in *Lord Jim*, quoted earlier in Chapter 2: '[…] we are only on sufferance here and got to pick our way in cross lights, watching every precious minute and every irremediable step, trusting we shall manage yet to go out decently in the end […]' (35). The cautiousness of the Assistant Commissioner's thought process suggests that he is 'not certain of anything in this world of contradictions' (84).

The Assistant Commissioner has 'an adventurous disposition' (113) for, unlike Verloc, who is intimidated by the view of London from his bedroom window, the Assistant Commissioner is not intimidated by the view from his office window. What he finds 'trying to his sensitive liver' (100) in the view from the window is the English weather, and if possible he would have much preferred to work in a tropical colony. The view from his office window is not only disagreeable to his liver, but has the effect of '[augmenting] his general mistrust of men's motives and the efficiency of their organisation' (100).

> It was a very trying day, choked in raw fog to begin with, and now drowned in cold rain. The flickering, blurred flames of gas-lamps seemed to be dissolving in a watery atmosphere. And the lofty pretensions of a mankind oppressed by the miserable indignities of the weather appeared as a colossal and hopeless vanity deserving of scorn, wonder, and compassion. (100)

The sight of the miserable weather oppresses him, but at the same time it also makes him more lenient and sympathetic to the 'lofty pretensions of a mankind,' for example, to the pretentions of Chief Inspector Heat, for he later speaks of him to Sir Ethelred with empathetic insight: '[…] he is an old departmental hand. They have their own morality. My line of inquiry would appear to him an awful perversion of duty' (142). Hogan maintains:

> In the case of anger and fear, the most obvious inhibitions come from empathy. […]. It alters the dynamics of our emotion systems by aligning them with the emotions of someone else […]. As such, it tends to inhibit our tendencies toward punitive or preventive violence […]. (2011: 239)

When he feels oppressed by the view of the miserable weather from the window, the Assistant Commissioner does not turn away from the window, but instead, '[h]e [ceases] to think completely for a time' and '[t]hat utter stillness of his brain lasted about three seconds' (100); that is to say, he shakes off the oppressive thought of the weather and reorients his thoughts into another channel, so that after three seconds, his mind refreshed by the temporary cessation of thought, we find him addressing Heat with a new question. This ability to switch from a negative to a positive train of thought demonstrates the Assistant Commissioner's resilience to the contradictions inherent in life.

The Assistant Commissioner is 'not easily accessible to illusions'; however, he has one sore spot, which is his marital relationship with his wife who is 'a woman devoured by all sorts of small selfishnesses, small envies, small jealousies' (112). He appears to experience some difficulty in retaining a harmonious relationship with his wife, and therefore he relies on the beneficial influence that his wife's friend and the patroness of Michaelis exercises on her. The patroness is infatuated with Michaelis, and therefore when the Assistant Commissioner hears Chief Inspector Heat abruptly mention Michaelis as a possible suspect in the bomb explosion, he experiences a surprise 'resembling a physical shock' (103), and suddenly '[becomes] alarmed at the convict Michaelis's possible fate' (112). Even though he is aware that, as an officer of the police force, he should not allow himself to be affected by his own personal prejudices, he cannot overcome this alarm because, if Michaelis is arrested, his patroness may break off her friendship with him, and then the precarious peace of his conjugal life will be affected. This alarm is soon replaced by 'unreasonable resentment' (115) when he begins to suspect Heat of conspiring to arrest Michaelis in order to avoid the arrest of Verloc, because Verloc is indispensable to him as a police informer; the 'unreasonable resentment' reflects also the frustration of the Assistant Commissioner at being forced in such a circumstance to depend on his subordinates, such as Heat, instead of acting on his own initiative. The Assistant Commissioner may not usually be accessible to illusions, but on this occasion he is seized by the illusion that preserving the friendship with the patroness by preventing Michaelis's arrest will assure the future peace of his conjugal life.

The strength of this illusion becomes irresistible when its fascination is augmented by the temptation introduced by the possibility of his own direct intervention in the affair. This is because, if he were to intervene, it could offer him the longed-for opportunity to fulfill his strong desire to 'exercise his considerable gifts for the detection of incriminating truth' (117), and to satisfy the instinct of 'a born detective' (117). On this occasion, the Assistant Commissioner gives in to the illusion, which, if temporarily, suspends his strong sense of insecurity and allows him to act out the role of an undercover police agent. By the end of the day, he feels he has had 'a very full evening' (228), because he has succeeded in preventing Heat from arresting Michaelis by drawing out a confession from Verloc that he was involved in the bomb affair.

In spite of their difference of world view, the two officers go through the same emotional sequence of surprise, followed by anger and then angry thought; and ironically, they seem to exchange places: while Heat behaves sceptically, the Assistant Commissioner behaves with self-assurance; that is to say, while Heat seems to have learnt to think 'as though words had been the stepping-stones for his intellect picking its way across the waters of error' (98), the Assistant Commissioner seems to have learnt to behave like a tight-rope performer who performs as if he places full confidence in his manager.

SELFLESSNESS AND SELFISHNESS: STEVIE AND WINNIE

Stevie and Winnie Verloc are siblings and have always lived under the same roof. They resemble each other in their emotional and thinking habits, perhaps because they share the memory of domestic violence and carry its trauma. However, they differ considerably in their exposure to the stern realities of life; while Stevie is constantly exposed to the severities of life, Winnie hides herself behind her façade of indifference. This becomes apparent particularly after Chapter 8.

Structurally, Chapter 8 takes the narrative back to the end of Chapter 3 through a brief description of Stevie and Winnie's mother, who, like the Assistant Commissioner, is not easily accessible to illusions: she '[reflects] stoically that everything decays, wears out, in this world' (161), and, therefore, 'in considering the conditions of her daughter's married state, she [rejects] firmly all flattering illusions' (162) and moves out of her son-in-law's house to an almshouse, so that she can entrust Stevie's future to the Verlocs more securely. Her weak point may be that in doing so she gives way to the illusion that Stevie will always be safe if he stays with the Verlocs, just because her son-in-law inspires her 'with a sense of absolute safety' (8) and her daughter shows 'fondness for her delicate brother' (8).

The courageous attitude of the mother in thinking things out, even at the expense of her own emotional pain, is inherited by her son, not her daughter. Stevie is mentally retarded, but he has the ability to think; only 'his thoughts [lack] clearness and precision' (171), so he tends to lose the thread of a train of thought and to confuse disparate ideas. He is literate, but he cannot use words skillfully enough, so he '[mutters] half words, and even words that would have been whole if they had not been made up of halves that did not belong to each other' (171). For Stevie, thinking entails '[fitting] all the words he could remember to his sentiments in order to get some sort of corresponding idea' (171): the sentiments come first, then the idea which corresponds to them. He relies more on his sentiments than on his ideas, because while his thoughts lack clearness and precision, his feelings are more complete and profound. For instance, when Winnie observes, 'This isn't a very good horse' and then just looks away (157), Stevie senses the physical pain of the infirm horse and protests, 'Don't whip' (157); while Winnie judges the horse by its value as a cab horse, Stevie views it as a fellow sentient creature like himself. Then when he realizes that it is no use protesting, he climbs down from the cab on the spur of the moment to lighten the weight of it for the infirm horse. Generally, Stevie is 'wise in knowing his own powerlessness,' but on this occasion he climbs down from the cab, well aware of his power to take effective action: 'No physical impossibility stood in the way of his whim. Stevie could have managed easily to keep pace with the infirm, dancing horse without getting out of breath' (158). Nevertheless, as Stevie has a 'fundamentally docile disposition' (158), he obediently climbs back on the box when Winnie rebukes him; and his 'face of despair' (158) expresses the frustration he feels in his failure to exercise his power as a boy already in his adolescence.

Stevie's disposition is also marked by his morbid fear of pain, the traumatic effect of domestic violence, which is often accompanied by righteous indignation. When the office-boys work upon his feelings by abruptly telling him tales of injustice and oppression, he gives vent to his indignation by letting off fireworks, which figuratively signifies 'an outburst of anger' (*OED*); incidentally, as the typical shape of the fireworks displayed in the sky is circular, it reminds us of the circles which he draws, perhaps to give vent to his minor frustrations. Again, when he hears Karl Yundt and Michaelis mention the sizzled human skin, he is so shocked at first that he temporarily becomes motionless 'as if rooted suddenly to the spot by his morbid horror and dread of physical pain' but then '[h]is scared eyes [blaze] with indignation' (49). The indignation develops into an angry train of thought, so that he is still 'gesticulating and murmuring' (55) over the matter when Verloc happens to catch sight of him in the kitchen long after the visitors have left; Stevie is '[prowling] round the table like an excited animal in a cage' (55), just as we all tend to walk around a room when we are wrapped in thought. Likewise Stevie, according to Winnie, sometimes 'gets a red face' when he reads the newspapers in the window; she says that once when he had read a story about a cruel German soldier in an anarchist weekly presumably edited by Ossipon, he was holding a carving knife and 'shouting and stamping and sobbing' (60). Stevie's anger is almost always caused by his consideration for not himself but for others, such as the infirm cab horse, Mrs. Neele's starving children, or the socially oppressed 'poor people.'

Ironically, Stevie, who 'can't stand the notion of any cruelty,' tends to grow pitiless when he hears of cruel incidents: 'The tenderness of his universal charity had two phases as indissolubly joined and connected as the reverse and obverse sides of a medal. The anguish of immoderate compassion was succeeded by the pain of an innocent but pitiless rage' (169). Stevie may be able to feel 'with greater completeness and some profundity' (171), but he cannot 'restrain his passions' (169), and therefore his 'immoderate compassion' is often succeeded by 'an innocent but pitiless rage.' This tendency is most manifest in the scene in which Stevie is taken aback by the definition that Winnie incautiously gives him of the police. Stevie, unlike his sister whose safeguard in life is 'distant and uninquiring acceptance of facts' (153), possesses sufficient curiosity and courage to question the unpleasant facts of life, and therefore, when Winnie tells him that the police are not there to help the poor, he presses her for an explanation: '[…] he wished to go to the bottom of the matter. He carried on his inquiry by means of an angry challenge. "What are they for then, Winn? What are they for? Tell me"' (173). When she tells him that the police are there 'so that them as have nothing shouldn't take anything away from them who have' (173), Stevie is taken by surprise, and then becomes angry: 'He had been always easily impressed by speeches. He was impressed and startled now, and his intelligence was very alert' (173). His anger serves to start off a train of thought and he eventually manages to fit his sentiments to a corresponding idea by fitting the words 'bad' and 'poor' into a logical phrase, 'Bad world for poor people'(171); it indicates that his intellectual understanding has improved considerably, but at the same time it has aggravated his anger, and as a result he grows pitiless:

Directly he had expressed that thought he became aware that it was familiar to him already in all its consequences. This circumstance strengthened his conviction immensely, but also augmented his indignation. Somebody, he felt, ought to be punished for it – punished with great severity. Being no sceptic, but a moral creature, he was in a manner at the mercy of his righteous passion. (171–72).

According to Hogan, 'Anger-based moral orientations tend to be highly punitive and oriented toward violence,' and, moreover, '[t]he tendencies are enhanced when the fear system is activated as well' (2011:238). Stevie becomes pitiless and grows more punitive, because his thought has been evoked by anger, accompanied by strong fear.

When Verloc decides to make use of Stevie in the attempted bomb outrage, he takes advantage of Stevie's urge to punitive action as a result of righteous indignation: 'Though not much of a psychologist, Mr Verloc had gauged the depth of Stevie's fanaticism' (229). Even Winnie notices the change that has come over Stevie and becomes concerned when she sees him muttering to himself in corners 'in a threatening tone' (187), clenching his fists 'without apparent cause' (187), and 'scowling at the wall instead of drawing circles as he used to do' (187); his behaviour suggests that Stevie, like Verloc, has become obsessed with his angry thoughts and is determined to deal out a punishment 'with great severity' on whoever is responsible for the '[b]ad world for poor people.'

Stevie, though mentally retarded, goes through the same emotional sequence of surprise, anger, and resentful thoughts as that of the other characters. However, there is one characteristic which distinguishes him from the rest: Stevie never exploits others. In contrast, Verloc takes advantage of Stevie in the attempted bomb outrage, the Professor is ready to sacrifice any number of people to carry out his mission, Chief Inspector Heat is willing to make use of Verloc as a police informer, the Assistant Commissioner does not mind imposing on the friendship of Michaelis' patroness to preserve his marital serenity, and Winnie Verloc makes use of Verloc to secure Stevie's livelihood.

Exploiting others, that is to say, making use of a person unfairly so as to benefit oneself requires having a clear understanding of the situation and planning a line of action. Stevie's thoughts, however, lack 'clearness and precision,' and therefore he is not good at making assumptions based on facts or even remembering them long enough, unless he is incited to do so by another person. All the other characters make assumptions and therefore they live in constant danger of their assumptions being challenged in the world of contradictions. For instance, Verloc is afraid of

5 SURPRISE, ANGER, AND OBSESSIVE THOUGHT: ... **101**

losing his job as an *agent provocateur*, the Professor is fearful of failing in his mission, Heat is apprehensive about losing his occupation as a police officer, the Assistant Commissioner is afraid of losing the precarious peace of his conjugal life, and Winnie Verloc is terrified by the prospect of being hanged on the gallows. Stevie, on the other hand, is not afraid of what may happen, although what is happening before his eyes may arouse fear in him at any moment. He is constantly exposed to whatever may impinge on his emotions, because he has no assumptions or attachments strong enough to shield him emotionally from the stern realities of life; moreover, ironically, because he is mentally retarded, he has to rely more on his feelings than on his intellect to grasp what is going on. However, looked at from a different point of view, it may be said that Stevie, because he is intellectually disadvantaged, is able to live with a constant sense of insecurity in the world of contradictions, responding wholeheartedly to everything he encounters.

Stevie's sister, Winnie Verloc, also goes through the same emotional sequence as the rest of the characters we have examined. In his 'Author's Note' to *The Secret Agent*, Conrad refers twice to Winnie Verloc, once to her 'maternal passion' and 'the days of her childhood' (xii), and once to her story's 'anarchistic end of utter desolation, madness and despair' (xv), which suggest that Winnie Verloc's potentially reckless and desperate emotional life plays an important role in the narrative. Her disposition is first indicated in Chapter 1: she is 'in charge of' her brother, Stevie, who is 'an object of quasi-maternal affection' (8) for her; that is to say, she is in control of her brother and apparently holds motherly feelings towards him. Winnie may be called maternal because she has taken it on herself to protect her brother by exercising close control over him; however, she shows very little motherly care or attentiveness for Stevie, as can be observed in the following scene which takes place just before dinner on the day Verloc visits the Embassy:

> An hour or more later she took the green baize apron off her brother Stevie, and instructed him to wash his hands and face in the peremptory tone she had used in that connection for fifteen years or so [...]. She spared presently a glance away from her dishing-up for the inspection of that face and those hands which Stevie, approaching the kitchen-table, offered for her approval with an air of self-assurance hiding a perpetual residue of anxiety. (38)

She orders Stevie to wash his hands and face in a 'peremptory tone,' inspects them and offers her 'approval,' but fails to notice his underlying 'perpetual residue of anxiety.'

Likewise, Winnie fails to notice the two phases of Stevie's emotionality under the surface of excitement:

> The tenderness of his universal charity had two phases as indissolubly joined and connected as the reverse and obverse sides of a medal. The anguish of immoderate compassion was succeeded by the pain of an innocent but pitiless rage. Those two states expressing themselves outwardly by the same signs of futile bodily agitation, his sister Winnie soothed his excitement without ever fathoming its twofold character. Mrs Verloc wasted no portion of this transient life in seeking for fundamental information. (169)

The cause of Winnie Verloc's inattention towards her brother's emotional expressions is complex and far-reaching. Her 'quasi-maternal affection' is rooted in the 'protecting compassion' engendered by the domestic violence in which she had to protect Stevie from her father's blows 'often with her own head' (242); her father, 'wounded in his paternal pride,' had declared himself 'obviously accursed since one of his kids was a "slobbering idjut and the other a wicked she-devil"' (242). That is to say, the domestic violence has left a trauma not only on Stevie, who was affected directly, but also on Winnie, who was involved closely in it and therefore affected indirectly. In addition to the domestic violence that she had witnessed and experienced, the miseries she has suffered since, the drudgery at the boarding house and the disappointment of a love affair, seem to have made her fearful of facing up to reality of the moment.

Compared with some other traumatized women in Conrad's novels, such as Flora de Barral in *Chance* and Arlette in *The Rover*, Winnie is desolate, because she has neither a sympathetic friend nor a solicitous lover to watch over her. As a result, she has conceived a fixed idea which the narrator proclaims to be a philosophy that 'consisted in not taking notice of the inside of facts' (154). In other words, she has acquired an obstinate habit of making use of her position as a protector of Stevie as an excuse for consciously disregarding the harsh realities of life. Her attitude marked by 'distant and uninquiring acceptance of facts' (153) functions as the 'force and her safeguard in life' (153). Winnie is '[s]teady-eyed like her husband' (5), because she too is habitually on guard against an unexpected event which may affect her false security and threaten her mental indolence.

For nearly 15 years, Winnie's philosophy has guarded her from the awkward and unexpected events that are bound to happen in the world of contradictions; however, it has also made her emotionally vulnerable to unforeseen events, should they happen, and such an event does happen, with a vengeance, when Chief Inspector Heat unexpectedly informs her of the death of her brother. As the intensity of a surprise depends on the circumstances of the receiver, in Winnie's case the cumulative effect of her philosophy, her emotional vulnerability, and the impact of the sudden loss of her brother who has been her safeguard in life must have been devastating. The surprise quickly turns into anger as she sits at the counter, even before Chief Inspector Heat has left the shop: 'The perfect immobility of her pose expressed the agitation of rage and despair, all the potential violence of tragic passions [...]' (212).

However, Winnie does not act violently immediately; she goes through a variety of thoughts, which are, according to the narrator, more like 'visions' than 'words,' when even her mentally retarded brother thinks in 'half words' (171):

> The exigencies of Mrs Verloc's temperament, which, when stripped of its philosophical reserve, was maternal and violent, forced her to roll a series of thoughts in her motionless head. These thoughts were rather imagined than expressed. Mrs Verloc was a woman of singularly few words, either for public or private use. With the rage and dismay of a betrayed woman, she reviewed the tenor of her life in visions concerned mostly with Stevie's difficult existence from its earliest days. (241)

Winnie, who is unused to using words 'either for public or private use,' that is to say, in either speech or thought, sees 'in visions' the scenes of domestic violence, the drudgery at the boarding house, the frustrated love affair, 'the visions of 7 years' security for Stevie,' meaning her married life with Verloc, down to 'the vision of her husband and poor Stevie walking up Brett Street side by side away from the shop,' when she had been so deceived that she had even thought that they '[m]ight have been father and son' (244).

This 'supreme illusion of her life' has the effect of occupying her mind with a 'paralysing atrocity of the thought.' As Winnie is so used to thinking in terms of visions rather than words, the vision of the two walking away is translated, not into a logical thought, but into a simplistic idea which torments her: 'This man took the boy away to murder him. He took the boy away from his home to murder him. He took the boy away from me to murder him!' (246): 'Mrs Verloc's whole being was racked by that inconclusive and maddening thought. [...]. The protection she had extended over her brother had been in its origin of a fierce and indignant complexion' (246). She becomes more and more obsessed by the idea till she is unable to think of anything else:

> Mrs Verloc's mental condition had the merit of simplicity; but it was not sound. It was governed too much by a fixed idea. Every nook and cranny of her brain was filled with the thought that [...] the man whom she had trusted, took the boy away to kill him! (249)

The narrator asks, 'What could words do to her for good or evil in the face of the fixed idea?' (250).

Nevertheless, at this point, Winnie is still not ready yet to kill her husband, as her thought process has not been completed. Just as Stevie had to struggle to fit his half words into a sentence, Winnie also has to struggle to incorporate the visions into her thought process. Verloc's words, 'Lie low for a bit' (250) have, at first, the effect of evoking in Winnie the habitual question, 'And what of Stevie?' but when he goes on to tell her, 'I can't let you go out, old girl' (255), the declaration forces her thoughts into another channel:

> Mrs Verloc's mind got hold of that declaration with morbid tenacity. The man who had taken Stevie out from under her very eyes to murder him in a locality *whose name was at the moment not present to her memory* would not allow her to go out. (255–56, emphasis added).

Just as Stevie's indignation develops into an urge to punish the offender when he manages to complete his thought, 'Bad world for poor people,' Winnie's urge to murder her husband is unleashed when her vision is completed: 'Greenwich Park. A park! That's where the boy was killed. A park—smashed branches, torn leaves, gravel, bits of brotherly flesh and bone, all spouting up together in the manner of a firework. She remembered now what she had heard, and she remembered it pictorially' (260). She manages to complete her thought consisting of visions by restoring the missing information on the location of her brother's death. It is then

5 SURPRISE, ANGER, AND OBSESSIVE THOUGHT: ... 105

that she manifests a 'subtle change on her features, in the stare of her eyes, giving her a new and startling expression' and 'her wits, no longer disconnected, were working under the control of her will' (261), ready to stab her husband: 'the resemblance of her face with that of her brother grew at every step, even to the droop of the lower lip, even to the slight divergence of the eyes' (262). The 'resemblance of her face with that of her brother' (262) is a sign of the resemblance of her thought process with that of her brother; yet in contrast to Stevie's thought, which may be simple but logical, her characteristic reasoning has 'all the force of insane logic' (256), as her thoughts are reckless and anarchistic.

After she kills her husband, Winnie is compelled to look into the depths of the immediate reality for the first time; and the first thing which she perceives is the sound then the sight of the blood trickling down from her husband's wound, reminding her that it is herself who committed the murder. Characteristically, she becomes haunted by a vision: 'She saw there an object. That object was the gallows' (267); and then becomes obsessed by the hackneyed journalistic phrase: 'The drop given was fourteen feet' (268). This does not suggest that she becomes capable of thinking rationally, for Conrad says, 'The printed page of the Press makes a sort of still uproar, taking from men both the power to reflect and the faculty of genuine feeling [...]' (*Notes on Life and Letters* 90); it suggests, rather, that she becomes obsessed with the monotonous phrase because it elaborates her vision of the gallows; she is again governed by a fixed idea. Unfortunately, the first (and the last) acquaintance whom she chances to communicate with after she kills her husband is Ossipon, whose blind acceptance of the ideas of scientists, such as Lombroso, has deprived him also of his ability to observe what Conrad calls '[d]irect vision of the fact' or feel 'genuine emotion' (*Notes on Life and Letters* 84); and therefore he is also fixated by a cliched journalistic sentence in the newspaper reporting the incomprehensible circumstances of Winnie's disappearance from the deck of a cross-Channel boat and presumed suicide: '*An impenetrable mystery seems destined to hang for ever over this act of madness or despair*' (307, emphasis original). In conclusion, as Conrad indicates at the end of the 'Author's Note,' Winnie Verloc is driven to her death friendless, obsessed by the vision of the gallows and, unable to shut the vision out of her mind, she desperately takes her own life; thus Conrad succeeds in telling Winnie Verloc's story 'to its anarchistic end of utter desolation, madness and despair.'

Stevie may be mentally retarded, but he is able to think verbally and logically, at least to a certain extent, and responds spontaneously to what is taking place before his eyes. In contrast, Winnie is not mentally retarded, but she thinks in terms of visions rather than words, and responds more to the fixed illusionary vision in her mind than what is actually taking place in front of her. However, in spite of these differences, both Stevie and Winnie share with other characters the propensities to follow the emotional sequence of surprise, anger, and obsessive thought, when their assumptions are contradicted by the world.

Part II on *Nostromo* and *The Secret Agent* examined the common emotional tendencies manifested by the characters when their sense of identity was threatened by contingencies. The next part looks at the emotions of the protagonists in 'The Duel' and 'The Secret Sharer' through the entire process of their emotional maturation.

PART III

Maturing in Adversity

CHAPTER 6

A 'Pilgrimage of Emotions': 'The Duel'

> It's extraordinary how in one way or another this man has managed
> to fasten himself on my deeper feelings. ('The Duel')

Part III focuses on the psychological process that a protagonist undergoes in the course of an intense one-to-one engagement with another character. Chapter 6 on 'The Duel' traces D'Hubert's shifting emotions, of which he is seldom aware, and analyses how his opponent's tenacious and irrational challenges to fight the duels draw a certain calm courage out of him. On the other hand, Chapter 7 on 'The Secret Sharer' examines how Leggatt's close and precarious bodily presence awakens in the captain the sense of physicality that is essential for commanding a ship; the chapter approaches Conrad's works from a slightly different angle to the other chapters in this book, in that it attempts to elucidate the captain's course of learning in the narrative by applying a religious principle extrinsic to the text.

'The Duel' first appeared in *Pall Mall Magazine* from January to May 1908, and was included in *A Set of Six*, published by Methuen on 6 August 1908. In the 'Author's Note' to the volume, Conrad maintains that in writing 'The Duel' he was trying to capture 'the Spirit of the Epoch'—a spirit 'almost childlike in its exaltation of sentiment—naively heroic in its faith' (ix), which is somewhat suggestive of emotional immaturity.

© The Author(s), under exclusive license to Springer Nature   109
Switzerland AG 2024
Y. Okuda, *Emotions and Contingencies in Conrad's Fiction*,
https://doi.org/10.1007/978-3-031-66723-7_6

110   Y. OKUDA

Although Conrad seems to emphasize the psychological element in the story, some critics have felt that he had not succeeded in developing the theme. Lawrence Graver observes:

> Planning to call the tale 'The Masters of Europe,' Conrad wished to make the exuberant singularity of Feraud and D'Hubert exemplary of the 'child-like exaltation of sentiment,' the naïve heroism, so characteristic of early nineteenth century France. Putting aside the question of whether such feelings were actually a major element in the *Zeitgeist*, one can still fault Conrad for his banal treatment of the theme [...]. (1969: 145)

Similarly, Addison Bross asserts that 'the separate dueling incidents which make up the plot, though they are exciting, do not work together to complicate and develop the psychological and moral conflict beyond its very simple dimensions at the beginning of the tale' (Bross in Carabine 1992: 115).

Does Conrad really fail to develop the psychological aspect of this tale? John Stape observes that the flaws of 'The Duel' 'expose some of Conrad's fundamental psychological preoccupations' (42), adding that 'as the story moves towards its conclusion the duel itself dwindles in importance, and psychological interests increasingly emerge as the focus of Conrad's attention' (41). More recently, Nidesh Lawtoo calls the reader's attention to the binary opposition between D'Hubert's psychology and Feraud's, and maintains that Conrad's focus on the duel is 'as personal and psychological as it is collective and historical': 'their opposed physical appearance reflects their opposed psychological disposition [...]. North versus south, reason versus passion, mind versus body, culture versus instinct: the opposition could not be more clearly drawn' (7).

This chapter attempts to demonstrate Conrad's psychological preoccupations in 'The Duel' by tracing the emotionality of the main characters through a thematic and stylistic examination of the narrative,[1] with close attention to D'Hubert's love and resignation.

---

[1] For the definitions of stylistic terms used in this chapter, see *A Dictionary of Stylistics* edited by Katie Wales (Pearson Education, 2001).

SHIFTING EMOTIONS

'The Duel' is a story told by an omniscient narrator who maintains an ironic distance from the duelists, by consistently referring to them by their titles, especially their rising military ranks, and by their last names.[2] The story consists of four parts, in the course of which five duels take place over a period of about 14 years: the first duel is fought in a private garden in Strasbourg, and Feraud is slashed on the arm; the second duel is fought in a field, and D'Hubert is wounded in his side; in the third duel, fought in Silesia, both officers are badly wounded, and so the fight has to be broken off; the fourth duel is fought on horseback outside the town of Lübeck, and Feraud is cut on the forehead; and finally, the fifth and last duel is fought with pistols in a pine wood somewhere in Provence, and D'Hubert wins without firing a single shot. The discourse time allocated to the description of each episode, including what happens just before and after each duel, differs considerably. The first duel is allocated the whole of Part 1; the second, third, and fourth duels all take place in Part 2; no duel as such occurs in Part 3, and the final duel takes up most of Part 4.

Armand D'Hubert has arrived in Strasbourg lately as a lieutenant of hussars with the position of *officier d'ordonnance* of the general. According to the narrator, D'Hubert and Feraud have known each other 'but slightly' (169) before D'Hubert is sent to arrest him and they meet in Madame de Lionne's salon. In spite of this fact, even before he meets Feraud in the salon, D'Hubert has already developed an unconscious prejudice against him. He refers to Feraud as 'a lunatic' (167), whose conduct in showing himself off in his best uniform after wounding a well-connected civilian in a duel is 'positively indecent' (168). The information offered to D'Hubert by the Alsatian maid, telling him that Feraud has gone to pay a visit to Madame de Lionne, brings out more clearly D'Hubert's social prejudice against Feraud, whom he does not believe to be 'specially worthy of attention on the part of a woman with a reputation for sensibility and elegance' (170). This prejudice, combined with his own position, as being 'attached to the person of the general commanding the division,' makes him unconsciously assume that he is justified in appearing uninvited at Madame de Lionne's salon:

---

[2] Mick Short maintains that 'someone to whom you refer with "title + last name" would be remote socially, and you would normally refer to those with whom you are close by their first name' (272).

112   Y. OKUDA

> He clanked and jingled along the streets with a martial swagger. To run a comrade to earth in a drawing-room where he was not known did not trouble him in the least. A uniform is a passport. His position as *officier d'ordonnance* of the general added to his assurance. Moreover, now that he knew where to find Lieut. Feraud, he had no option. It was a service matter. (171)[3]

As this is his view, D'Hubert could not imagine that 'in the innocence of his heart and simplicity of his conscience Lieut. Feraud took a view of his duel in which neither remorse nor yet a rational apprehension of consequences had any place' (172). Myrtle Hooper maintains: 'the shift in focalization that occurs from "D'Hubert could not imagine" to "Feraud took a view" is important, [...] it marks D'Hubert's incapacitating inability to grasp Feraud's view of things and hence his own danger' (113).[4]

Likewise, Feraud, unconscious of any misbehaviour, reacts at first with 'astonishing indifference' (172), then with 'profound wonder' (172) when he hears that he is to be placed under house arrest. As Feraud has 'not the slightest doubt of being himself the outraged party' (172), it is natural that he should respond in a way that D'Hubert never expected. It is only when Feraud tries and fails 'to reconcile the information with his feelings' (174) that 'his choler at the injustice of his fate' (174) begins to rise. The changes that come over Feraud's feelings, from indifference to wonder, and from wonder to choler, are presented directly by the narrator or through Free Indirect Thought, which indicates that, as in D'Hubert's case earlier, Feraud is not quite conscious of his own shifting emotions. The only way Feraud can account for his feelings is to blame the injustice of fate. What Feraud calls injustice is anything outrageous that he cannot reconcile with the state of his own feelings, and it has nothing to do

---

[3] According to Mick Short, Free Indirect Thought suggests that the character is not conscious of what he is thinking (290); if so, as such sentences as 'A uniform is a passport' and 'It was a service matter' are presented as D'Hubert's Free Indirect Thought, we can assume that D'Hubert is unconscious of the prejudice and arrogance underlying his behaviour.

[4] In her *Narrative Fiction: Contemporary Poetics*, Shlomith Rimmon-Kenan refers to the psychological facet of focalization (point of view) in the following words: 'Whereas the perceptual facet has to do with the focalizer's sensory range, the psychological facet concerns his mind and emotions [...]. Knowledge, conjecture, belief, memory – these are some of the terms of cognition' (79–80).

with reason or memory; thus, concerning his duel with a civilian, Feraud has 'no clear recollection how the quarrel had originated' (172). What is important for him is not the cause but the fact that his feelings are 'outraged' (172). In his view, he himself is always 'the outraged party' (172), and therefore the victim of injustice. Ironically, it is D'Hubert himself who suggests to Feraud this pretext verbally, saying, 'Of course, I don't know how far you were justified [...]. And the general himself may not be exactly informed' (174).

Absurd as it may seem, this is invariably Feraud's pretext for challenging someone to a duel. He challenges D'Hubert in Strasbourg because he is not 'a man to submit tamely to injustice' (175), and chafes 'at the systematic injustice of fate' (203) when he learns that he cannot challenge D'Hubert because D'Hubert has attained a higher rank. To the very last he challenges D'Hubert in order to minister to his own feelings, whether of anger, envy, or simply boredom. The analysis of Feraud's emotionality supports Conrad's remark in his 'Author's Note' (viii): 'I have made it [the pretext] sufficiently convincing by the mere force of its absurdity.' The pretext is based on emotion, not reason.

Although Feraud's emotional characteristics remain fairly constant throughout the story, D'Hubert's undergo a considerable change. His initial arrogant contempt towards Feraud quickly shifts to vexation at finding him so unreasonable. This vexation turns to anxiety for the fear of being exposed to social ridicule, and then this anxiety turns to disgust at being forced to fight a duel. He is preoccupied with the prospects of his future even after the first duel has begun, though such anxieties are 'misplaced in view of the solemnity of the moment' (180). As a result, he is kept on the defensive against Feraud's truculent attack. It is not until he perceives Feraud's 'fixity of savage purpose' (180) that his interest is sufficiently roused that he can throw off his preoccupations and fight back.

Even though he wins the duel, once he is back in his own quarters his dread of 'discredit and ridicule' (184) returns, and he ends up becoming 'frightfully harassed' (186). The narrator says that D'Hubert is harassed because he is 'without much imagination, a faculty which helps the process of reflective thought' (186). Up to this point in Part 1, not being imaginative or reflective, D'Hubert takes no delight in 'the infinite variety of the human species,' as Madame de Lionne does (173). Neither does he find that 'the diversity of opinion is amusing,' as the surgeon does

(187). It never occurs to him that 'there could be two opinions on the matter' (187).

Out of the remaining four duels, three take place in Part 2. Just before the second duel, which takes place in 'a convenient field,' D'Hubert declares, 'There's a crazy fellow to whom I must give a lesson' (193). The declaration sounds patronizing, and being overconfident, he naturally loses.

The third duel, fought in Silesia, ends with the two officers being 'disheveled, their shirts in rags, covered with gore and hardly able to stand' (204). It has the appearance of deadly animosity, because it is a collision between two totally opposing desires: 'a rational desire to be done once for all with this worry' (204) on the part of D'Hubert, and 'a tremendous exaltation of his pugnacious instincts and the incitement of wounded vanity' (204) on the part of Feraud (204). Neither Feraud nor D'Hubert has changed much since the second duel. D'Hubert is still trying to escape from the absurd situation he has found himself in instead of accepting it.

Compassionate Love: Léonie and Feraud

What brings about a change in D'Hubert's emotional attitude is the threat posed to his love for his sister and his love for his fiancée. Love for another person can assume various forms, such as a passionate love or a compassionate love. An attachment in the form of passionate love is defined as '"a state of intense longing for union with the other [...]" and may be associated with a confusion of feelings: elation and pain, tenderness and sexuality, anxiety and relief, altruism and jealousy' (Sander and Scherer 243–44). On the other hand, a compassionate love is 'a far less intense emotion,' and is defined as 'the affection and tenderness we feel for those with whom our lives are deeply intwined, and is characterized by affection, commitment, intimacy, and concern for the welfare of the other' (Sander and Scherer 244). Individuals who are securely attached are 'more contented [...] and have a more flexible and adaptable mindset,' in contrast, individuals who are anxiously attached are 'more likely to interpret life events in pessimistic, threatening fashion' (Sander and Scherer 243).

D'Hubert may have thought that he was securely attached to his sister Léonie, but a day before the fourth duel, over-tired from his work as an aide-de-camp, he receives a letter from his sister informing him of her forthcoming marriage. He and his sister had been 'great friends and confidants' since childhood but he is to be 'ousted from the first place in her thought' (207). He realizes that his attachment to his sister is about to undergo a change in its nature, and this threat, coming on top of the impending fourth duel, upsets him so much that he breaks off writing the letter of congratulation that he had started. This incident, however, has the effect of stimulating his imagination, and offers him his first opportunity for philosophical reflection. He reflects on the possibility of his own death, and starts to write his last will and testament. He becomes temporarily 'pessimistic,' because he perceives that his attachment to 'old Léonie' is threatened. What is important, however, is that on this occasion D'Hubert not only begins to reflect, but also learns to dismiss his unpleasant reflections: he '[jumps] up, pushing his chair back,' and '[yawns] elaborately in sign that he didn't care anything for presentiments' (207)[5]; D'Hubert is learning to cope physically with his negative emotions. The scene anticipates the close relationship between the mind and the body that Conrad is to explore in the future.

Although D'Hubert succeeds in repulsing his pessimistic thoughts, as soon as he reaches the open ground outside the town of Lübeck to fight his fourth duel, 'the imbecility of the impending fight [fills] him with desolation' (268), and he is reminded of the presentiments of death that had come to him earlier and had made him want to write his will; but subsequently the unexpected result of winning the duel frees him from anxious presentiments and restores his sense of security. He therefore destroys the will and testament that he had started and finishes writing the congratulatory letter to Léonie, even asking her to find him a spouse.

D'Hubert wins the fourth duel partly because he has learned to separate reflection and action, and partly because Feraud is carried away by his vanity: 'For some obscure reason, depending, no doubt, on his psychology, he imagined himself invincible on horseback' (206). However, after the duel, on the rebound from his previous unpleasant reflection, D'Hubert suddenly becomes contemptuous of Feraud's influence on him: 'He didn't care a snap for what that lunatic could do. He

---

[5] In *Victory* (1915), Lena repulses the numbness in her head by jumping to her feet: 'The girl unexpectedly got up from the chair, swaying her supple figure and stretching her arms above her head [...]. She had jumped to her feet to react against the numbness, to discover whether her body would obey her will [...]. Though not physiologist, she concluded that all that sudden numbness was in her head, not in her limbs' (288).

116   Y. OKUDA

had suddenly acquired the conviction that his adversary was utterly power-less to affect his life in any sort of way [...]' (209). The statement 'He didn't care a snap for what that lunatic could do' is presented in Free Indirect Thought, which suggests that he is not consciously analysing his own feelings and thoughts. The conviction that Feraud is powerless to affect his life is of course mistaken, and therefore the incident suggests that D'Hubert still has a lot to learn.

The Russian campaign which follows, by expending 'all their store of moral energy [...] in resisting the terrific enmity of nature and the crushing sense of irretrievable disaster,' seems at first sight to put the two officers on an equal footing. However, from the point of view of emotion, it widens their differences, as their respective attitudes towards Napoleon indicate. While Feraud, characteristically, '[accuses] fate of unparalleled perfidy towards the sublime Man of Destiny' (214), D'Hubert, having learnt to imagine and to reflect, begins to grow sceptical:

> The early buoyancy of his belief in the future was destroyed. If the road of glory led through such unforeseen passages, he asked himself – for he was reflective – whether the guide was altogether trustworthy. It was a patriotic sadness, not unmingled with some personal concern, and quite unlike the unreasoning indignation against men and things nursed by Colonel Feraud. (215)

D'Hubert, who once lacked the imagination to help 'the process of reflec-tive thought' (186), has matured to some degree: his letters to his sister begin to contain 'some philosophical generalities upon the uncertainty of all personal hopes' (216). Unlike Feraud, who remains 'irreconcilable' (218) after Napoleon's downfall, D'Hubert, provided that his sister cares for him, finds resignation 'an easy virtue' (219).

A significant change comes over this passive attitude, however, when, on hearing two retired officers in a café speak of the potential danger that threatens Feraud's life; D'Hubert is suddenly seized by 'an irrational tenderness towards his old adversary' (223), which is then followed by an impulse of 'almost morbid need to attend to the safety of his adver-sary' (224). D'Hubert's feeling of 'irrational tenderness' for Feraud is in some ways analogous to his compassionate love for his sister. After all, by this time, D'Hubert has known Feraud for nearly 15 years and, because of Feraud's obsession with the duel, their lives have become inextricably entwined. Although their attachment may not be exactly

6 A 'PILGRIMAGE OF EMOTIONS': 'THE DUEL'

characterized by 'love,' it is still characterized by 'commitment,' 'intimacy,' and even 'a concern for the welfare of others,' which are said to be characteristic of compassionate love; not only have they confronted each other in duels, but they have retreated together from Moscow in snow and wind, leant on each other in fatigue, and fought jointly as comrades-in-arms against the Cossacks (212). They have become so intimate that they appear to their comrades as 'two indomitable companions in activity and endurance' (213–14). When he finds himself becoming earnestly concerned for Feraud's welfare, D'Hubert, for the first time, '[appreciates] emotionally the murderous absurdity their encounter had introduced into his life' (223); that is to say, he recognizes emotionally that Feraud's irrationality, far from being powerless to affect his life, as he had thought when he won the fourth duel, is powerful enough to affect his life considerably. Meanwhile, intellectually, he is still looking for a rational explanation: 'I fancy it was being left lying in the garden that had exasperated him so against me from the first' (223). The thought is presented in quotation marks, so it implies that it is a conscious thought. Subsequently, this 'irrational tenderness' drives D'Hubert to commit an impulsive act: he abruptly obtains a private audience from the Minister of Police, Fouché, and makes a plea to exclude Feraud from the operations of the Special Court. It indicates that he has accepted the situation with fatalistic resignation, as he tells his sister afterwards, 'It had to be done. But I feel yet as if I could never forgive the necessity to the man I had to save' (230).

In 'A Familiar Preface' to *A Personal Record* (1911), Conrad denies thinking that resignation is the last word of wisdom. He says, 'I am too much the creature of my time for that,' however, he goes on to say:

> But I think that the proper wisdom is to will what the gods will, without perhaps being certain what their will is – or even if they have a will of their own. And in this matter of life and art it is not the Why that matters so much to our happiness as the How. (xix)

D'Hubert has accepted his intimate relationship with Feraud, but he is still looking for a rational explanation and concerned with 'the Why' of his situation, which suggests that he still has not attained 'the proper wisdom.'

Passionate Love: Adèle

Part 4 of 'The Duel' begins with the narrator making a distinction between Feraud's vanity and D'Hubert's pride:

> No man succeeds in everything he undertakes. In that sense we are all failures. The great point is not to fail in ordering and sustaining the effort of our life. In this matter vanity is what leads us astray. It hurries us into situations from which we must come out damaged; whereas pride is our safeguard, by the reserve it imposes on the choice of our endeavor as much as by the virtue of its sustaining power. (234).

It is wounded vanity that incites Feraud to the third duel in Silesia, and it is his vain conceit that he is 'invincible on horseback' (206) that makes him jump at the idea of the fourth, which he loses. Similarly, the prospect of a final duel with D'Hubert gives him the illusion of his own 'marvelous resurrection' (233), ironically recalling Fouché's allusion to Napoleon: 'Luckily one never does begin all over again, really' (228). Prior to the last duel, Feraud says to his seconds, 'We must have pistols. He's game for my bag. My eyes are as keen as ever' (233)—a boast undermined by the narrator's report which precedes it: 'General Feraud sat erect, holding the folded newspaper at arm's length in order to make out the small print better' (231). It suggests that his eyesight has deteriorated with age and he needs a pair of reading glasses. Finally, it is his vanity that convinces Feraud he has killed D'Hubert:

> The first view of these feet and legs determined a rush of blood to his head. He literally staggered behind his tree, and had to steady himself against it with his hand. The other was lying on the ground, then! On the ground! Perfectly still, too! Exposed! What could it mean? [...]. The notion that he had knocked over his adversary at the first shot entered then General Feraud's head. Once there it grew with every second of attentive gazing, overshadowing every other supposition – irresistible, triumphant, ferocious.
>
> 'What an ass I was to think I could have missed him,' he muttered to himself. 'He was exposed *en plein* – the fool! – for quite a couple of seconds.'
>
> General Feraud gazed at the motionless limbs, the last vestiges of surprise fading before an unbounded admiration of his own deadly skill with the pistols.

6 A 'PILGRIMAGE OF EMOTIONS': 'THE DUEL'   119

> 'Turned up his toes! By the god of war, that was a shot!' he exulted mentally. 'Got it through the head, no doubt, just where I aimed, staggered behind that tree, rolled over on his back, and died!' (254)

The first two sentences are the narrator's Representation of Action. However, the next five are presented as Free Indirect Thought. Then come two sentences of Representation of Action, followed by five sentences of Feraud's Direct Thought enclosed in quotation marks, with a Representation of Action in between them. They are the only examples in the story where Feraud's thoughts are recorded extensively in both Free Indirect and Direct Thought, leaving no doubt of his vanity.

In contrast, D'Hubert is ruled by his pride. When Feraud challenges him to the first duel, he answers 'I won't be made ridiculous,' and after the duel, we are informed that '[h]e dreaded the discredit and ridicule above everything' (184). Once he falls passionately in love with his fiancée Adèle, the intensity of his love adds to his emotional trials. For the first time, he experiences irrational feelings and impulses which he may have recognized in Feraud but has not been familiar with in himself. He goes through 'variations of his inward state' (236), characteristic of passionate love which is 'associated with a confusion of feelings' (Sander and Scherer 243): 'A watchful deference, trembling on the verge of tenderness was the note of their intercourse on his side' (236); and he walks home 'sometimes intensely miserable, sometimes supremely happy, sometimes pensively sad, but always feeling a special intensity of existence' (230). Moreover, his 'pride' (234) demands more than just 'no insurmountable dislike' (235) from his fiancée Adèle, whom he loves 'enough to kill her rather than lose her' (235), but he doubts whether his love is reciprocated:

> Her violet eyes laughed while the lines of her lips and chin remained composed in admirable gravity. All this was set off by such a glorious mass of fair hair, by a complexion so marvellous, by such a grace of expression, that General D'Hubert really never found the opportunity to examine with sufficient detachment the lofty exigencies of his pride. In fact, he became shy of that line of inquiry since it had led once or twice to a crisis of solitary passion in which it was borne upon him that he loved her enough to kill her rather than lose her. (235)

In witnessing her youth and beauty, General D'Hubert becomes not only 'acutely aware of the number of his years, of his wounds, of his many moral imperfections, of his secret unworthiness,' but also '[learns] by experience the meaning of the word funk' (235).

It is Feraud's challenge to the last duel that gives D'Hubert the opportunity to overcome his cowardice; he gets over his disgust at being forced to fight another duel and accepts Feraud's challenge, because he realizes that he cannot escape the absurdity which Feraud has imposed on him as 'a fatality' (246). It gives him the opportunity to experience the irrational 'instinctive fury of his menaced passion' and 'a sentiment of melancholy despair' (247), which eventually compels him to go through an emotional crisis. For the first time, D'Hubert faces his own emotions in their full variety and intensity:

> That night, General D'Hubert [...] made the full pilgrimage of emotions. Nauseating disgust at the absurdity of the situation, doubt of his own fitness to conduct his existence, and mistrust of his best sentiments [...] – he knew them all in turn. [...]. And he tasted the torments of jealousy too. She would marry somebody else. His very soul writhed. The tenacity of that Feraud, the awful persistence of that imbecile brute, came to him with the tremendous force of a relentless destiny. [...]. General D'Hubert was tasting every emotion that life has to give. He had in his dry mouth the faint sickly flavour of fear, not the excusable fear before a young girl's candid and amused glance, but the fear of death and the honourable man's fear of cowardice. (247–248)

His 'pilgrimage of emotions' is presented mainly as the narrator's Representation of Action. D'Hubert has been compelled to go through this crisis because of the emotional pressure exerted on him by his passionate love for Adèle, compounded by the pressure of Feraud's tenacity. Having tasted 'every emotion that life has to give,' including 'the fear of death and the honourable man's fear of cowardice,' D'Hubert comes to realize 'the tremendous force of a relentless destiny' that Feraud has imposed on him, and his genuine resignation draws from him 'true courage': 'if true courage consists in going out to meet an odious danger from which our body, soul, and heart recoil together, General D'Hubert had the opportunity to practice it for the first time in his life' (248).

Not 'the Why' but 'the How'

Once he has overcome his cowardice, D'Hubert is no longer concerned with 'Why' he has to meet his destiny, but with 'How' to cope with it. On his way to the pine wood, he picks two oranges and sucks one to quench the thirst in 'his dry mouth' that has 'the sickly flavour of fear' (248); this has the effect of making '[that] temperamental good-humoured coolness in the face of danger' assert itself (248–49). He is no longer concerned with the past or the future but only with how to respond to the immediate circumstances. This revived coolness is reflected in the way he neatly folds his coat (250), but more importantly, it subsequently draws out from him his innate resourcefulness. It inspires him to use a hand mirror to see both ways, and indirectly makes Feraud waste his second shot. As a result, Feraud loses the duel and D'Hubert is henceforth able to hold him at bay.

D'Hubert's newly gained courage not only enables him to free himself from Feraud's tenacity, but also to ascertain the depth of Adèle's love; for if he had failed to summon enough courage to fight the duel and had not confided it to the Chevalier, declaring to him, 'I must kill him!' (246), Adèle would never have known that D'Hubert had gone to fight a deadly duel. Then she would not have taken such an impulsive and unseemly action as running two miles over the fields with her hair down, betraying her passionate love for D'Hubert. Returning home from the duel, D'Hubert experiences a 'staggering emotion' (260) on finding Adèle in his room 'in distress.' (260). When he realizes what it implies, D'Hubert gives way to his elation, and '[makes] an aggressive movement towards the divan which nothing could check' (263). It may be said that it was Feraud who gave him the chance to release his irrational feelings of passionate love, which D'Hubert acknowledges in the words: 'It's extraordinary how in one way or another this man has managed to fasten himself on my deeper feelings' (266).

In 'The Duel' Conrad explores the possible effects of an intense emotional engagement imposed by a vainglorious and aggressive opponent on a proud and reserved character.[6] In the course of five duels,

---

[6] In 'The Plot of Conrad's *The Duel*,' J. DeLancey Ferguson mentions one of the sources of the plot of 'The Duel' which appeared in the September 1858 issue of *Harper's Magazine*, and he maintains that 'the discovery of the source does not affect the artistic validity of the finished work,' because 'the intense emotional engagement' with the fiction that Conrad has created is lacking in this source. (389)

D'Hubert refines his sensitivity and grows more imaginative, reflective, and courageous. As John Stape suggests, the psychology presented in 'The Duel' may not be without flaws. Comparisons between, for instance, Feraud's 'choler at the injustice of his fate' (191) and Jim's sense of being tried 'more than is fair' in *Lord Jim* (97), or between the discovery that D'Hubert makes at the end of 'the full pilgrimage of emotions' (247) and the discovery that Razumov makes at the end of *Under Western Eyes* may suggest a lack of perspicacity into the psychology of the characters, so the theme of emotions in 'The Duel' is perhaps not so thoroughly explored as in some other works. Nevertheless, 'The Duel' demonstrates that the thematic issue of emotions is an overarching issue that Conrad addresses not only in novels and novellas, but also in short stories.

In 'The Duel,' the physical effects of intense emotional engagement on D'Hubert are referred to only sporadically. However, in 'The Secret Sharer,' which also traces the process of the protagonist's emotional maturation through an intense one-to-one engagement with another character, the theme of emotions is addressed in closer relation to the theme of the body.

CHAPTER 7

'The Feel of the Ship': 'The Secret Sharer'

I had come creeping quietly as near insanity as any man who has not actually gone over the border. That gesture restrained me, so to speak.

('The Secret Sharer')

'The Secret Sharer' was composed in December 1909 during a break in the composition of *Under Western Eyes*. It was published in *Harper's Magazine* in America from August to September 1910, and then collected in the volume *'Twixt Land and Sea*, published by Dent in Britain on 14 October 1912, and by Hodder & Stoughton in America on 3 December 1912.

In his essay, 'Memorandum on the Scheme for Fitting Out a Sailing Ship,' Conrad stresses the importance of physical exertion in seamen's work: 'In its essence life at sea has been always a healthy life, and part of that was owing to the very nature of the physical exertions required' (*Last Essays* 71). He maintains that the physical work that seamen do brings them into intimate contact with the physical aspect of the ship, such as its machinery, and enables them to 'learn the feel of [the ship]' (71). Moreover, he claims that 'any physical work intelligently done develops a special mentality; in this case it would be the sailor mentality' (71); it is through physical exertion that seamen develop their typical way of thinking.

© The Author(s), under exclusive license to Springer Nature Switzerland AG 2024
Y. Okuda, *Emotions and Contingencies in Conrad's Fiction*,
https://doi.org/10.1007/978-3-031-66723-7_7

123

Although in this essay Conrad emphasizes the physical aspect of seamen's life, 'The Secret Sharer' is often read with a focus on the mental aspect of the story, reflecting, perhaps, the traditionally dominant Western view of the body. In the 'Introduction' to *The Cambridge Companion to the Body in Literature*, David Hillman and Ulrika Maude maintain:

> The body has always been a contested site. In the Christian and Humanist traditions, it has often been seen as a mere auxiliary to the self, a vehicle or object that houses the mind or the soul. In these views of embodiment, the self is seen as a transcendent entity whose existence depends only contingently on the body, which the 'true' self will eventually shed like a defunct item of clothing. (2015: 1)

Criticisms of 'The Secret Sharer' have also tended to dismiss the theme of the body, and read it at its non-literal level. Albert Guerard, for instance, regards 'The Secret Sharer' as the 'most frankly psychological of Conrad's shorter works' (21); C. B. Cox asserts that '[…] the captain's quest for self-identification will not be helped by his perceptions of exterior objects. He must seek to find himself in his subjective consciousness […]' (144); and Barbara Johnson and Marjorie Garber maintain that '"The Secret Sharer" seems an ideal […] text on which to base an introduction to the varieties of psychoanalytic criticism' (628).

On the other hand, a few critics emphasize the importance of reading the novella at its literal level. Ian Watt calls into question the non-literal approach to the work by drawing the reader's attention to the emotional attributes of Leggatt, namely his conspicuous self-possession—his composure, calmness, and the ability to control his feelings:

> The reader can enjoy the narrative at its literal level, and must decide for himself how much more Conrad intends; and this must include why, if he intends Leggatt to represent the captain's unconscious, he makes him so conspicuously self-possessed. (1985: 31)

Similarly, Cedric Watts criticizes the psychoanalytic approach by saying that '[t]he stress on strange kinship has encouraged some critics to see Leggatt as some kind of Freudian "id" or Jungian "anima," as a repressed part of the hero's psyche, but this endeavor is resisted by the tale's predominant realism which establishes fully the external existence of Leggatt' (134).

7 'THE FEEL OF THE SHIP': 'THE SECRET SHARER' 125

Does Conrad intend the story to be read at a literal or a non-literal level? This chapter addresses the narrative at its literal level, with special focus on the potential of the body to express, to communicate, and above all, to learn. First, it examines the characters' physical potential to express and communicate, in reference to what Jeremy Hawthorn calls 'bodily communication'; second, it discusses the physical potential of the captain to learn, by citing the learning processes discussed by J. K. Kadowaki; and finally it argues that 'The Secret Sharer' can be interpreted at its literal level by focusing on the physical aspect of the characters and suggests an answer to Ian Watt's question as to why Conrad makes Leggatt 'so conspicuously self-possessed.'

The Body's Potential to Express and Communicate

As 'The Secret Sharer' was composed during a break in the composition of *Under Western Eyes*, it reflects some features of the longer work. One such feature is the theme of the body. In *Joseph Conrad: Narrative Technique and Ideological Commitment*, Jeremy Hawthorn professes his concern for a lack of critical attention to what he calls 'bodily communication':

> *Under Western Eyes* is reiteratively preoccupied with these three areas of human communication, with human word language, facial expression and eye-contact, and what we can call bodily communication. Conrad's concern with language and with 'seeing' in the novel has received considerable critical attention already, but it has not always been recognized that the communicative and expressive potentialities of the physical human body are also closely scrutinized in this work. (1990: 236)

According to Hawthorn, *Under Western Eyes* is full of references to 'the expressive physical disposition of the human body: posture, gesture, movement, touch, expression' (236), and it is necessary to pay close attention to them because 'such detailing is easy to miss, for it is rarely foregrounded, and often takes place in the context of fuller description' (240).

Hawthorn's concern for the lack of critical attention to 'bodily communication' in *Under Western Eyes* applies also to the criticisms of 'The Secret Sharer.' As in *Under Western Eyes*, there are many references to posture, gesture, movement, touch, and expression, including eye-contact, in the novella. For example, there is a reference to touch in the opening scene of the story when the captain is resting his hand lightly on the rail of the ship, feeling as if he were putting his hand 'on the shoulder of a trusted friend' (92). Likewise, there are references to posture, gesture, movement and expression in the scene in which Leggatt narrowly escapes detection by the steward: there is a reference to posture in the way Leggatt stands, a reference to gesture and movement in the way he raises his hands to convey the feeling of relief, and a reference to facial expression in the look of concern on his face. (130) Finally, there are references to eye-contact; for instance, when the captain and Leggatt part in the stateroom, they look into each other's eyes: 'Our eyes met; several seconds elapsed, till, our glances still mingled, I extended my hand and turned the lamp out' (138).

Of the three areas of human communication with which Hawthorn maintains that *Under Western Eyes* is preoccupied—'word language,' 'facial expression and eye-contact,' and 'bodily communication,' 'The Secret Sharer' is least preoccupied with word language. This is because Leggatt is a stowaway, and therefore he and the captain have to keep their oral communication to a minimum to avoid detection by the crew. These strained circumstances, on the other hand, could have propelled them to develop the other two areas of communication: 'facial expression and eye-contact,' and 'bodily communication.'

The Body's Potential to Learn

'The Secret Sharer' not only features the potential of the body to express and communicate, but also the potential of the body to learn. Jacob Lothe maintains that the story 'definitely dramatizes an important learning process on the part of the narrator,' but indicates that 'problems arise if we enquire into the terms and possible results of this learning' (69). In 'The Secret Sharer,' the terms of learning are just as important as the results of learning; moreover, they reflect the learning process suggested by Conrad in the essay quoted earlier. The learning process proceeds from physical exertion to mentality, in other words, from the body to the mind.

Learning first through the body is not just typical of seamen, but is characteristic also of certain forms of religious training, such as the Zen meditation. In *Zen and the Bible*, J. K. Kadowaki, a Japanese Jesuit priest who is also trained in practicing the Zen way of meditation, contrasts the learning process of Zen with the learning process of Christianity:

Learning through the body is a fundamental of Zen. It is a way which proceeds 'from the body to the mind.' We can call it a method of practising with the whole body. Christianity took the opposite direction as it developed in the West. The Western way is to first reflect rationally, make a judgment, will to do something, and finally use the body to carry out the act. This way of proceeding can be called 'from reason to the body.' (1980:10)

According to Kadowaki's definition, the body is 'the whole person as seen from its physical nature,' and it ultimately covers 'the conscious and the unconscious' (31). Kadowaki maintains that the word 'body' is often used in this sense even in the Bible, as the Bible 'does not separate the body from the soul as the Greeks did, nor does it hold that the soul is noble and the body is base [...]' (122). Although the two learning processes take opposite directions, they both cover the mind and the body.

In Zen, the direction of the learning process proceeds 'from the body to the mind,' and it is practiced in the form of meditation: '[...] by first adjusting one's posture in a proper position, regulating the breath and composing the mind' (Kadowaki 10). It is analogous to the learning process identified by Conrad in seamen,[1] in the sense that it proceeds from physical procedure to mental state, which follows the direction 'from the body to the mind.'

The analogy between the learning process of seamen and that of Zen practitioners, of course, does not suggest that Conrad was a Zen Buddhist! However, an attempt to interpret 'The Secret Sharer' in terms of the learning process which proceeds 'from the body to the mind,' developed in the East, is not so implausible as it may seem. In his essay, 'Autocracy and War,' occasioned by the Russo-Japanese War of 1904, Conrad remarks:

[...] it is from the East that wonders of patience and wisdom have come to a world of men who set the value of life in the power to act rather than in the faculty of meditation. (*Notes on Life and Letters* 88)

---

[1] In 'Memorandum on the Scheme for Fitting Out a Sailing Ship,' Conrad emphasizes the physical exertion seamen put forth in performing their work. In Zen Buddhism also, the physical exertion put forth in performing one's work (*samu*), such as cleaning the temple and tending the gardens, is considered to be almost as important as practicing meditation (*zazen*).

128   Y. OKUDA

The allusion to 'the faculty of meditation' suggests that Conrad knew something about the Eastern way of meditation, and the words, 'wonders of patience and wisdom' indicate that he appreciated its value. Thinking about the Russo-Japanese War has somehow reminded Conrad of 'the faculty of meditation' valued in the East, and he was moved to contrast it with 'the power to act' valued in the West. The purpose of this chapter, however, is not to discuss the effects of meditation or the merits and demerits of the two contrasting learning processes. It is to examine whether or not 'The Secret Sharer' can be interpreted at its literal level.

We perceive the physical presence of ourselves and others through our five senses: sight, hearing, smell, taste, and touch. Of the five senses, the predominant sense is sight; Jacob Lothe remarks that, in 'The Secret Sharer,' '[v]isual impression constitutes the narrator's primary source of information' (60).[2] It should be noted, however, that sight is a physical sense; Kadowaki reminds us that 'when you look at a view, the principal role is played by the seeing eyes, so it would be more correct to say that it is the body that is seeing' (12). The sights we see are the impressions received by the sense of the bodily eyes.

'The Secret Sharer' opens with the captain alone on the deck of his ship, allowing his eyes to roam across the scenery of the sea and the land that surrounds him. First, his eyes wander from the mysterious 'lines of fishing-stakes' on the right to 'a group of barren islets' on the left (91). He then glances at the receding tug and notes the dividing line between the land and the sea, broken only by the estuary of the river Meinam with the Great Pagoda in its background. Finally, his eyes rest on the deck of his ship, his first command, whose fitness for the task of accomplishing the long journey is not yet known to him. He puts his hand lightly on the ship's rail and for a moment all his senses seem to be focused on the ship; however, not for long. The next minute, the captain's eyes wander off the deck of his ship to the islands, and catch sight of a ship anchored between them (92). In this scene, the captain is seeing things with his bodily eyes, and his attention is fixed on the fishing-stakes, the islets, the Meinam, the Pagoda, then the deck of the ship, and finally on a ship anchored between the islands.

However, when the captain returns to the deck after supper, to take the self-imposed five hours' anchor-watch occasioned by his sense of

---

[2] Daniel R. Schwarz in '"The Secret Sharer" as an Act of Memory,' discusses what he calls 'retrospective seeing' (1997:97).

strangeness, he very soon ceases to see with his bodily eyes. The feeling of strangeness arises from his unfamiliarity with the ship, the crew, and his anxiety about his fitness for the task of his first command; it provokes him to indulge in reassuring imaginings which soothe the feeling of strangeness. This indicates that the captain is trying to solve the problem of strangeness by approaching it first from the mind:

> I descended the poop and paced the waist, *my mind picturing to myself* the coming passage out through the Malay Archipelago, down the Indian Ocean, and up the Atlantic. All its phases were familiar enough to me, every characteristic, all the alternatives which were likely to face me on the high seas – everything! ...except the novel responsibility of command. But I took heart from the reasonable thought that the ship was like other ships, the men like other men, and that the sea was not likely to keep any special surprises expressly for my discomfiture. (96; emphasis added)

He imagines the phases of the coming passage, which reassures him that he is 'familiar enough' with them, and regains self-assurance by the rather dubious 'reasonable thought' that no unexpected occurrence is likely to happen. This 'comforting conclusion,' in its turn, emboldens him to go down to his cabin to get a cigar, neglecting his task as a watch. Downstairs, his sense of security is strengthened when he finds everybody sleeping profoundly, and it is further strengthened when, back on the deck, he observes that the riding-light is burning 'clear' and 'untroubled' (96).

However, as I discussed in detail in Chapter 2, indulging in a sense of security is a sign of negligence and inattention in Conrad's fiction: 'a sense of security [...], even the most warranted, is a bad counsellor. It is the sense which [...] precedes the swift fall of disaster.' (*The Mirror of the Sea* 30); an undue sense of security is often a sure sign that something unforeseen is going to happen, and that is precisely what happens in the next scene.

The first unexpected object that upsets the captain's sense of security is a rope ladder. When the captain returns to the deck with his cigar, he notices that a rope side-ladder has been left unhauled. Barbara Johnson and Marjorie Garber suggest that the rope side-ladder can be regarded as either symbolizing 'vulnerability to castration,' if it is interpreted as a sign of the captain's Oedipal complex, or as 'an umbilicus,' if Leggatt is compared to a newly-born infant:

130   Y. OKUDA

> [...] viewed mythically or archetypally, the dangling rope ladder, though it
> may in one way signal vulnerability to castration, in another resembles an
> umbilicus, and the scene is a birth scene, the naked infant emerging from
> the water clinging to the cord. (635)

But what does a rope side-ladder signify literally? A rope ladder is 'a ladder
made of two long pieces of rope connected at intervals by short cross-
pieces of rope, wood, metal, etc.' (*OED*). It is such a rope ladder that the
captain tries to draw in, but surprisingly he fails to do so:

> I proceeded to get the ladder in myself. Now a side-ladder of that sort
> is a light affair and comes in easily, yet my vigorous tug, which should
> have brought it flying on board, merely recoiled upon my body in a totally
> unexpected jerk. (97)

Anyone who has taken part in a tug of war, a contest in which two teams
pull at opposite ends of a rope, will be familiar with the physical sense
of such a jerk. What it signifies is that the captain's first encounter with
Leggatt is tactile, and therefore physical.

After this, the captain and Leggatt learn about one another by
responding physically to each other. When the captain fails to draw in
the rope ladder, he looks over the rail and sees with his bodily eyes 'a
naked body of a man'—the very body that only a moment ago 'recoiled
upon [his] body.' He then perceives Leggatt's body part by part: 'a pair
of feet, the long legs, a broad livid back' and 'the neck' (97). When he
notices that the head is lacking, his amazed reaction is also physical: his
mouth loses hold of his cigar. To this Leggatt also responds physically, by
raising his head at the sound made by the cigar dropping into the water,
and the sight of his 'black-haired head' (97–98) prevents the captain from
making exclamations. The first stage of the communication between the
captain and Leggatt is almost entirely physical and non-verbal.

Even after they begin to talk with each other, they still continue to
communicate non-verbally, especially through the tone of their voices. For
instance, when the captain, prompted by the disquieting suspicion that
Leggatt does not want to come on board, asks him in a composed tone
'What's the matter?' Leggatt answers nonchalantly, 'cramp.' However, he
acknowledges later that it was the captain's unexpected tone of composure that had prevented him from recklessly swimming away: '[...] you
speaking to me so quietly [...] made me hold on a little longer' (110).

Instead of swimming away, therefore, Leggatt announces his name. The captain is impressed by the sense of self-possession that Leggatt's voice carries, and finds himself becoming more self-possessed:

> The voice was calm and resolute. A good voice. The self-possession of that man had somehow induced a corresponding state in myself. It was very quietly that I remarked: 'You must be a good swimmer.' (99)

The captain's self-possession, in its turn, provokes Leggatt to confess to him the dilemma he is in—whether he should swim away or come on board. However, instead of responding verbally to Leggatt's confession, the captain perceives that Leggatt must be young enough to face such a dilemma. The concatenation of successful non-verbal communication makes the captain realize that 'A mysterious communication [has been] established already' between them (99). The upshot of which is that, as if he too had perceived the mysterious communication, Leggatt suddenly climbs up the ladder; and this spontaneous physical reaction prompts the captain to hasten away from the rail to fetch clothes for him. It is to be noted that this mysterious communication between the two has been established *before* the captain learns that Leggatt is the son of a parson in Norfolk, that he was a *Conway* boy, or that he has unwittingly killed a man on the ship anchored inside the group of islets. Physical communication entails alertness to the immediate circumstances; in other words, it entails self-possession. In this scene the captain and Leggatt induce in each other a sense of self-possession which enables them to communicate effectively physically. An examination of the captain's first encounter with Leggatt demonstrates that the learning process it follows is 'from the body to the mind.'

The Mind's Eye Versus the Bodily Eye

As we have seen, the captain regains the faculty of his bodily eyes and develops his physical senses through his chance meeting with Leggatt. However, just before this encounter he was indulging himself in his visual memory, picturing to himself in his mind 'the coming passage out through the Malay Archipelago, down the Indian Ocean, and up the Atlantic' (96). Interestingly, there is a scene which closely resembles this

132   Y. OKUDA

scene in *The Shadow-Line*, published in 1917. The captain of *The Shadow-Line* also pictures to himself the expected passage before he embarks on the journey of his first command:

> I was familiar enough with the Archipelago by that time [...]. The road would be long [...]. But this road *my mind's eye* could see on a chart, professionally, with all its complications and difficulties. (*The Shadow-Line* 44; emphasis added)

In this scene, the captain of *The Shadow-Line* sees the coming passage in detail with '[his] mind's eye.' Seeing with one's mind's eye in *The Shadow-Line* corresponds to picturing in the mind in 'The Secret Sharer.' Etymologically, the early form of 'one's mind's eye' is 'the eye of the mind,' and there is an example in *OED* from Geoffrey Chaucer's 'Man of Law's Tale' in *The Canterbury Tales*.[3] The examples of the later form, 'one's mind's eye,' are found in William Shakespeare's *Hamlet*. In Act I of *Hamlet*, Horatio says, 'A mote it is to trouble the mind's eye' (I. i. 112), and in a later scene, when Hamlet says 'My father, methinks I see my father,' and Horatio asks 'Where, my lord?,' Hamlet answers 'In my mind's eye, Horatio' (I. ii. 184–186). As 'one's mind's eye' refers to one's visual memory or imagination, it signifies something quite different from what is signified by bodily vision.

The concept of the mind's eye reflects a similar concept in psychoanalytic criticisms, which often focus their attention on such expressions as 'the double' or 'the other self.' For example, Joan E. Steiner discusses the novella in terms of the concepts of the doubling by duplication and the doubling by division (1980). However, such concept of the doubling relationship seems applicable to the captain only when he is seeing Leggatt in his mind's eye. Examined closely, however, such expressions as 'the double' and 'the other self' in the text signify not Leggatt in the captain's mind's eye, but Leggatt seen through his bodily eyes. When the captain, as a narrator, refers to Leggatt as a 'double,' 'the other self,' or 'the secret sharer,' these words are often followed by a qualifying phrase which signifies physical space. For example, when the captain refers to Leggatt as 'my double' for the first time, he does not just say 'my double,' but 'like my double *on the poop*' (100; emphasis added). It implies that Leggatt is

---

[3] 'It were with thilke eyen of his mynde, With whiche men seen, after that they been blynde' (*OED*).

7 'THE FEEL OF THE SHIP': 'THE SECRET SHARER' 133

physically occupying a space on the poop. The same thing can be said about such phrases as 'the secret self [...] *sleeping in that bed*' (114; emphasis added), 'the secret sharer *of my cabin*' (119; emphasis added), and 'my double there *in the sail-locker*' (141; emphasis added). The qualification of space added to these expressions indicates that the captain was conscious of Leggatt's physical presence. It corroborates Ian Watt's assertion that the 'narrative interest and psychological realism' of the story 'may well supply a sufficient reason for all these emphases on the captain's identification with his "other self"' (1985: xi).

Although the captain does not seem to be indicating that Leggatt is a doppelganger of himself, it must however be admitted that the captain's awareness of Leggatt's physical presence weakens, if temporarily, in the course of the story. This is due partly to the stress placed on him by the fact that Leggatt is a stowaway in hiding from the rest of the crew, added to the stress placed on him by the visit of the skipper of the *Sephora* in search of the fugitive. For example, immediately after the captain draws the curtains of his bed-place for Leggatt, he loses control over his physical sense: 'I sat there [...] trying to clear my mind of the confused sensation of being in two places at once' (111). Similarly, when he is breakfasting with his two mates, he says: 'all the time the dual working of my mind distracted me almost to the point of insanity' (113–14). Again, during the interview with the skipper of the *Sephora*, he admits that he is obsessed with Leggatt's image in his mind; he reflects later, 'I should have sympathized with him if I had been able to detach my mental vision from the unsuspected sharer of my cabin [...]' (117); and finally he confesses that even his professional ability to respond alertly to certain conditions as a seaman has been affected by his 'mental feeling of being in two places at once' (125). What these words, 'clear my mind,' 'working of my mind,' 'mental vision,' and 'mental feeling,' indicate is that the captain is not split between his 'double' and himself, his 'other self' and himself, or his conscious and unconscious selves, but between what he is seeing with his mind's eye and what he is seeing with his bodily eyes. What the captain has to do to solve this problem is to learn to see with the bodily eyes without the interference of the mind's eye.

The captain solves this problem in the climactic scene in which he faces Leggatt immediately after he has escaped the steward's detection. When the steward suddenly opens the door of the bathroom to hang up the captain's coat, Leggatt's self-possession enables him to squat down at once so as not to be seen by him. However, the captain in the dining room becomes temporarily convinced that Leggatt has been detected by the steward, so when he sees Leggatt safe in the cabin he cannot believe his bodily eyes: 'an irresistible doubt of his bodily existence flitted through my mind' (130). Fortunately, he is called back to reality by the sight of the bodily communication that Leggatt makes: he gestures to the captain by raising his hands slightly to express his relief at having so closely escaped detection. The captain says, 'I think I had come creeping quietly as near insanity as any man who has not actually gone over the border. That gesture restrained me, so to speak' (130): this appeal to his bodily eyes strikes out the illusory sight in the captain's mind's eye and revives his awareness of physical presence. When Leggatt tells him what really happened, the captain is impressed by Leggatt's self-possession which has enabled him to respond physically with such resilience and alertness to sudden changes of circumstances.

The Art of Handling Man and Ship

It is significant that just as the captain's bodily senses have been revived by this incident, two things occur that forebode further difficulties ahead: one is that Leggatt suddenly announces his wish to leave the ship by having himself marooned, and the other is that the wind changes, so the mate puts the ship on the off-shore tack. These two things are incompatible, because to enable Leggatt to swim safely to the shore, the captain has to put the ship not on the off-shore tack but on the shoreside tack; moreover, to do this, he first has to learn how to handle the ship.

The learning process that the captain undergoes with the ship is reminiscent of the learning process that he undergoes with Leggatt. At one point, the captain becomes so affected by the strain of the manoeuvre that he briefly shuts his eyes: 'The strain of watching the dark loom of the land grow bigger and denser was too much for me. I had shut my eyes—because the ship must go closer' (139); he feels that 'Already she [the ship] was [...] gone too close to be recalled, gone from me altogether' (140). It reminds us of the scene in which the captain becomes temporarily convinced that Leggatt is 'Lost! Gone!' (129). Fortunately, however, the strain placed on the captain is dispelled by physical exertion when he has to shake his mate several times to bring him back to his senses.

By this time, the captain has forgotten all about Leggatt, but he has not yet 'learnt the feel' of the ship, so he cannot tell whether she is coming-to or not. Conrad says that there is 'something sentient which seems to dwell in ships' (*A Personal Record* xv), and also that '[...] the art of handling ships is finer, perhaps, than the art of handling man' (*The Mirror of the Sea* 28). The captain, however, overcomes this crisis when he detects a hat drifting forward in the shadow of the ship. It turns out to be the hat that he rammed on Leggatt's head, seized suddenly by 'pity for his mere flesh' (142), just as he was leaving, and so the sight of the hat may have sharpened his physical sense.[4] Helped by the hat, he learns to feel the ship gather sternway and completes his learning process with the ship, attaining the 'perfect communion of a seaman with his first command' (143); in other words, he attains the physical state that Conrad describes as a state in which the seaman's sense 'were like her [the ship's] sense, that the stress upon his body made him judge of the strain upon the ship's masts' (*The Mirror of the Sea* 33).

As Ian Watt and Cedric Watts have indicated, 'The Secret Sharer' can be interpreted literally; the two main characters, the captain and Leggatt, communicate with each other predominantly through the senses of their bodies, and the captain awakens to the physical presence of Leggatt and the ship through a process 'from the body to the mind.' What enables the captain to learn through the body in the first place is the self-possession that Leggatt inspires in him. Bodily communication of the kind depicted in this story entails response on the spur of the moment; if one is preoccupied with one's thoughts or distracted by one's personal feelings, it is not possible to respond alertly enough through the body. It is for this reason that, as Ian Watt indicates, Leggatt's self-possession—of being in control of his emotions—plays an important role in this narrative. Leggatt had to look 'always perfectly self-controlled, more than calm—almost invulnerable' (127), so that the captain can learn from him how to communicate with his ship through the body.

Traditionally, as Kadowaki indicates, the body is more foregrounded in the Eastern culture than in the Western culture. However, Kadowaki's concept of the body as 'the whole person as seen from its physical nature' (31) is by no means an unfamiliar concept in Conrad's fiction, which depicts the body as something which has 'a force, subtlety and sophistication that goes beyond the reaches of language' (Hawthorn 236). The thematic issue of the body is inextricable from the issue of emotions,

---

[4] The hat may have reminded the captain of Leggatt's physical presence and his self-possession.

because the body participates in crucial ways in feeling. The theme of the body is suggested tentatively in 'The Duel,' but it begins to assume prominence in 'The Secret Sharer,' and culminates in *Under Western Eyes*.

PART IV

Emotion and the Body

CHAPTER 8

The Body, the Theatre of Emotions: *Under Western Eyes*

'And even my person, too, is loathsome to you perhaps […].'
(*Under Western Eyes*)

Part IV of this book comprises only one novel, *Under Western Eyes*, which began as a short story entitled 'Razumov,' and was composed between December 1907 and January 1910. The serial version of the narrative was published from December 1910 to October 1911 in the *English Review* and the *North American Review*, and was then published in book form by Methuen on 5 October 1911 and by Harper and Brothers in New York 2 weeks later. In his letter to Macdonald Hastings, dated 24 December 1916, Conrad says, 'These pages represent 2 years of constant artistic preoccupation, much mental effort and about 18 months of actual writing work' (*CL* 5: 695). He refers to *Under Western Eyes* as 'the most deeply meditated novel that came from under my pen,' and asks Hastings specifically to read it 'with detachment and with no idea at the back of your head' (*CL* 5: 695).

In a typewritten text of *Under Western Eyes*, later cut on revision, Conrad had written:

He [Razumov] had for years, read, thought, lived pen in hand fixing his conquered knowledge of facts, theories, systems, speculations in the shape of notes. And now he was trying perhaps to fix in the familiar way and with

© The Author(s), under exclusive license to Springer Nature Switzerland AG 2024
Y. Okuda, *Emotions and Contingencies in Conrad's Fiction*, https://doi.org/10.1007/978-3-031-66723-7_8

140   Y. OKUDA

> the idea of serving a practical purpose another kind of knowledge – the knowledge of impulses emotions and thoughts altogether his own [...].
> (Osborne and Eggert 451–2)

The deleted passage confirms Conrad's interest in the issues of impulses, emotions, and thoughts. Razumov's intellectual pursuit of 'the knowledge of impulses emotions and thoughts' is gradually superseded by his experience of impulses, emotions, and thoughts, leading to the awareness of the living body that signifies his true identity; in *Under Western Eyes*, the issues of emotion and of identity are explored in close association with the issue of the body.

The criticism of *Under Western Eyes* ranges widely from the psychological and the political, to the autobiographical,[1] but the earliest psychosomatic criticism is Tony Tanner's 'Nightmare and Complacency: Razumov and the Western Eye' (1962). Tanner maintains that '[t]he narrator brings home to us the physical symptoms with a calmness that makes those very symptoms stand out in arresting relief [...]' (Tanner in Carabine 1992: 149). Likewise Jeremy Hawthorn, as mentioned earlier in Chapter 7, discusses 'the communicative and expressive potentialities of the physical human body' (1990: 236), pointing out: 'how important non-verbal communication is in this novel, a novel full of references to gestures, posture and expressions [...]' (57).

If addressing the issue of emotion is a comparatively new approach in literary criticism, addressing the issue of the body is also fairly new.[2] Its late appearance in the field of literary criticism may be attributed to the traditionally Western tendency to make light of the body and its role, as noted in Chapter 7.[3] However, as David Hillman and Ulrika Maude point out, there is now in the West 'an alternative way of understanding the body, supported by more recent discoveries in science, medicine and

---

[1] See, for instance, Bruce E. Johnson's *Conrad's Models of Mind* (1971), Eloise Knapp Hay's *Political Novels of Joseph Conrad* (1963), and Keith Carabine's '"The Figure Behind the Veil": Conrad and Razumov in *Under Western Eyes*' (Carabine in Smith: 1991).

[2] According to Hillman and Maude, 'over the last three or four decades, critics and theorists have found myriad ways of addressing the representation of the body and embodied experience in literature' (2015: 3). For example, William A. Cohen discusses 'the convergence of literary and other kinds of writing on a set of ideas about embodiment' (xiii) in his *Embodied: Victorian Literature and the Senses* (2009).

[3] In *Poets of Reality*, J. Hillis Miller maintains that '[f]rom the point of view of consciousness, the fact that men are in one sense part of nature is the most shocking

philosophy,' and according to this understanding, the body 'participates in crucial ways in thinking, feeling and the shaping of our personalities [...]' (1). One interesting example of recent discoveries which supports this alternative way of understanding the body is the discoveries made in cognitive science. For instance, Antonio Damasio states:

> [...] our very organism rather than some absolute external reality is used as the ground reference for the constructions we make of the world around us and for the construction of the ever-present sense of subjectivity that is part and parcel of our experiences; [...] our most refined thoughts and best actions, our greatest joys and deepest sorrows, use the body as a yardstick. (2006: xxvi)

Damasio's emphasis on the body's influence on thoughts, actions, and emotions is curiously reminiscent of Conrad's emphasis in his works.

According to Damasio, besides thoughts, actions, and emotions, the body is also associated closely with the aspect of the mind we call consciousness, which serves 'the critical biological function that allows us to know sorrow or know joy, to know suffering or know pleasure [...]' (1999:4); emotions are, therefore, induced by consciousness and 'played out in the theatre of the body' (1999:8). Interestingly, in a letter to R. B. Cunninghame Graham, Conrad also indicates that it is consciousness that induces emotions:

> Egoism is good, and altruism is good, and fidelity to nature would be the best of all, and systems could be built, and rules could be made – if we could only get rid of consciousness. What makes mankind tragic is not that they are the victims of nature, it is that they are conscious of it. To be part of the animal kingdom under the conditions of this earth is very well – but as soon as you know of your slavery the pain, the anger, the strife – the tragedy begins. (31 January 1898; *CL2*: 30).

Becoming aware of the conditions of the living universe induces various emotions. Conrad does not state positively that the emotions are 'played out in the theatre of the body,' but in works like *Under Western Eyes* he depicts in detail how emotions are staged in terms of the living body.

---

evidence of the strangeness of matter. If a man exceeds his body by reason of his knowledge, his intentions, memories, and thoughts, in another way he is trapped in his body. He is just this piece of matter here, so many pounds of flesh and blood [...]' (1965: 50).

142 Y. OKUDA

In literature, as in real life, it is consciousness that allows the characters to know themselves and the conditions of the surrounding world. David Lodge claims that 'literature is a record of human consciousness, the richest and most comprehensive we have':

> Works of literature describe in the guise of fiction the dense specificity of personal experience, which is always unique, because each of us has a slightly or very different personal history, modifying every new experience we have; and the creation of literary texts recapitulates this uniqueness. (2002:10)

This chapter examines how Conrad depicts Razumov's unique psychosomatic experience and demonstrates how closely the body is interwoven with consciousness, emotions, thoughts, and identity in a world subject to change and chance.

IMPRESSIONS AND CONSCIOUSNESS

The word 'impression' (168), together with such words as 'representation' (170) and 'mental image' (170), conveys a special significance for the narrator of the novel, the teacher of languages, for he maintains, 'After all, one has to fall back on that word. Impression!' (170). In Part 1 of *Under Western Eyes*, two kinds of images of Haldin are impressed upon Razumov's consciousness: a concrete image and an abstract image. The first kind of impression is visible and tangible, and it reflects the bodily presence of Haldin as Razumov witnessed it at a specific time and place:

> All black against the usual tall stove of white tiles gleaming in the dusk, stood a strange figure, wearing a skirted, close-fitting, brown cloth coat strapped round the waist, in long boots, and with a little Astrakhan cap on its head. (14)

This image presents Haldin as Razumov discovers him just as he enters his rooms. Razumov, at this point, has neither recognized the figure as Haldin nor is aware that he has committed a crime that morning, and therefore the chief emotion he feels is that of surprise. Another example of this kind of impression is the image of Haldin lying down on the bed just before Razumov leaves the rooms to take a message to Ziemianitch. By this time Razumov has already learnt what Haldin has done, and is full of anger at him for involving him in the affair; yet Haldin in this image seems quite harmless and even resigned, and perhaps for that reason Razumov's emotions of fear, hate, and anger are not reflected in the description of this image:

> He threw himself full length on Razumov's bed and putting the backs of his hands over his eyes remained perfectly motionless and silent. Not even the sound of his breathing could be heard. (23)

In contrast to these two images, the second kind of impression is conceptual and verbal, as it reflects the presence of Haldin, not as Razumov witnessed it at a specific time and place, but as he conceived it verbally in reaction to his disturbing realization that Haldin has wrought an irrevocable change in his life by what he has done: 'the appalling presence of a great crime and the stunning force of a great fanaticism' (24). This impression of Haldin is, in fact, a projection of Razumov's emotion of fear, especially the fear for his future, and this 'fear engenders in him [Razumov] a peculiarly *verbal* mode of thought' (Hawthorn 1990: 48; emphasis original); the train of thought triggered by fear engenders an abstract image which is superimposed on the concrete image. The thoughts are made up of words, and, as the narrator says at the opening of the narrative, 'Words [...] are the great foes of reality' (3); words are 'foes of reality' because they can obscure reality:

> The record of the thoughts which assailed him in the street is [...] minute and abundant. They seem to have rushed upon him with the greater freedom because his thinking powers were no longer crushed by Haldin's presence – the appalling presence of a great crime and the stunning force of a great fanaticism. (24)

It should be noted, however, that the real reason that the impression of Haldin's presence becomes repulsive to Razumov is not because it reminds him of Haldin's crime and fanaticism, but because it reminds him that Haldin has wrought an unexpected and irrevocable change on his otherwise uneventful daily life; and it engenders in Razumov a fear of losing his conceptual identity, which at that time is based on his assumptions of the bright future that the silver medal promises. This is why, when going up the stairs to his rooms after reporting Haldin to the police, Razumov defies the changed circumstances mentally, both the change that has taken place in the immediate past—'Nothing was changed' (53)—and the change that is bound to follow—'Nothing would change (53)':

> The sense of life's continuity depended on trifling bodily impression. The trivialities of daily existence were an armour for the soul. And this thought reinforced the inward quietness of Razumov as he began to climb the stairs familiar to his feet in the dark, with his hand on the familiar clammy banister. The exceptional could not prevail against the material contact which makes one day resemble another. Tomorrow would be like yesterday. (53–54)

However, in an impermanent world, each day, each moment is unique, so tomorrow is never like yesterday.

The abstract image intensifies the emotions of fear, hate, and anger in Razumov, which in their turn evoke 'a tumult of thoughts' that in the end convinces Razumov that Haldin's presence signifies 'disruption' (34)—'violent dissolution of continuity' (*OED*):

> On looking through the pages of Mr. Razumov's diary I own that a 'rush of thoughts' is not an adequate image.
> The more adequate description would be *a tumult of thoughts – the faithful reflection of the state of his feelings*. (24, emphasis added)

Likewise, during the walk after he leaves Ziemianitch, when Razumov happens to look up to the 'clear black sky of the northern winter, decorated with the sumptuous fires of the stars' (33), he receives 'an almost physical impression of endless space and of countless millions' (33), but here again the material sight of 'the black sky' and 'the stars' is supplanted by the abstract image of 'space and numbers,' which seems to him to offer 'a guarantee of duration, of safety' (33); it then convinces him of 'the one great historical fact of the land,' and engenders his belief in 'the man who would come at the appointed time' to guarantee duration and safety. (34).

It is not very surprising that Razumov should be attracted by the abstract image rather than the concrete, because he has inherited the 'peculiarity of Russian natures that, however strongly engaged in the drama of action, they are still turning their ear to the murmur of abstract ideas' (294). However, in the case of Razumov, personal experience plays an even more important role than racial inheritance because, as Lodge says, 'each of us has a slightly or very different personal history, modifying every new experience we have.' Razumov has been 'brought up in

8 THE BODY, THE THEATRE OF EMOTIONS: ...   145

an educational institute' where, he says, 'they did not give us enough to eat' (60). Therefore, he has had no experience of the filial relation and has 'never heard a word of warm affection or praise in his life' (61). More importantly, he has never been familiar with emotional communication through direct physical contact. This can be inferred from his extravagant emotional reactions to Prince K. when he meets him for the first time:

> To his intense surprise Razumov saw a white shapely hand extended to him. He took it in great confusion (it was soft and passive) and heard at the same time a condescending murmur in which he caught only the words "Satisfactory" and "Persevere." But the most amazing thing of all was to feel suddenly a distinct pressure of the white shapely hand just before it was withdrawn; a light pressure like a secret sign. The emotion of it was terrible. Razumov's heart seemed to leap into his throat. (12)

Razumov's lack of experience of direct physical contact and its emotional effects is demonstrated also in the following scene in which Razumov finds the physical contact with Haldin repulsive, whereas Haldin, who has known filial relations, seems to embrace it:

> His [Razumov's] hand fell lightly on Haldin's shoulder, and directly he felt its reality he was beset by an insane temptation to grip that exposed throat and squeeze the breath out of that body [...].
> Haldin did not stir a limb, but his overshadowed eyes moving a little gazed upwards at Razumov with wistful gratitude for this manifestation of feeling. (57–58)

Subsequently, when Haldin notices Razumov's nervous attention to his watch, and hears his reproachful appeal to sympathize with his solitary existence, as well as such telling words as 'No doubt you shall be looked upon as a martyr someday' (61), he responds to the sight and the words first by '[turning] over on his side and '[looking] on intently' (59), next by '[raising] himself on his elbow' (60), and finally by throwing his arms forward as if to keep Razumov off, crying out: 'I understand it all now [...]. I understand—at last' in 'awestruck dismay' (62). He has guessed not only what Razumov has done, but also why he has done it, for he says in 'a subdued, heartbroken attitude':

> 'I see now how it is, Razumov – brother. You are a magnanimous soul, but my action is abhorrent to you – alas... [...]. *And even my person,*

146   Y. OKUDA

too, is loathsome to you perhaps,' Haldin added mournfully, after a short
pause, looking up for a moment, then fixing his gaze on the floor. 'For
indeed, unless one...' He broke off, evidently waiting for a word. Razumov
remained silent. (62; emphasis added)

Razumov remains silent, because he has not understood the significance
of Haldin's reference to his own person. The word 'person' in this context
means '[t]he living body or physical appearance of a human being' (*OED*:
4.a.). The word 'person' is not commonly used in this sense, yet in *Under
Western Eyes* it appears repeatedly in this sense, as I will discuss in detail
later.

In Part 1, Razumov fails to respond sensitively to the body of Haldin
because, having led a solitary life, his sensitivity to the body has not developed sufficiently. His solitary life may reflect the national history of the
Russians. Being constantly exposed to dangers of existence and to fear
through 'the means by which a historical autocracy represses ideas, guards
its power, and defends its existence' (25)—such as torture and impris-
onment—makes people predisposed to disbelief in human sincerity and
goodness, that is to say, it makes people susceptible to 'cynicism'; the
narrator says, 'the spirit of Russia is the spirit of cynicism' (67). Razumov
therefore may have retreated from 'the irremediable life of the earth as
it is' (104) to a solitary life. However, such fear is the fear for what may
or may not happen in the future, whereas Razumov's failure to respond
sensitively to the physical presence of Haldin is the failure to respond
to what is before his eyes at that moment. The fact that the teacher
of languages repeatedly refers to this unique aspect of Razumov's background suggests that he is well aware of its significance in Razumov's
personal life:

That I should, at the beginning of this retrospect, mention again that Mr.
Razumov's youth had no one in the world, as literally no one as it can be
honestly affirmed of any human being, is but a statement of fact from a
man who believes in the psychological value of facts. (293)

The concrete and physical image of Haldin impressed on Razumov's
consciousness is quickly supplanted by an abstract and verbal image,
because one's consciousness is also subject to impermanence, shifting
from moment to moment. Razumov, in his solitary life, has rarely been
put in a situation in which he has noted the physical symptoms or

emotional expressions on the body of others, whereas he has often noted and responded to words, especially in writing and thought.[4]

It may be inferred from the depiction of these impressions and Razumov's reactions to them that Conrad was aware of two kinds of human consciousness which reflect two different kinds of images. The concept of dual consciousness is advocated also by Antonio Damasio in *The Feeling of What Happens: Body and Emotion in the Making of Consciousness* (1999); in this book he discusses two kinds of consciousness—core consciousness and extended consciousness—, and also two kinds of situations in which emotions are induced.

As to consciousness, Damasio maintains that:

> [...] consciousness is not a monolith, at least not in humans: it can be separated into simple and complex kinds, and the neurological evidence makes the separation transparent. (1999: 16)

He then defines the first kind of consciousness as follows:

> The simple kind, which I call *core consciousness*, provides the organism with a sense of self about one moment – now – and about one place – here. The scope of core consciousness is the here and now. Core consciousness does not illuminate the future, and the only past it vaguely lets us glimpse is that which occurred in the instant just before. (1999: 16; emphasis original)

The physical impression of Haldin imprinted on Razumov's mind, the image of Haldin with his brown cloth coat, long boots, and Astrakhan cap, standing in front of the stove, is provided by this consciousness, as Razumov senses it at the moment of his return—now—and on a certain spot facing the stove in the hallway—here. The same can be said about the image of Haldin lying on the bed, as Razumov perceives it on a spot facing the bed—here—a moment before he leaves the rooms to take a message to Ziemianitch—now.

On the other hand, the second, complex, kind of consciousness is defined by Damasio in these words:

---

[4] In the 'Introduction' to his book (1990), Hawthorn discusses words as the language of thought from a narrative point of view, and Yael Levin, in 'The Interruption of Writing: Uncanny Intertextuality in *Under Western Eye*,' discusses the novel as 'a story of writing.'

148   Y. OKUDA

> [...] the complex kind of consciousness, which I call *extended consciousness* and of which there are many levels and grades, provides the organism with an elaborate sense of self – an identity and a person, you or me, no less – and places that person at a point in individual historical time, richly aware of the lived past and of the anticipated future, and keenly cognizant of the world beside it. (1999: 16; emphasis original)

The abstract image of Haldin as 'the appalling presence of a great crime and the stunning force of a great fanaticism' (18) is provided by what Damasio calls 'extended consciousness'; the image arouses a sense of self which incorporates both 'the lived past' and 'the anticipated future' of Razumov, and makes him keenly aware of its precariousness.

Next, Damasio's idea of the two situations which induce emotions may also be applied to Razumov's situations in the narrative; Damasio says that the first kind of situation occurs:

> [...] when the organism processes certain objects or situations with one of its sensory devices – for instance, when the organism takes in the sight of a familiar face or place' (1999: 56).

This kind of situation corresponds to the situation in which Razumov responds to Haldin's physical presence with his visual sense. Damasio goes on to say:

> The second type of circumstance occurs when the mind of an organism conjures up from memory certain objects and situations and represents them as images in the thought process – for instance, remembering the face of a friend and the fact she has just died. (1999: 56)

This second type of situation corresponds to the situation in which Razumov conjures up Haldin's image from memory after leaving the eating-house, and is seized by 'a tranquil, unquenchable hate' (31) for Haldin, which starts 'the thought process' in his mind that eventually convinces him that 'Haldin means disruption' (34):

> For a train of thought is never false. The falsehood lies deep in the necessities of existence, in secret fears and half-formed ambitions, in the secret confidence combined with a secret mistrust of ourselves, in the love of hope and the dread of uncertain days. (33–34)

8 THE BODY, THE THEATRE OF EMOTIONS: ... 149

It is Razumov's unacknowledged emotions, such as his fears, ambitions, and confidence, that falsify his train of thought.

Conrad's depiction of these situations indicates that, for better or worse, it is what Damasio calls 'extended consciousness' that induces complex emotions, which in their turn evoke positive or negative thought processes. As a result, the embodied image of Haldin's figure 'left lying on his bed' (37), provided by core consciousness, is reduced to no more than a 'distinct but vanishing illusion' (55) on the snow; and as it is devoid of substance, Razumov easily walks over it; however, in doing so he betrays not Haldin, but himself; that is to say, he determines to disregard the concrete image of Haldin provided by core consciousness and chooses to embrace the abstract image provided by extended consciousness. It is only when he subsequently informs the police that he actually betrays Haldin.

This comparison of Conrad's psychosomatic depiction of Razumov and the recent ideas in cognitive science indicates Conrad's remarkably keen insight into human consciousness and emotions. The next section will examine how Razumov's consciousness undergoes a subtle change in the course of the face-to-face conversations he holds with several other characters after he arrives in Geneva.

Conversation and the Body

The word 'conversation' originally meant '[t]he action of living or having one's being *in* a place or *among* persons.' (*OED* 1: Obsolete; Italics original); today it means '[i]nterchange of thoughts and words' (*OED* 7.a.), but before the invention of the telephone and the Internet, holding conversations with others entailed face-to-face contact. In *Under Western Eyes*, Razumov holds conversations with several characters, which demand his physical presence '*in* a place,' or '*among* persons'; they offer him fresh opportunities to familiarize himself with the physicality of his interlocutors, and as a result his sense of the body of himself and others begins to sharpen. On examining the subtle changes that occur in Razumov's consciousness and the sense of the body, the following three conversations will be discussed in the order that they take place in the novel, beginning with the conversation with the teacher of languages, followed by the conversation with Sophia Antonovna, and ending with the conversation with Natalia Haldin.

150 Y. OKUDA

As conversations assume the interlocutors' physical presence, these scenes are depicted dramatically; that is to say, not enacted as in drama, but told visually. Jeremy Hawthorn says that in the novel:

> If our first impression is that we are witnessing a scene directly, a second glance will confirm that we are actually being *told* about the scene. The telling is such that we can visualize what is described [...]. (1985: 10; Italics original)

The dramatic scenes in the novel are similar to what we witness onstage:

> Onstage, bodies constantly engage with one another, characters revealing themselves through their gestures and trying to read each other's bodily signs. (Hillman 2015: 46)

In the novel also, characters reveal themselves 'through gestures' and try 'to read each other's bodily signs.' The dramatic effect is precisely what Conrad aimed at in *Under Western Eyes*. In the letter addressed to Macdonald Hastings mentioned earlier, Conrad refers to the artistic aim of this novel in these words:

> My artistic aim was to put as much dramatic spirit into the form of a novel as was possible without apparently departing from the form. It is the dramatization of the inner feelings – and also of *ideas*, brought out in scene and dialogue as near as possible without the novel ceasing to be a novel and becoming a hybrid and unsatisfactory freak of presentation. I tried to keep close to scenic effects all the time. (*CL5* 696)

The word 'dramatization' confirms the importance of dramatic effects suggested by Tanner and Hawthorn, and the phrase 'inner feelings' recalls the same phrase used in Conrad's letter to Edward Noble, indicating that, in *Under Western Eyes*, the dramatic effects are closely connected with the issue of emotions.

The first prolonged conversation that Razumov holds with a stranger is his interview with Councilor Mikulin at the General Secretariat in St. Petersburg; apart from Mikulin's dim gaze, which is 'almost without expression' (86), and the inscrutable gestures of raising his hand and passing it down his face deliberately (96) or glancing rapidly down his beard (88), the conversation is predominantly verbal and there are few references to the body. In contrast, the conversation between Razumov and the teacher of languages which takes place on the Bastions in Geneva is surprisingly full of 'the communicative and expressive potentialities of the physical human body.'

The teacher of languages is often discussed by critics in the role of a narrator, sometimes as an impercipient narrator who 'never achieves any sympathetic insight into Razumov's inner predicament' (Tanner in Carabine 1992: 140–41), and at other times as 'a dynamic character who grows in stature as he is drawn into situations requiring personal commitment and moral discrimination' (Schwarz 1980: 195). He is a homodiegetic narrator, like Marlow, a narrator but also a character in the situations and events he recounts. In the scene in which the teacher of languages is engaged in a long conversation with Razumov on the Bastion, he is first and foremost a character; he is depicted as sharing the same time and space as Razumov, and he sometimes suspends his role as a narrator and tells us only the things he could have known as a character.

The teacher of languages as a character demonstrates certain features: he is English, so he is not as partial to words and abstract ideas as the Russians are; on the contrary, he values physicality, as can be inferred from the following words he uses:

> Life is a thing of *form*. It has its *plastic shape* and a definite intellectual aspect. The most idealistic conceptions of love and forbearance must be *clothed in flesh* as it were before they can be made understandable. (106, emphasis added)

Neither could he be as imperceptive and unimaginative as he sets himself up to be, as he is after all not just a teacher of languages but, as Razumov puts it more accurately, 'a teacher of English literature' (188) who has been 'reading English poetry' with Natalia Haldin (188), and reading poetry requires a certain amount of perception and imagination.[5]

The teacher of languages' interest in Razumov is not official, like the interest of Councilor Mikulin who, as an officer in power, is interested in how Razumov could be made serviceable to the Tsarist regime; the teacher of languages' interest in Razumov is personal, as it arises from his complex but only half-admitted affection for Natalia Haldin and also his mistrust of Peter Ivanovitch: he has a 'fear of seeing the girl surrender

---

[5] Natalia Haldin expresses a wish to 'go through a course of reading the best English authors with a competent teacher' (101).

152   Y. OKUDA

to the influence of the Chateau Borel revolutionary feminism' (164–65). Not being an officer in power or a revolutionist, the teacher of languages does not suspect Razumov of being a revolutionary opponent of the Tsarist regime, as does General T., but neither does he share Sophia Antonovna's admiring opinion of him, an opinion based on a view of him as the hero of a successful revolutionary plot, although he may have suspected him of having been involved in the plot.

When the teacher of languages becomes aware that Natalia Haldin wants him to prepare the ground for her next meeting with Razumov by informing him about her mother's state of mind, he seizes the opportunity to probe Razumov's personality. On this occasion, the teacher of languages, characteristically, pays more attention to Razumov's body than to his enigmatic words, and draws his own inferences. The teacher of languages is sensitive, both in the sense that he is quick to detect the physical symptoms of others and in the sense that he appreciates the feelings of others. He detects Razumov's physical symptoms even before he is introduced to him; he observes Razumov's 'faint commencement of a forced smile, followed by the suspicion of a frown' (179), and says: 'I detected them, though neither could have been noticed by a person less intensely bent upon divining him than myself,' which shows how keen he is on finding out about Razumov's personality for the sake of Natalia Haldin. He also notices Razumov's brusque movements, often followed by a totter (184), and 'the convulsive start' of his body (189). When he observes the quiver on Razumov's lips which seems to suggest that he was 'wickedly amused' by Natalia Haldin's assumption about his ability to understand her, he says:

> I looked at him rather hard. Was there a hidden and inexplicable sneer in this retort? No. It was not that. It might have been resentment. Yes. But what had he to resent? He looked as though he had not slept very well of late. I could almost feel on me the weight of his unrefreshed, motionless stare, the stare of a man who lies unwinking in the dark, angrily passive in the toils of disastrous thoughts. Now, when I know how true it was, I can honestly affirm that this *was* the effect he produced on me. It was painful in a curiously indefinite way […]. (183; emphasis original)

By observing Razumov's physical symptoms, the teacher of languages successfully divines his feelings and even feels the impression of Razumov's 'toils of disastrous thoughts' as a 'weight' on his own body; as a

8 THE BODY, THE THEATRE OF EMOTIONS: ... 153

result, he experiences an empathetic feeling for the 'painful' situation that Razumov is in. (183).

In addition to this capacity for empathy[6], the teacher of languages has the ability to refrain from forming hasty conclusions when he is drawn into situations which require personal engagement and moral discernment. For instance, when Razumov offensively charges him with expecting him to understand so much, he at first remains 'silent, checked between the obvious fact and the subtle impression' (184), and then, valuing 'the subtle impression' above 'the obvious fact,' tells himself: 'he seems a sombre, even a desperate revolutionist; but he is young, he may be unselfish and humane, capable of compassion [...]' (184). Again, when the teacher of languages happens to mention the peculiar circumstances of Haldin's arrest, he has his arm suddenly gripped by Razumov:

> I felt my arm seized above the elbow, and next instant found myself swung so as to face Mr. Razumov.
> "You spring up from the ground before me with this talk. Who the devil are you? [...] Why! What for!" (186)

He is surprised at 'this display of unexpectedly profound emotion' (187), but again refrains from making hasty judgement and, feeling 'sorry for him' (187), invites Razumov to sit down at one of the vacant tables. The teacher of languages' responses to Razumov's offensive speeches, aggressive behaviour, and outbursts of emotion during their conversation demonstrate not only that he has a considerable fund of empathy, but also that he has a latent capacity for what John Keats calls 'negative capability'; that is to say, he is capable of accepting uncertainties without making further inquiry.

From Razumov's point of view, the teacher of languages is 'a stranger, a foreigner, an old man' (189–90). Razumov cannot fathom his English way of thinking, and consequently he cannot frame his own thoughts about him verbally; he therefore stares at him all the time, on the alert for any physical signs. He is so perplexed that he is even driven to ask him outright, "'What are you at? What is your object?'" (185). On the

---

[6] According to Hogan, empathy is fundamentally 'a process that—when successful—allows a person to achieve some explicit or implicit knowledge of the mental states of other people' (2022: 159).

154   Y. OKUDA

other hand, this new experience of essentially non-verbal communication has the benefit of stimulating Razumov's dormant sense of the body.

Razumov is a very sensitive character, and therefore he could not have been totally unaware of the teacher of languages' enigmatic tolerance of his offensive speeches and sympathetic concern for his emotional outbursts. This is indicated in an incident in which the teacher of languages tells Razumov that Mrs. and Miss Haldin's implicit belief in his judgement and the truthfulness of his word makes it impossible for him 'to pass them by like strangers' (140). The teacher of languages is deeply disconcerted by Razumov's piteous cry, '"Must I go then and lie to that old woman!"':

> It was not anger; it was something else, something more poignant, and not so simple. I was aware of it sympathetically, while I was profoundly concerned at the nature of that exclamation. (190–91)

Subsequently the teacher of languages is irritated by Razumov's ambiguous attitude to the reported circumstances of Haldin's arrest, and pronounces, '"Either the man is a hero to you, or..."' (191). At first, Razumov responds aggressively: 'He approached his face with fiercely distended nostrils close to mine so suddenly that I had the greatest difficulty in not starting back' (191); however, the next moment Razumov unexpectedly makes an appeal to him for sympathy:

> '" [....] Look here! I am a worker. I studied. Yes, I studied very hard. [...] Don't you think a Russian may have sane ambitions? Yes – I had even prospects. Certainly! I had. And now you see me here, abroad, everything gone, lost, sacrificed. You see me here – and you ask! You see me, don't you? – sitting before you."' (191)

This is one of the most poignant scenes in the narrative. Razumov made a similar appeal for sympathy to Haldin, but that was understandable because by then Haldin had become vaguely aware of the circumstances in which Razumov found himself. However, what is the point of making such an unreasonable appeal for sympathy to a stranger and a foreigner like the teacher of languages, who at this juncture does not know the circumstances of his despair? The only possible answer is that Razumov has been driven to make the appeal because he is moved by the teacher of languages' sympathetic and tolerant attitude towards him. The misdirected appeal for sympathy is poignant because it exposes the depth of Razumov's moral solitude, and ironic because such an unreasonable appeal is usually made only to one's family or intimate friends. However, what is most ironic in this scene is that by appealing to the teacher of languages in such words as, 'You see me here—and you ask! *You see me* [...] *sitting before you*' (emphasis added), Razumov is inadvertently appealing to him to acknowledge his visible and tangible presence and accept him as a whole being there and then. This is the very thing he failed to do when he was appealed to do so by Haldin, as he finished telling him the circumstances of his escape that morning: 'And so...*here I am*' (18; emphasis added).

This incident is followed by another incident in which Razumov responds with a gesture, unaccompanied by speech, when the teacher of languages casually mentions Natalia Haldin's suspicion of betrayal.

> "[...]. As to Miss Haldin herself, she at one time was disposed to think that her brother had been betrayed to the police in some way."
>
> To my great surprise Mr. Razumov sat down again suddenly. I stared at him, and I must say that he returned my stare without winking for quite a considerable time. (193)

What crossed their minds while they thus stared at each other? The teacher of languages does not tell us even what crossed his own mind, but this scene is one of the most effective illustrations of dramatic irony in the novel. Moreover, it should be noted that on this occasion Razumov's reaction is curiously free from his usual expression of resentment and aggressiveness, which may have surprised the teacher of languages, and that may be why he quickly adds, "'Some unforeseen event, a sheer accident might have done that, [...] the folly or weakness of some unhappy fellow-revolutionist'" (193), not realizing that Razumov is that 'unhappy' person, if not a 'fellow-revolutionist.' Razumov's subsequent question, "'But what do you think?'" (194) is not defiant but yielding; and his response to the teacher of languages' answer, "'I like what you said just now'" (194), sounds like an acceptance of the view that the betrayal was the result of '[s]ome unforeseen event, a sheer accident.' It is even suggestive of an awakening sense of trust in him.

156   Y. OKUDA

On this occasion, the teacher of languages comes closest to the truth about the circumstances of Haldin's arrest, yet he refrains from ascertaining the facts of the situation and directs his attention to Razumov himself, because he values physically manifested subtle impressions over verbally expressed facts. The teacher of languages enters into Razumov's feelings by sensing something 'painful' in his stare (183), something 'pitiful' in his voice (184), something 'poignant' in his cry (191), something distressing in the clasping of his hands (195), and something shocking in the queer expression on his face:

> What strange thought had come into his head? What vision of all the horrors that can be seen in his hopeless country had come suddenly to haunt his brain? If it were anything connected with the fate of Victor Haldin, then I hoped earnestly he would keep it to himself for ever. (196)

The teacher of languages detects a reflection of horror on Razumov's face, but does not wish to have a glimpse into his vision to ascertain its cause. Here again, the teacher of languages restricts his report to what he experienced as a character. The passage is somewhat reminiscent of the impression of horror Marlow detects on Kurtz's face and his cry of 'The horror! The horror!' in 'Heart of Darkness.'

The conversation between Razumov and the teacher of languages ends here, but there is an epilogue to it at the beginning of Part 3. As soon as the teacher of languages walks away and Razumov finds himself alone by the bridge, he shows signs of scorn and resentment towards him, calling him 'that meddlesome old Englishman,' which exhibits a striking contrast to the yielding attitude he had manifested towards him at the end of the conversation. This abrupt change of attitude is reminiscent of the change that suddenly comes over him when he leaves Haldin behind in his rooms to find Ziemianitch; on that occasion, too, he suddenly starts to attack Haldin verbally in his thoughts, because 'his thinking powers were no longer crushed by Haldin's presence' (24); he does the same thing here as soon as his thinking powers are no longer suppressed by the presence of the teacher of languages. If we applied Damasio's theory in interpreting this scene, Razumov's sudden change of attitude might be explained as a switch from core consciousness to extended consciousness: the impression of the physical presence of the teacher of languages provided by core consciousness weakens, and the impression provided by extended consciousness, the thought which reflects Razumov's feelings heightens. However, there is one difference between Razumov's reaction in the earlier scene and his reaction in this scene; in this scene Razumov at first tries to dismiss what happened as 'insignificant,' if 'not absurd,' but then, on reflection, he decides that in fact '[t]here is nothing, no one, too insignificant, too absurd to be disregarded' (198). It suggests that Razumov has become less attached to his thoughts and is now capable of reflecting on them more dispassionately. The change that has come over him is reflected in a curious experience he has, which will be discussed later.

The second conversation, the long conversation with Sophia Antonovna, takes place on the grounds of the Chateau Borel on a 'day of many conversations' (237), a couple of weeks after the conversation with the teacher of languages. The teacher of languages is not physically involved in the scene, and therefore he may have gained the details of this conversation from Razumov's diary. If so, the report manifests an improvement in Razumov's acuteness of vision and insight, compared with the report on the conversation with Mikulin.

Sophia Antonovna is a revolutionist with white hair, who has been involved in revolutionary activities since she was sixteen, and who has sacrificed most of her life to the revolutionary cause, even her love: she is Peter Ivanovitch's 'right hand, as it were,' (253), and as we learn from Razumov's train of thought, '[s]tripped of rhetoric, mysticism and theories, she was the true spirit of destructive revolution' (261). Although she is Russian, she has spent more than 20 years shuttling in and out of Russia, so in some ways she is not typically Russian. For instance, although she shares the Russian partiality to words and abstract ideas, she is also capable of detecting physical symptoms in others, and once she even responds to Razumov by looking at him not 'as a listener looks at one, but as if the words he chose to say were only of secondary interest' (242).

Sophia Antonovna's interest in Razumov is twofold. On the one hand, as a revolutionist with power, she is interested in how Razumov can be made serviceable to the revolution, especially in the approaching insurrection in the Balkans. She tells Razumov that he is 'likely to turn out an invaluable acquisition for the work in hand,' and seems even to 'be already apportioning him, in her mind, his share of the work' (258). On the other hand, as a private individual she is puzzled by the physical symptoms she observes in Razumov and his enigmatic remarks: '[…] it was a special— a unique case. She had never met an individuality which interested and puzzled her so much' (269).

158   Y. OKUDA

For Razumov, the accidental meeting with Sophia Antonovna at the gates of the Chateau Borel is not as bewildering as his totally unexpected encounter with the teacher of languages on the Bastions was, because he has spent three days with her in Zurich before coming to Geneva, and also because she is a Russian who comes from the same cultural background as he does. He even shares, to a certain extent, the regard shown to her by other revolutionists:

> He knew nothing of her parentage, nothing of her private history or political record; he judged her from his own private point of view, as being a distinct danger in his path. "Judged" is not perhaps the right word. It was more of a feeling, the summing up of slight impression aided by the discovery that he could not despise her as he despised all the others. (242)

Here Razumov, like the teacher of languages, depends on 'a feeling, the summing up of slight impression' to make her out. It may be that he feels a regard for her because he is impressed by 'the simple, brisk self-possession of the mature personality,' which in its turn suggested that 'in her revolutionary pilgrimage she had discovered the secret, not of everlasting youth, but of everlasting endurance' (264).

In the first half of this conversation, Sophia Antonovna also seems to judge Razumov by 'a feeling, the summing up of slight impressions,' that is to say by giving her attention to Razumov's physical symptoms and emotional expressions. She detects his lassitude under his sarcastic remark, and asks him frankly, "'What is the matter with you?'" (240). She sees through his affected smile and exclaims, "'What are you trying to insinuate?'" On some occasions she embarrasses Razumov by voicing her doubts about him: she says "'What are you flinging your very heart against? Or perhaps you are only playing a part",' (251) and also "'One does not know what to think, Razumov. You must have bitten something bitter in your cradle'" (253). Like the teacher of languages, who is checked between 'the obvious fact' of Razumov's verbal 'sally' and 'the subtle impression' of 'his voice' (184), she is checked between the obvious fact of his bitter and sarcastic replies and the subtle impressions of his physical symptoms.

However, Sophia Antonovna is a Russian, who shares 'the Russians' extraordinary love of words' (4), and therefore in the second half of the conversation Sophia Antonovna's Russian predisposition for words seems to revive, especially after she begins to question Razumov about a letter she received from St. Petersburg three days earlier. She was pleased to have come upon Razumov on the grounds of the Chateau Borel, because she wanted to question him about the letter. When Sophia Antonovna asks him abruptly whether he attended the lecture at the university on the morning of the assassination, Razumov tries to restrain his alarm by gripping a bar of the gate, and answers, '"Lectures—certainly […]. But what makes you ask?"' On this occasion Sophia Antonovna expresses no suspicion at what he says. She just says, 'I call such coolness superb' and even adds that 'It is a proof of uncommon strength of character' (255). Again, when Razumov begins to enlarge on the circumstances of his escape, and says that he felt inclined to lie down and sleep in the side-street, telling her what he had actually heard from Haldin, she '[clicks] her tongue at that symptom, very struck indeed' (256). She is so convinced that she says, 'If you have luck as well as determination, then indeed you are likely to turn out an invaluable acquisition for the work in hand"' (258). Ironically, in this scene, Sophia Antonovna mentions the word 'hand' a couple of times, but fails to notice that Razumov's hand is gripping the bar of the gate or that his lips are trembling. She seems to have become suddenly more easily swayed by the words spoken by Razumov, as well as the words in her own thoughts:

> " […] You are not an enthusiast, but there is an immense force of revolt in you. I felt it from the first, directly I set my eyes on you – you remember – in Zurich. Oh! You are full of bitter revolt. That is good. […] that uncompromising sense of necessity and justice which armed your and Haldin's hands to strike down that fanatical brute…for it was that – nothing but that! *I have been thinking it out.*" (260–61; emphasis added)

Sophia Antonovna is easily persuaded also by what Razumov tells her about the suspicion raised against Ziemianitch. When Razumov tells her that Haldin tended to take fancies on insufficient grounds, she forms a hasty conclusion, saying, "That, to my mind, settles it"' (274), adding, '"Every word you say confirms to my mind the suspicion communicated to me in that very interesting letter".' Razumov, however, is able to perceive that '[i]t was really the idea of her correspondent, but Sophia Antonovna had adopted it fully' (275). Finally, alluding to the subject that Razumov is most uneasy about, that is whether or not his own visit to the eating-house had passed unnoticed, Sophia Antonovna again agrees

160   Y. OKUDA

with the writer of the letter and draws her conclusion from the words in the letter: "'Some scoundrelly detective was sent to fetch him along, and being vexed at finding him so drunk broke a stable fork over his ribs'" (282).

In the course of this long conversation, Sophia Antonovna undergoes a subtle change of attitude: at first she seems to value subtle impressions over words, but later she seems to become less sensitive to bodily impressions and more sensitive to words, both to the words which Razumov utters and to the words in the letter; in other words, she becomes more Russian than she was at the beginning of the conversation, and ends up drawing a mistaken conclusion by 'keeping so close to the truth, departing from it so far in the verisimilitude of thoughts and conclusions,' consequently giving Razumov 'the notion of the invincible nature of human error, a glimpse into the utmost depths of self-deception' (282).

'Person,' or the Living Body

Razumov's perception of human susceptibility to verbal self-deception indicates that he has matured a little emotionally. When he was 'assailed' by thoughts which reflected his feelings in St. Petersburg (24), he was not able to resist them; however, in the course of the conversations with various characters in Geneva, his sense of the body sharpens, and he becomes more capable of responding to reality with his body. This process is marked in the narrative by the constant, if not frequent, use of the word 'person,' in the sense of 'the living body.' .

The word 'person' is used in this sense for the first time when Haldin says to Razumov, 'even my person, too, is loathsome to you perhaps' (62). Although Razumov fails to appreciate the significance of the word in the earlier scene, it does not necessarily indicate that he is innately incapable of responding to the physicality of others. When he meets Natalia Haldin for the first time below the terrace of the Chateau Borel, at first, he responds spontaneously to her physical presence:

> Coming up with Peter Ivanovitch, he did observe her; their eyes had met, even. He had responded, as no one could help responding, to *the harmonious charm of her whole person, its strength, its grace, its tranquil frankness* [...]. (167, emphasis added)

However, this impression does not last long, for, when Natalia Haldin stretches out her hand and Razumov fully recognizes that she is Haldin's sister, the abstract impression he has had of her brother is superimposed on her image and he experiences a powerful emotional reaction of hate and dismay: the recognition 'nearly suffocated him physically with an emotional reaction of hate and dismay, as though her appearance had been a piece of accomplished treachery' (167). This indicates that at this stage Razumov has not yet matured, which is understandable, as the event takes place only several days after Natalia Haldin learns of his arrival in Geneva, so he has not yet held any significant conversations, although he does so subsequently.

The first subtle change that leads to a change in his reaction to the living body or 'person' can be detected soon after his long conversation with the teacher of languages.

> Razumov felt a faint chill run down his spine. It was not fear. He was certain that it was not fear – not fear for himself – but it was, all the same, a sort of apprehension as if for another, for some one he knew without being able to put a name on the personality. (199)

Who is this personality that he knows but cannot identify? It seems as though the unexpected and excruciating conversation he has just had with the teacher of languages, whose cultural and communicative assumptions are so different from those of his fellow countrymen, has somehow extended his mental horizons so that he has become capable of noticing things that he had never noticed before about himself. The last word, 'personality,' signifies a person considered as the possessor of individual characteristics or qualities. Who is this familiar but anonymous personality, who can affect him physically by sending a chill down his spine? It is an aspect of Razumov's own personality whose individual characteristics and qualities have hitherto remained unnoticed by him; it represents what the narrator calls 'that side of our emotional life to which his solitary existence had been a stranger' (357–58).

About a week later, Razumov receives a similar but more distinct impression just after he has had a conversation with Madame de S—. Madame de S—is 'presented to the reader in the form of a set of relatively discrete body-parts whose sum does not necessarily merit the privilege of a personal pronoun' (Hawthorn 1990: 243). During the conversation,

162   Y. OKUDA

Razumov is fascinated by the symptoms and expressions of the 'body-parts,' but is not much concerned with the emotions that they convey. In contrast, when Tekla comes into the room to pour more tea, he notices her anxious and scared face, and becomes concerned at how she is treated by Peter Ivanovitch and Madame de S—. This is the first time Razumov gives his full attention to someone else's feelings, forgetful of his own; and it is interesting to note that this altruistic reaction strengthens his grasp of reality:

> He was calming down, getting hold of the actuality into which he had been thrown – for the first time perhaps since Victor Haldin had entered his room...and had gone out again. (218)

It is soon after this experience that Razumov receives another, more distinct, impression of the newly discovered aspect of his self on the terrace:

> He felt, bizarre as it may seem, as though another self, an independent sharer of his mind, had been able to view *his whole person* very distinctly indeed. (230, emphasis added)

This time, the familiar but unidentified 'personality' not only shares his mind but seems to have acquired a body, because the personality has gained the visual sense with which to view Razumov's 'whole person very distinctly indeed.' The episode indicates that Razumov has become more sensitive to his own body—an indispensable step to achieving the ultimate goal of confessing to Natalia Haldin. The constant appearance of the word 'person,' signifying the living body, demonstrates that the theme of the body runs throughout the narrative. It traces the development of Razumov's sensitivity to the body from the time he finds Haldin waiting for him in his rooms to the time he discovers Natalia Haldin waiting for him in the anteroom.

The theme of the body can be discerned in the scene of his encounter with Mrs. Haldin. Brief as this encounter is, it is made profound by the subtle layers of irony it possesses. First, Mrs. Haldin, who seems to embody filial relationship in opposition to Razumov's unfamiliarity with it, ironically shares his trait of allowing emotions to reflect on thoughts; Natalia Haldin says, 'At first poor mother went numb [...] then she began to think and she will go on now thinking and thinking in its unfortunate strain' (117). As a result, by the time Razumov visits her, she is possessed by the illusory thought that her son is still alive and even that he has returned; at first, therefore, she turns to him eagerly, but when she realizes that Razumov's story contradicts with her assumption that her son is still alive, she disregards both his words and his presence, and sits looking down on the illusory image of her son's head on her lap. (339) Razumov, who disregarded Haldin's physical presence in his rooms, and repulsed even the memory of its impression, now finds his own presence repulsed by Haldin's mother, as if in revenge.

Alarmed by this unexpected reaction, Razumov at first tries to persuade himself that 'the phantom's mother consumed with grief and white as a ghost [...] was of no importance. Mothers did not matter' (340), but very soon realizes that maternal affection cannot be disregarded as insignificant; and immediately the envy towards Haldin revives in the guise of 'the old anger' (341). As he leaves the drawing room, he broods on the chances of stealing his sister's soul to take his revenge on Haldin, which the teacher of languages detects as 'something consciously evil' (337) on his face.

Words, The Foes of Reality

The last long conversation, the conversation between Razumov and Natalia Haldin, begins with her unexpected presence in the ante-room, which takes Razumov by surprise. The word 'unexpected' appears 21 times in *Under Western Eyes*, compared with seven times in *Lord Jim*, 10 times in *Nostromo*, and 14 times in *The Secret Agent*. As I have discussed in previous chapters, in Conrad's works, the word is suggestive of a contingent world which intrudes suddenly through the layers of our assumptions. In *Under Western Eyes*, such significant intrusions play an important role in changing Razumov's consciousness: when he recognizes Haldin, Razumov cries out 'But this is indeed unexpected' (14); the presence of the teacher of languages at the Bastions was 'a very unexpected fact [...] to stumble on' (182); he had not 'expected to see her [Sophia Antonovna] so soon' (242); and he detects 'something he had not expected' in the obstinacy shown by Mrs. Haldin. (337)[7] On all these occasions, it may be said that what Damasio calls 'core consciousness' is temporarily enhanced in Razumov. According to Sue Zemka, human beings have always been fascinated with sudden events: 'With unexpected changes and turning points; with insights that arrive in a flash; with things that come in a moment: shocks, surprises, love, gods, ghosts, accidents, explosions and revelations' (1).

Natalia Haldin's presence in the anteroom was also 'as unforeseen as the apparition of her brother had been' (341), and it is the sudden and unexpected appearance of Natalia Haldin in the anteroom that enables Razumov to become fully conscious of her physical presence as well as his own. It signifies that he has gained an insight into the true nature of the identity of his whole being. At first glance, Razumov's emotional reaction to Natalia Haldin on this occasion seems like a repetition of what took place in the garden of Chateau Borel. However, there is one important difference; in this scene, Natalia Haldin's concrete image is not replaced by Haldin's abstract image which reflected his hate and anger for him:

> He raised his face, pale, full of unexpressed suffering. But that look in his eyes of dull, absent obstinacy, which struck and surprised everybody he was talking to, began to pass away. It was as though he were coming to himself in the awakened consciousness of that marvellous harmony of feature, of lines, of glances, of voice, which made of the girl before him a being so rare, outside, and, as it were, above the common notion of beauty. (342–43)

It is at this moment that Razumov acknowledges the significance of the living body; he frees himself from the emotion-based abstract image he has had of Haldin, the image that had given his eyes the look of 'dull, absent obstinacy,' and by accepting his sister's physical presence wholeheartedly, he belatedly acknowledges Haldin's physical presence, the 'person' that had once been so 'loathsome' to him. Razumov writes in his diary:

---

[7] Interestingly, Razumov tells Haldin that he imagined '[e]ternity' to be 'something quiet and dull,' because '[t]here would be nothing unexpected [...]. The element of time would be wanting' (59); it seems to suggests that Razumov was vaguely aware of 'the unexpected' in his personal life.

8 THE BODY, THE THEATRE OF EMOTIONS: ... 165

> Suddenly you stood before me! You alone in all the world I must confess.
> You fascinated me – you freed me from the blindness of anger and hate –
> the truth shining in you drew the truth out of me. (261)

He attains an insight into his own identity when he becomes aware that Natalia Haldin's identity resided in 'that marvellous harmony' of her person.

Razumov's conversation with Natalia Haldin in the anteroom is the most dramatic in the narrative, and it is meant to be so. There is the stage:

> The light of an electric bulb high up under the ceiling searched that clear square box into its four bare corners, crudely, without shadows – a strange stage for an obscure drama. (342)

There are the two performers—Razumov and Natalia Haldin—and the audience—the teacher of languages. In the letter to Hastings quoted earlier, Conrad says, '[...] it is in order to keep always before myself the effect of a "performance" that I invented the old teacher of languages' (*CR*5: 696), which indicates that Conrad had fully intended the scene to produce dramatic effects.

Natalia Haldin is a Russian, with the Russian partiality to words and abstract ideas. She is obsessed by her brother's words of praise for Razumov as one of the '[u]nstained, lofty, and solitary existences' (135). The teacher of languages calls it 'a confident exaggeration of praise' (169), and reflects that 'the character of the words which I perceived very well must tip the scale of the girl's feelings in that young man's favour' (169). The words 'unstained, lofty, and solitary existences' had evoked a 'representation of that exceptional friend, a mental image of him' (170) in her mind long before she even met Razumov. Haldin's words do not correspond with the physical impression she receives from Razumov when she meets him for the first time; what impresses her most when she meets him in the garden of Château Borel is that he is 'a man of such strong feeling' and that '[he] seems to be a man who has suffered more from his thought than from evil fortune' (168). These subtle physical impressions describe Razumov more accurately than her brother's words, but she continues to cling on to his words. This attachment to words on her part is what makes it so difficult for Razumov to convey to her the truth of the circumstances of her brother's arrest and his betrayal.

Razumov makes three attempts to convey the truth to Natalia Haldin, twice with words and once with the body. The first time that Razumov tries to make an oblique verbal confession is when Natalia Haldin tells him that he is the only person who could comfort her mother. He tries to make her understand that, as he has never had any experience of filial relationship, it is now too late for her to expect such a tenderness from him, but she interprets Razumov's bitterness and suppressed anger as 'the signs of an indignant rectitude' (345). She even says to him callously, if not intentionally, 'it is in you that we can find all that is left of his generous soul' (346), suggesting that she wishes him to remain true to her brother's words because, if it should be otherwise, it may cast a slur on her brother's character. The reader who is aware of the dramatic irony, understands why Razumov retorts 'as if speech were something disgusting or deadly' (346).

Then, when Natalia Haldin informs him of her mother's present condition, Razumov tells her that he did not tell her mother either that Haldin meant to escape or that his last conversation was with him:

> Of you he said that you had trustful eyes. [...] It meant that there is in you no guile, no deception, no falsehood, no suspicion – nothing in your heart that could give you a conception of a living, acting, speaking lie, if ever it came in your way. That you were a predestined victim...Ha! What a devilish suggestion!" (349)

This virtual confession, together with his sarcastic comments on the revolutionists, including Sophia Antonovna, and his indictment of words, 'the old Father of Lies—our national patron—our domestic god' (350), should have conveyed to her that he was not the man she believed him to ·be. Here he is virtually telling her that he himself was that 'living, acting, speaking lie' who had tried to deceive her, but Natalia Haldin continues to appeal to him to 'utter at last some word worthy of her exalted trust in her brother's friend' (351), blinded by her obsession with her brother's words; the physical impression that the teacher of languages perceives—the impression that Razumov 'had stabbed himself outside and had come in there to show it' (350)—may be a reflection of Razumov's impatience

8 THE BODY, THE THEATRE OF EMOTIONS: ... 167

at her obtuseness, an attempt to destroy her mental image of him.[8] The teacher of languages, who has discerned the truth, says:

> Utterly misled by her own enthusiastic interpretation of two lines in the letter of a visionary, under the spell of her own dread of lonely days, in their overshadowed world of angry strife, she was unable to see the truth struggling on his lips. (354)

Not only the teacher of languages, but Razumov also perceives that it is her obsession with words—the 'foes of reality'—that is hindering her from perceiving the truth that he is trying to convey to her. It is then, only then, that Razumov resorts to a confession by means of the body:

> "The story, Kirylo Sidorovitch, the story!"
> "There is no more to tell!" He made a movement forward and she actually put her hand on his shoulder to push him away but her strength failed her and he kept his ground though trembling in every limb. "It ends here – on this very spot." He pressed a denunciatory finger to his breast with force, and became perfectly still. (354)

The gesture indicates that Razumov has understood the nature of the curse that the teacher of languages had told him of (194), and has found the means to break it as well. The words, 'It ends here—on this very spot' indicate that he has finally found an answer to Mikulin's question, 'Where to?' (99), and realized that the only place he can retire to is his own 'person.'

When he breaks the curse laid on him by 'the old Father of Lies' and '[escapes] from the prison of lies' (363), he at the same time breaks the curse laid on Natalia Haldin and frees her from being held in captivity to her brother's words. As Hugh Epstein points out, Razumov's gesture is 'answered by another gesture: Natalia has not spoken, but "pointed mournfully at the tragic immobility of her mother [...]"' (2020: 268). Razumov had once asked, 'What is betrayal?' and prevailed on himself that

---

[8] According to Antonio Damasio, sometimes 'we use part of the mind as a screen to prevent another part of it from sensing what goes on elsewhere. [...]. One of the things the screen hides most effectively is the body, our own body [...]. Like a veil thrown over the skin to secure its modesty, but not too well, the screen partially removes from the mind the inner states of the body, those that constitute the flow of life as it wanders in the journey of each day' (1999: 28).

168   Y. OKUDA

'[a]ll a man can betray is his conscience' (37). Ironically, it is the betrayal of his conscience in turning away from Haldin's immediate physical presence that compels him to confess to Natalia Haldin till she finally divines its full significance. The word 'conscience' in this context may be defined not so much as an ability to make moral judgements in terms of right and wrong or good and bad, as the 'concentration of the consciousness on what is most central and essential' (Nakamura 108; my translation).

Razumov and Natalia Haldin awaken to the consciousness of their physical identity almost at the same time by freeing themselves from the abstract ideas in the mind—Razumov is freed from the abstract image of Haldin as he conceived it during his walk in St. Petersburg and Natalia Haldin from the verbal image of Razumov as she conceived it misled by her brother's words. When they accept each other's bodily presence, they identify themselves with their own body and thus free themselves from the world dominated by words and gain independence from it. Razumov proclaims to the revolutionists, 'today I made myself free from falsehood, from remorse—independent of every single human being on this earth' (368), and the teacher of languages detects 'the perfection of collected independence' in Natalia Haldin when he sees her for the last time (373); they have both matured by their 'open and secret experience' (373).

The teacher of languages has also matured by watching the drama. He may have 'raged at him [Razumov] like a disappointed devil,' seeing that his hopes that Razumov will be a guide for Natalia Haldin have been ruined, and even have felt a repulsion to Razumov's body, telling him ironically, 'Don't you understand that your presence is intolerable— even to me?' (355). When his rooms in St. Petersburg were searched by the police, Razumov had wondered whether he should continue to live, yet '[t]he idea of laying violent hands upon his body did not occur to Razumov,' because '[t]he unrelated organism bearing that label, walking, breathing, wearing these clothes, was of no importance to any one [...]' (77). However, at the end of the drama, the teacher of languages, as a sole member of the audience, affirms the significance of the living body:

> [...] my eyes fell on Razumov, still there, standing before the empty chair, as if rooted for ever to the spot of his atrocious confession. A wonder came over me that the mysterious force which had torn it out of him had failed to destroy his life, to shatter his body. It was there unscathed. I stared at the broad line of his shoulder, his dark head, the amazing immobility of his limbs. (355)

When we recall the sympathy he manifested to Razumov during their conversation on the Bastions, it may not be reading too much into the text to suggest that it might have been 'pity,' and not 'extreme astonishment,' that dimmed his eyes at seeing Razumov pick up the dropped veil and press it to his face.

In the 'Author's Note' to *Under Western Eyes*, Conrad claims that the book is 'an attempt to render not so much the political state as the psychology of Russia itself' (vii), based on 'the general knowledge of the condition of Russia and of the moral and emotional reactions of the Russian temperament to the pressure of tyrannical lawlessness' (viii). However, when read from the perspective of emotions and contingencies, *Under Western Eyes* seems to provide a framework that synthesizes the major emotional issues addressed in the preceding six chapters: the teacher of languages' attention to Razumov's emotional expressions is reminiscent of Marlow's in *Lord Jim* and 'Heart of Darkness'; the emotional propensities Razumov exhibits initially in clinging to his self-image reflect those exhibited by the characters in *Nostromo*; the emotional sequence that Razumov follows from surprise to anger and from anger to obsessive thought recalls the sequence that the characters in *The Secret Agent* follow; and the significant conversations that Razumov holds in Geneva remind us of the one-to-one emotional engagements in 'The Duel' and 'The Secret Sharer.' As Bruce E. Johnson maintains, the story is 'symbolic of our common experience' (1971: 151). Insisting that these emotional experiences are exclusively Russian may be a profound irony on the part of the author.

CHAPTER 9

Conclusion

> World, world, O world!
> But that thy strange mutation makes us hate thee
> Life would not yield to age. (*King Lear* IV. i.)

Contingencies and accidents are signs of impermanence. Paul B. Armstrong maintains that '[c]omplacency, the resolute refusal to recognize the threat of contingency, is for Conrad a fundamental feature of the human condition' (113). In Conrad's fiction, this 'resolute refusal to recognize the threat of contingency' is explored in terms of reactive emotions which induce egoistic and non-egoistic reactions to a reality that contradicts one's assumptions. Emotions and contingencies figure prominently and consistently in Conrad's works. However, past criticism has tended not to pay much attention to these issues. To fill this gap in Conrad criticism, this book has aimed to shed light on Conrad's unique insight into the workings of human emotions in the framework of a world subject to change and chance.

The theme of emotions runs right through all of Conrad's works from *Almayer's Folly* (1895) to *The Rover* (1923). In *Almayer's Folly*, Conrad explores how Almayer fails to penetrate the meaning of his life 'deceived by the emotional estimate of his motives' (102), and in *The Rover* (1923) he probes the effects of 'a kind of intimate emotion' aroused by Arlette in old Peyrol (88). However, Conrad says, even as late as 1918, that his

© The Author(s), under exclusive license to Springer Nature
Switzerland AG 2024
Y. Okuda, *Emotions and Contingencies in Conrad's Fiction*,
https://doi.org/10.1007/978-3-031-66723-7_9

writing career 'has been a time of evolution [...] and that the process is still going on' (To Barrett H. Clark, 4 May 1918; *CL6*: 210), and this applies to his exploration of emotions in his works as well; he looks at emotions from a fresh angle in each of his works.

This book has traced the development of Conrad's emotional insight from *Lord Jim* (1900) to *Under Western Eyes* (1911) against the background of a narrative world marked by contingencies. The chapter on *Lord Jim* highlighted Marlow's outlook on the world and examined the stress that the world placed on Jim, with a view to establishing the relationship between emotions and contingencies underlying Conrad's fiction. The next chapter on 'Heart of Darkness' compared and contrasted the emotional propensities of the Europeans and the indigenous people and analysed Kurtz's aberrant behaviour brought about by his abysmal ignorance of his own emotionality. This was followed by two chapters on *Nostromo* and *The Secret Agent* that revealed the common emotional propensities discernible among a group of characters who strived to renew their identity or to preserve their self-image in contingent circumstances. Chapters 6 to 8 traced the entire process of the emotional development of the respective protagonists stage by stage. The chapter on 'The Duel' attempted to elucidate how D'Hubert learnt to accept the irrational side of his own emotionality by accepting the irrationality of his opponent, and the following chapter on 'The Secret Sharer' demonstrated how the captain-narrator learnt to handle his first command by gaining self-possession and physical sensitivity through his involvement with a stowaway. Finally, the last chapter on *Under Western Eyes* revealed how Razumov gained an insight into his true identity by penetrating the familiar surface of his own emotions and discovering the physical side of his emotional life.

In approaching Conrad's fiction from the dual perspective of individual emotions and universal contingencies, this book follows a tradition in Conrad criticism begun by contemporary reviewers and critics who approached the author and his oeuvre from a similar perspective. This approach calls attention to Conrad's own dual perspective which reflects his view of the universe and his view of humanity. W. L. Courtney, as mentioned earlier in the Introduction, praises Conrad for his insight into the universe and humanity: 'He sees the world as a whole, and is under no misapprehension as to the insignificant part played therein by humanity' (1908; *CR2*: 451). Wilson Follett also emphasizes Conrad's dual perspective and maintains that 'the unifying principle [...] lying at the core' of

9 CONCLUSION   173

Conrad's achievement consists of 'his particular view of the world, and, standing in a somewhat paradoxical relation to that, his other view of what the world can be made to mean to the individual'; he calls them otherwise, 'his philosophy of the cosmos and [...] his philosophy of life' or 'his two strangely opposed visions of nature and of man' (1915: 13).[1] More recently, Ian Watt discusses Conrad in terms of 'a sense of alienation' and 'a sense of commitment.' He indicates that Conrad shared a sense of alienation with his Victorian contemporaries who felt that '[...] so far from being the eternal setting created by God for his favourite, man, the natural world was merely the temporary and accidental result of purposeless physical processes' (1964 / 2000: 3); nevertheless, he goes on to say that 'Conrad also gives us a sense of much wider commitment to the main ethical, social and literary attitudes, both of the world at large and of the general reader, than do any other of his great contemporaries' (1964/2000: 6). It is interesting to note that all these reviewers and critics evince an awareness of Conrad's dual perspective, referring to one perspective in such phrases as 'the world as a whole,' 'the cosmos,' or 'the natural world,' and to the other perspective as 'humanity,' 'life,' or 'the world at large.'

One possible way of accounting for Conrad's characteristic dual world view may be found in his seafaring career. Thomas Mann claims that 'this man's very deepest and most personal experience has been the sea, his perilous fellowship with that mighty element' (Mann in Watt 1973: 101–102); Ian Watt says that 'Conrad's years at sea were everything for his career as a writer' (2000: 7); and Zdzislaw Najder maintains that during his life at sea:

Conrad gained an immense range of experience, from stark, helpless fear, disgust, and boredom to the ecstatic enjoyment of beauty, a sense of the triumphant efficacy of his own body and spirit, to exhaustion relieved by the consciousness of victory in the struggle against an incomparably stronger elemental opponent. (2007: 189)

---

[1] In a letter to F. N. Doubleday, dated 10 April 1916, Conrad pays tribute to Follett's study saying, '[...] nothing ever written about me had come anywhere near it, in tone, in discernment, in comprehension. You may tell him that C. [Conrad] feels less lonely since he has read his pages' (*CL* 5: 575).

Conrad's overarching view of emotions, which sees them in the framework of contingencies, is essentially the view of a seaman. The origins of his sense of insecurity may be traced back to the tribulations he suffered as a child in Ukraine, such as the exile to Vologda and the subsequent loss of his parents. This sense of insecurity may later have been augmented by the perils of the sea he encountered as a seaman on various sailing vessels. Moreover, what Conrad calls 'the weather sense,' which is 'that touch with the natural phenomena of wind and sea which was the very breath of our professional life' (To Captain Arthur W. Phillips, 12 January 1924; *CL8*: 272), may have nurtured in him a strong sense of the mutability of Nature. Meanwhile 'the sailor mentality,' which is developed by 'physical work into which one puts all one's heart in association with others and for a clearly understood purpose' (*Last Essays* 70–71), may have enhanced his sensitivity of the body, cultivated in him a strong sense of solidarity, and developed a keen eye for the real aspect of things. On the other hand, the ego-centric and non-egocentric emotions expressed by his fellow-seamen, glimpsed while facing adversities at sea, may have given him a penetrating insight into the workings of human emotions. Therefore, it may be said that Conrad's views on emotions and contingencies were not the consequence of philosophical reflection, but the outcome of impressions he derived from his association with Nature.

It may be unfashionable to quote Conrad's early readers in Conrad criticism today, but it was the contemporary reviewers and critics, rather than their modern counterparts, who attached most importance to Conrad's views on Nature or the cosmos. One of these reviewers was John Galsworthy. Galsworthy knew Conrad intimately, and therefore he perhaps had a more penetrating insight into Conrad's view of a contingent and impermanent universe. He claims that '[i]n the novels of Joseph Conrad, Nature is first, man second,' and he even senses 'something of the unethical morality of Nature' in what he calls Conrad's 'cosmic spirit,' and claims that '[t]he virtues of this cosmic spirit are a daring curiosity and courageous resignation' (Galsworthy in Watt 1973: 91). To be curious, according to Galsworthy, is 'to be in love': 'The man who has the cosmic spirit knows that he will never understand; he spends his life, inquiringly, in love. Nothing is too squalid, too small, too unconventional or remote for him to gaze on and long to know' (Galsworthy in Watt 1973: 90). He seems to suggest that Conrad's moral vision is not so much based on the traditional moral principles of right and wrong as on 'daring curiosity' and 'courageous resignation.'

9 CONCLUSION 175

In *A Personal Record*, Conrad says:

> The ethical view of the universe involves us at last in so many cruel and
> absurd contradictions, where the last vestiges of faith, hope, charity, and
> even of reason itself, seem ready to perish, that I have come to suspect that
> the aim of creation cannot be ethical at all. I would fondly believe that its
> object is purely spectacular: a spectacle for awe, love, adoration, or hate,
> if you like, but in this view – never for despair! Those visions, delicious
> or poignant, are a moral end in themselves. [...]. And the unwearied self-
> forgetful attention to every phase of the living universe reflected in our
> consciousness may be our appointed task on this earth. A task in which
> fate has perhaps engaged nothing of us except our conscience, gifted with
> a voice in order to bear true testimony to the visible wonder, the haunting
> terror, the infinite passion and the illimitable serenity; to the supreme law
> and the abiding mystery of the sublime spectacle. (92)

In this passage, Conrad presents two opposing views: an ethical view that
offers a possible means to achieve a moral end and a non-ethical view that
constitutes a moral end in itself. Each of these views entails a particular
set of emotions. The former view is based on the traditional theological
virtues of 'faith,' 'hope,' and 'charity,' and looks forward to the future:
'faith' is a strong belief that something always exists or is true, 'hope' is
a feeling of wanting and expecting something to happen, and 'charity'
is a desire to promote the wellbeing of others hereafter. These emotions
assume security beyond the immediate present, and therefore entertaining
them involves the risk of exposing oneself to morally 'cruel and absurd'
contradictions in a contingent world. In contrast, the latter view entails
such emotions as 'awe, love, adoration, or hate,' which are more often
induced spontaneously and unthinkingly. Such emotional reactions are
more likely to be confined in time and space to the 'here and now,' and as
they do not assume security beyond the immediate present, entertaining
them does not involve the risk of facing contradictions in the future.
The emotional effects they produce are not 'cruel and absurd' but 'deli-
cious or poignant'; that is to say, they are pleasant or unpleasant effects
that make us either smile or weep. Such a view requires us to remain
attentive to each and every phase of what Conrad calls a 'purely spectacular universe' (94), and as there is no room for ethical consideration
or judgement, these visions of the universe are 'a moral end in themselves.' The 'appointed task' is in fact moral in nature, as it stipulates that
we should bear witness to 'wonder' and 'terror,' and to 'the supreme

law' and 'mystery.' The passage reflects Conrad's 'daring curiosity' about human emotions and 'courageous resignation' to the law governing the mysterious universe.

In a letter to Bertrand Russell, Conrad claims, 'I have never been able to find in any man's book or any man's talk anything convincing enough to stand up for a moment against my deep-seated sense of fatality governing this man-inhabited world' (23 October 1922; *CL7*: 543). This may sound rather mortifying to man, who, in Galsworthy's words, cannot 'bear to think that he is bound up with a Scheme that seems to him so careless of his own important life' (Galsworthy in Watt 1973: 89). However, submitting to contingencies does not always signify humiliating surrender. In *A Personal Record*, Conrad recounts an interesting experience of his own as a boy on the Furca Pass when 'a passing glance' of kindly curiosity and a friendly smile from a complete stranger, whom Conrad later calls 'the ambassador of my future,' '[turns] the scale at a critical moment' in his life (41). Just as he is 'feeling utterly crushed' (41) by his tutor's persuasiveness, the momentary glance and smile from the stranger revives his nearly extinguished hope of going to sea; the stranger's unconscious appeal to young Conrad's eyes triumphs over the tutor's verbal eloquence. The visual impression that Conrad receives from this man inspires adoration in him, and quite accidentally decides Conrad's future career as a seaman, and perhaps even his subsequent career as a writer. The passage seems to suggest that the very fact that the stranger existed and happened to pass by him at that exact moment was, for Conrad, one of the wonders and mysteries of the spectacular universe.

Conrad believed that, not only his life, but his art also had its roots in the spectacular universe, and his aim as an artist was 'to remain true to the emotions called out of the deep encircled by the firmament of stars [...]' (*A Personal Record* 93). It is on this basis that he declares:

Our captivity within the incomprehensible logic of accident is the only fact of the universe. From that reality flow deception and inspiration, error and faith, egoism and sacrifice, love and hate. [...]. To produce a work of art a man must either know or feel that truth—even without knowing it. It must be the basis of every artistic endeavour. (To T. Fisher Unwin, 22 August 1896: *CL1*:303)

References

Achebe, Chinua. *An Image of Africa/The Trouble with Nigeria*. London: Penguin Classics, 2010.

Almond, Philip C. *The British Discovery of Buddhism*. Cambridge: Cambridge University Press, 1988.

Armstrong, Paul B. *The Challenge of Bewilderment: Understanding and Representation in James, Conrad, and Ford*. Ithaca & London: Cornell University Press, 1987.

Asher, Kenneth. *Literature, Ethics, and the Emotions*. Cambridge: Cambridge University Press, 2017.

Berthoud, Jacques. *Joseph Conrad: The Major Phase*. Cambridge: Cambridge University Press, 1978.

Bloom, Harold. Ed. *Joseph Conrad*. New York: Infobase Publishing, 2010.

Booth, Wayne C. *A Rhetoric of Irony*. Chicago: The University of Chicago Press, 1974.

Bradshaw, Graham. *Joseph Conrad's 'Heart of Darkness.'* Cornell Publishing, 2018.

Bross, Addison. '*A Set of Six*: Variations on a theme.' *Joseph Conrad: Critical Assessments III*. Ed. Keith Carabine. East Sussex: Helm Information, 1992.

Bulson, Eric ed. *The Cambridge Companion to the Novel*. Cambridge: Cambridge University Press, 2018.

Buzzard, Laura & Don LePan eds. *The Broadview Pocket Glossary of Literary Terms*. Ontario: Broadview Press, 2014.

Carabine, Keith. 'The Figure Behind the Veil: Conrad and Razumov in *Under Western Eyes*.' *Joseph Conrad's Under Western Eyes*. Ed. David R. Smith Hamden, Connecticut.: Archon Books, 1991: 1–38.

© The Editor(s) (if applicable) and The Author(s), under exclusive license to Springer Nature Switzerland AG 2024
Y. Okuda, *Emotions and Contingencies in Conrad's Fiction*,
https://doi.org/10.1007/978-3-031-66723-7

178 REFERENCES

Carabine, Keith. Ed. *Joseph Conrad: Critical Assessments II & III*. East Sussex: Helm Information, 1992.

Carlyle, Thomas. *Past and Present*. London: J. M. Dent and Sons, 1960.

Cohen, William A. *Embodied: Victorian Literature and the Senses*. Minneapolis: University of Minnesota Press, 2009.

Conrad, Joseph. *The Last Essays*. London: J. M. Dent & Sons, 1955.

Conrad, Joseph. *Lord Jim: A Tale*. London: J. M. Dent & Sons, 1946.

Conrad, Joseph. *The Mirror of the Sea & A Personal Record*. London: J. M. Dent & Sons, 1946.

Conrad, Joseph. *Nostromo*. London: J. M. Dent & Sons, 1947.

Conrad, Joseph. *Notes on Life and Letters*. London: J. M. Dent & Sons, 1946.

Conrad, Joseph. *A Set of Six*. London: J. M. Dent & Sons, 1949.

Conrad, Joseph. *The Shadow-Line & Within the Tides*. London: J. M. Dent & Sons, 1950.

Conrad, Joseph. *The Secret Agent*. London: J. M. Dent & Sons, 1946.

Conrad, Joseph. *'Twixt Land and Sea*. London: J. M. Dent & Sons, 1947.

Conrad, Joseph. *Under Western Eyes*. London: J. M. Dent & Sons, 1947.

Conrad, Joseph. *Victory*. London: J. M. Dent & Sons, 1949.

Conrad, Joseph. *Youth, Heart of Darkness, The End of the Tether*. J. M. Dent & Sons, 1946.

Cox, C. B. *Joseph Conrad: The Modern Imagination*. London: J. M. Dent & Sons, 1974.

Cox, C. B. Ed. *Conrad: Heart of Darkness, Nostromo and Under Western Eyes*. London: Macmillan Press, 1981.

Cuddon, J. A. & M. A. R. Habib eds. *Literary Terms & Literary Theory*. London: Penguin Books, 2014.

Daleski, H. M. *Joseph Conrad: The Way of Dispossession*. London: Faber and Faber, 1977.

Damasio, Antonio. *Descartes' Error*. New York: G. P. Putnam's Sons, 1994; reprinted. London: Vintage Books, 2006.

Damasio, Antonio. *The Feeling of What Happens: Body and Emotion in the Making of Consciousness*. San Diego, New York, and London: Harcourt, 1999.

Davies, Laurence, Frederick R. Karl & Owen Knowles eds. *The Collected Letters of Joseph Conrad*. 6. Cambridge: Cambridge University Press, 2002.

Davies, Laurence & J. H. Stape eds. *The Collected Letters of Joseph Conrad*. 7. Cambridge: Cambridge University Press, 2005.

Davies, Laurence & Gene M. Moore eds. *The Collected Letters of Joseph Conrad* 8. Cambridge: Cambridge University Press, 2008.

The Encyclopedia of Cultural Anthropology [Bunka-Jinruigaku-Jiten] (in Japanese). Eds. E. Ishikawa et al. Tokyo: Koubundo, 1962.

Epstein Hugh. 'Conrad and Nature, 1900–1904' *Conrad and Nature*. Eds. Lissa Schneider-Reboso et al. London: Routledge, 2019: 173–195.

REFERENCES **179**

Epstein, Hugh. *Hardy, Conrad and the Senses*. Edinburgh: Edinburgh University Press, 2020.

Evans, Ifor. *A Short History of English Literature*. London: Penguin Books, 1976.

Federico, Annette. *Engagements with Close Reading*. London: Routledge, 2016.

Ferguson, J. Delancey. 'The Plot of Conrad's *The Duel*.' *Modern Language Notes*. 50.6. 1935: 385–390.

Follett, Wilson. *Joseph Conrad: A short study of his intellectual and emotional attitude toward his work and of the chief characteristics of his novels*. Darby, Pa.: Darby Books, 1915; reprinted. New York: Doubleday, Page & Company, 1969.

Foster, Paul. *Beckett and Zen*. London: Wisdom Publications, 1989.

Frye, Northrop. *Anatomy of Criticism: Four Essays*. Princeton: Princeton University Press, 1957.

Fussel, Susan R. and Mallie M. Moss. 'Figurative Language in Emotional Communication.' *Language in Emotional Communication* 3. 1998: 1–31.

Galsworthy, John. 'Joseph Conrad: A Disquisition.' *Conrad: The Secret Agent*. Ed. Ian Watt. London: The Macmillan Press, 1973: 89–98.

Garnett, Edward. 'Mr. Conrad's Art.' *Joseph Conrad: Contemporary Reviews* 2. Ed. John G. Peters. Cambridge: Cambridge University Press, 2012: 202–07.

Garret, Peter K. *Scene and Symbol from George Eliot to James Joyce*. New Haven: Yale University Press, 1969.

Graver, Lawrence. *Conrad's Short Fiction*. Berkeley & Los Angeles: University of California Press, 1969.

Guerard, Albert. *Conrad the Novelist*. Cambridge, Massachusetts: Harvard University Press, 1958.

Hampson, Robert, ed. *Heart of Darkness*. London: Penguin Books, 2007.

Hampson, Robert. *Conrad's Secrets*. London: Palgrave Macmillan, 2012.

Hawthorn, Jeremy. *Studying the Novel: An Introduction*. London: Edward Arnold, 1985.

Hawthorn, Jeremy. *Joseph Conrad: Narrative Technique and Ideological Commitment*. London: Edward Arnold, 1990.

Hay, Eloise Knapp. *The Political Novels of Joseph Conrad: A Critical Study*. Chicago and London: University of Chicago Press, 1963.

Herman, David ed. *The Cambridge Companion to Narrative*. Cambridge: Cambridge University Press, 2007.

Hillman, David & Maude, Ulrika, eds. *The Cambridge Companion to the Body in Literature*. Cambridge: Cambridge University Press, 2015.

Hogan, Patrick Colm. *What Literature Teaches Us about Emotion*. Cambridge: Cambridge University Press, 2011.

Hogan, Patrick Colm. *Literature and Emotion*. London: Routledge, 2018a.

180 REFERENCES

Hogan, Patrick Colm. 'Complexities of Social Cognition: Dorothy Richardson's *Pointed Roofs*.' An unpublished paper read at the 2nd International Conference of the Modernist Studies in Asia at the Education University of Hong Kong, June 2018b.

Hogan, Patrick Colm. *Literature and Moral Feeling: A Cognitive Poetics of Ethics, Narrative, and Empathy*. Cambridge: Cambridge University Press, 2022.

Holland, N. Norman. 'Style as Character: *The Secret Agent*' *Joseph Conrad*. Ed. Harold Bloom. New York: Infobase Publishing, 2010: 53–62.

Hooper, Myrtle. 'The Ethics of Negativity: Conrad's "The Duel".' *L'Epoque Conradienne* 31. 2001: 107–117.

Jacob, Robert G. 'Comrade Ossipon's Favorite Saint: Lombroso and Conrad.' *Nineteenth Century Fiction* 23:1: 74–84.

Johnson, Barbara & Marjorie Garber 'Secret Sharing: Reading Conrad Psychologically.' *College English* 49, 1987: 628–40.

Johnson, Bruce E. *Conrad's Models of Mind*. Minneapolis: University of Minnesota Press, 1971.

Johnson, Bruce E. 'The Psychologist of Self-Image.' *Conrad: Heart of Darkness, Nostromo, and Under Western Eyes*. Ed. C. B. Cox. London: Macmillan Press, 1981: 112–30.

Kadowaki, J. K. *Zen and the Bible*. Trans. Joan Rieck. London: Routledge & Kegan Paul, 1980.

Kenko and Chomei. *Essays in Idleness and Hojoki*. Trans. Meredith McKinney. London: Penguin Classics, 2014.

Karl, Frederick R. & Laurence Davies eds. *The Collected Letters of Joseph Conrad* 1. Cambridge: Cambridge University Press, 1983.

Karl, Frederick R. & Laurence Davies eds. *The Collected Letters of Joseph Conrad* 2. Cambridge: Cambridge University Press, 1986.

Karl, Frederick R. & Laurence Davies eds. *The Collected Letters of Joseph Conrad* 3. Cambridge: Cambridge University Press, 1983.

Karl, Frederick R. & Laurence Davies eds. *The Collected Letters of Joseph Conrad* 5. Cambridge: Cambridge University Press, 1996.

Kirschner, Paul. *Conrad: The Psychologist as Artist*. Edinburgh: Oliver & Boyd, 1968.

Lawtoo, Nidesh. *Conrad's Shadow: Catastrophe, Mimesis, Theory*. East Lansing: Michigan State University Press, 2016.

Lester, John. *Conrad and Religion*. London: Macmillan Press, 1988.

Lodge, David. *Consciousness and the Novel*. London: Secker & Warburg, 2002.

Lothe, Jacob. *Conrad's Narrative Method*. Oxford: Clarendon Press, 1989.

Mann, Thomas. 'Joseph Conrad's *The Secret Agent*.' *Conrad: The Secret Agent*. Ed. Ian Watt. London: The Macmillan Press, 1973: 99–112.

Margolin, Uri. 'Character.' *The Cambridge Companion to Narrative*. Ed. David Herman. Cambridge: Cambridge University Press, 2007: 66–79.

REFERENCES   181

Martinière, Nathalie. 'Exploring the Unexpected with Marlow in *Lord Jim*.' *L'Epoque Conradienne* 39. 2013–2014: 45–66.

McCarthy, Jeffrey Mathes. 'A Choice of Nightmares: The Ecology of *Heart of Darkness*.' *Modern Fiction Studies* 55.8. 2009: 620–48.

Merton, Thomas. *The Seven Storey Mountain*. London: Sheldon Press, 1975.

Miller, J. Hillis. *Poets of Reality: Six Twentieth-Century Writers*. Cambridge, Massachusetts: Harvard University Press, 1965.

Moser, Thomas C. ed. *Lord Jim* (2nd edition). New York: W. W. Norton & Company, 1996.

Najder, Zdzislaw. *Joseph Conrad: A Life*. Trans. Halina Najder. Rochester, New York: Camden House, 2007.

Nakamura, Hajime. *In Search of Self* [*Jiko-no Tankyu*] in Japanese. Tokyo: Seidosha, 1987.

Oatley, Keith. *Emotions: A Brief History*. Oxford: Blackwell, 2004.

Oatley, Keith, Dacher Keltner and Jennifer M. Jenkins eds. *Understanding Emotions*. Oxford: Blackwell Publishing, 2006.

Orr, Leonard. 'The Semiotics of Description in Conrad's *Nostromo*.' *Critical Essays on Joseph Conrad*. Ed. Ted Billy. Boston, Massachusetts: G. K. Hall, 1987: 113–28.

Osborne, Roger and Paul Eggert, eds. *Under Western Eyes*. Cambridge: Cambridge University Press, 2013: 451.

Oxford Dictionary of Proverbs. Ed. Jennifer Speake. Oxford: Oxford University Press, 2015.

The Oxford English Dictionary, 2nd ed. Oxford: Oxford University Press, 1989.

The Oxford English Dictionary Online. www.oed.com

Peters, John G. *Conrad and Impressionism*. Cambridge: Cambridge University Press, 2001.

Peters, John G. ed. *Joseph Conrad: Contemporary Reviews* 2. Cambridge: Cambridge University Press, 2012.

Peters, John G. 'Environmental Imperialism in Joseph Conrad's *Nostromo*.' *College Literature* 46.3, 2019: 603–626.

Prickett, David. 'No Escape: Liberation and the Ethics of Self-Governance in *The Secret Agent*. Allan H. Simmons & J. H. Stape eds. *The Secret Agent: Centennial Essays*. Amsterdam: Rodopi, B. V. & The Joseph Conrad Society, 2007.

Rahula, Walpola. *What the Buddha Taught*. London: The Gordon Fraser Gallery, 1982.

Rimmon-Kenan, Shlomith. *Narrative Fictions: Contemporary Poetics*. London & New York: Methuen, 1983.

Roussel, Royal. *The Metaphysics of Darkness*. Baltimore: The Johns Hopkins Press, 1971.

182 REFERENCES

Royce, Anya Peterson. *The Anthropology of Dance*. Bloomington and London: Indiana University Press, 1977.

Sachs, C. *World History of the Dance*. New York: Norton & Co., 1937, 1965.

Said, Edward. *Culture and Imperialism*. London: Chatto & Windus, 1993.

Said, Edward. 'The Novel as Beginning Intention: *Nostromo.' Joseph Conrad*. Ed. Elaine Jordan. London: Macmillan Press, 1996: 103–15.

Sander, David and Klaus R. Scherer eds. *The Oxford Companion to Emotion and the Affective Sciences*. Oxford: Oxford University Press, 2009.

Schloegl, Irmgard. *The Zen Way*. London: Sheldon Press, 1977.

Schneider-Reboso, Lissa, Jeffery Mathes McCarthy and John G. Peters eds. *Conrad and Nature*. London: Routledge, 2019.

Schwarz, Daniel R. *Conrad: Almayer's Folly to Under Western Eyes*. London: The Macmillan Press, 1980.

Schwarz, Daniel R. '"The Secret Sharer" as an Act of Memory.' *The Secret Sharer*. Ed. Daniel R. Schwarz. Boston: Bedford Books, 1997: 95–111.

Shakespeare, William. *The Tragedies of Shakespeare*. Ed. W. J. Craig. London: Oxford University Press, 1956.

The Shambhala Dictionary of Buddhism and Zen. Eds. Ingrid Fischer-Schreiber et al. Trans. Michael H. Kohn. Boston: Shambhala Publication, 1991.

Short, Mick. *Exploring the Language of Poems, Plays and Prose*. Harlow, England: Pearson Education, 1996.

Simmons, Alan H. & J. H. Stape eds. *The Secret Agent: Centennial Essays*. Amsterdam: Rodopi, B. V. & The Joseph Conrad Society, 2007.

Skolik, Joanna. '"It shouldn't have been like that…" Between the Reasons and the Results: Unexpected Consequences of Protagonists' Conscious Choices in Conrad's Fiction.' *L'Epoque Conradienne* 39. 2013–2014: 33–44.

Smith, David R. ed. *Joseph Conrad's Under Western Eyes: Beginnings, Revision, Final Forms*. Hamden: Archon Books, 1991.

Stape, John H. 'Conrad's "The Duel": A Reconsideration.' Keith Carabine ed. *Joseph Conrad: Critical Assessments III*. East Sussex: Helm Information, 1992: 122–126.

Stein, William Bysshe. 'Buddhism and the "Heart of Darkness."' *Western Humanities Review* XI, 1957: 281–85.

Steiner, Joan E. 'Conrad's "The Secret Sharer": Complexities of the Doubling Relationship.' *Conradiana* 12.3 (1980):173–86.

Thorndike English Dictionary. London: The English Universities Press, 1948.

Tanner, Tony. 'Butterflies and Beetles—Conrad's Two Truths.' *Lord Jim* (2nd edition). Thomas C. Moser ed. New York: W. W. Norton & Company, 1996.

Wales, Katie, ed. *A Dictionary of Stylistics* (2nd edition). London: Pearson Education, 2001.

Warren, Robert Penn. 'Conrad: *Nostromo.' Joseph Conrad: Critical Assessments II.* Ed. Keith Carabine. Mountfield, near Robertsbridge, East Sussex: Helm Information, 1992: 572–589.

Watt, Ian. *Conrad: The Secret Agent.* London: The Macmillan Press, 1973.

Watt, Ian. *Conrad in the Nineteenth Century.* London: Chatto & Windus, 1980.

Watt, Ian. Introduction. *The Secret Sharer: An Episode from the Coast.* New York: The Limited Editions Club, 1985.

Watt, Ian. *Nostromo.* Cambridge: Cambridge University Press, 1988.

Watt, Ian. *Essays on Conrad.* Cambridge: Cambridge University Press, 2000.

Watts, Cedric. *A Preface to Conrad.* London: Longman, 1993.

Zemka, Sue. *Time and the Moment in Victorian Literature and Society.* Cambridge: Cambridge University Press, 2012.

INDEX

Note: The page numbers followed by 'n' represents footnotes.

A

accident(s), 1, 9
Achebe, Chinua, 18, 39, 49
action, 65–67, 72, 75, 84, 88, 100, 115
    practical action, 61, 64, 65, 76, 80
Adler, Alfred, 15n
affect, 3–4
Affect Studies, 3–4
Almond, Philip C., 13
anger, 89–91, 89n, 92, 98–100, 106.
    See also indignation; resentment
anxiety, 113, 114
Armstrong, Paul B., 11, 36, 76n, 171
Arnold, Edwin, 14
Asher, Kenneth, 45n

B

basic emotions, 89n
Beck, Aaron T., 87n
Berrong, Richard M., 1n
Berthoud, Jacques, 29–32, 41, 74
Blackwood, William, 84n

body, 125–136, 149–165
    bodily eye, 128–134
    communication and, 125–128, 151–157
    communion and, 135
    conversation and, 149–159, 167
    emotion and, 140–142, 162
    'from the body to the mind', 128–131
    identity and, 164–169
    person (the living body), 160–162
    physical contact, 145
    physical exertion, 123
    physical presence, 128, 133, 135, 146, 148–150, 156, 160, 163, 164, 168
    physical symptoms, 146, 152, 157, 158
    sense of, 144–147
    words and, 151–160, 165–169
Booth, Wayne, 85n, 86
Bradshaw, Graham, 40, 40n
Bross, Addison, 110

© The Editor(s) (if applicable) and The Author(s), under exclusive   185
license to Springer Nature Switzerland AG 2024
Y. Okuda, *Emotions and Contingencies in Conrad's Fiction*,
https://doi.org/10.1007/978-3-031-66723-7

186 INDEX

Buddha, Gautama, 14
Buddhism, 12–17, 57
    Buddha posture, 14, 57
    karuṇā, 57
    Three Signs of Being, 13
    Zen, 12, 12n, 15, 126–128
Buzzard, Laura, 3

C
Carabine, Keith, 140n
Carlyle, Thomas, 43, 44, 44n
    Past and Present, 43–44
change, 9, 11, 13, 63–64, 80, 142,
    144
Chaucer, Geoffrey, 132
    Canterbury Tales, 132
Clark, Barrett H., 2, 12, 172
Clifford, Hugh, 16, 87
close reading, 15
Cohen, William A., 140n
communication
    body and, 125–128, 151–157, 167
    non-verbal, 125–128, 151–157,
        167
compassion, 55–57, 56n. *See also* pity;
    sympathy
Conradian, 8n
Conrad, Joseph
    ESSAYS
        'Author's Note' to *The Secret
            Agent*, 83, 101
        'Author's Note' to *A Set of
            Six*, 109
        'Author's Note' to *Under
            Western Eyes*, 169
        'Autocracy and War' in *Notes
            on Life and Letters*, 65n,
            105, 127
        'The Censor of Plays' in *Notes
            on Life and Letters*, 92
        'A Familia Preface' to *A
            Personal Record*, 5, 117

Last Essays, 123, 127n, 174
'The Life Beyond' in *Notes on
    Life and Letters*, 57
'Memorandum on the Scheme
    for Fitting Out a Sailing
    Ship' in *Last Essays*, 123,
    127, 174
The Mirror of the Sea, 29, 63n,
    71, 129, 135
Notes on Life and Letters, 57,
    65n, 92, 105, 127
A Personal Record, 19, 56n,
    64, 71, 135, 175, 176
'Preface' to *The Nigger of the
    'Narcissus'*, 15, 33
NOVELS AND STORIES
    Almayer's Folly, 2, 171
    Chance, 17, 102
    'The Duel', 19, 109–122, 169,
        172
    'Heart of Darkness', 8, 14, 17,
        39–57, 80n, 156, 169
    Lord Jim, 11, 17, 23–37, 94,
        172
    Nostromo, 17–18, 61–81, 172
    The Rover, 17, 102, 171
    The Secret Agent, 6, 18,
        83–106, 169
    'The Secret Sharer', 19,
        123–136, 172
    'The Shadow Line', 51n, 132
    Under Western Eyes, 17, 19,
        139–169, 172
    Victory, 17, 115n
conscience
    as concentration of consciousness,
    168
consciousness, 141–149
    core consciousness, 147–149, 156
    extended consciousness, 147–149,
    156

INDEX 187

contingency (contingencies), 9–12, 17. *See also* accident; change; impermanence; insecurity
destructive element and, 31–32
unexpected and, 25–27
conversation
body and, 149–157
conviction, 64–65. *See also* identity
cosmos, 6–9. *See also* universe; world
courage, 120–121
Courtney, W.L., 6, 12, 43, 172
cowardice, 120
Cox, C.B., 124
Cuddon, J.A., 86
cynicism, 146

D
Daleski, H.M., 24
Damasio, Antonio, 54n, 140–141, 147–149, 156, 164, 167n
Dawson, F. Warrington, 10
daydreaming, 29
Deleuze, Gilles, 4
disruption, 144. *See also* change
dramatic effect(s), 150, 165
dual perspective, 19, 172

E
Eckman, Paul, 89n
emotion(s), 1–6, 13, 37, 84–85, 147–150
awareness of, 37, 53–54
definition (philosophical), 4–5
definition (psychological), 5
emotionality, 18n
emotional maturation, 19, 106, 122
emotional reaction(s), 3, 39–57
emotional sequence, 92, 97, 101, 169
intellect and, 52–53, 74–75
reactive emotion(s), 5–6

sensation, 1n
empathy, 153, 153n
English
adoption of, 16n
Epstein, Hugh, 8, 62n, 167
Evans, Ifor, 3
event(s), 1, 5, 84–85

F
faith, hope, and charity, 175
fear, 89n, 90–92, 101, 120, 121, 143, 146
Federico, Annette, 3, 15
Follett, Wilson, 172, 173n
Ford, Ford Maddox, 14n, 23
Foster, Paul, 15
Freud, Sigmund, 4, 15
Frye, Northrop, 84n
Fussel, Susan R., 41

G
Galsworthy, John, 6, 64, 174–176
Garber, Marjorie, 124, 129
Garnett, Edward, 6, 10, 61–63
Garret, Peter K., 62
Graham, R.B. Cunningham, 9, 49, 51–53
Graver, Lawrence, 110
Guerard, Albert J., 24, 39, 75, 124

H
Hampson, Robert, 24, 48n
Hastings, Macdonald, 139, 150, 165
Hawthorn, Jeremy, 125–126, 135, 140, 147n, 150, 161
Hay, Eloise Knapp, 140n
Hillman, David, 124, 140, 140n, 150
Hogan, Patrick Colm, 2, 2n, 3, 4n, 19, 88, 93, 95, 100, 153n
Holland, Norman N., 84n
Hooper, Myrtle, 112

188 INDEX

I
idea, 44, 49–54, 67, 144
  fixed idea, 49, 67, 71, 102–105
identity, 9–12, 64–81, 164–169
  conviction and, 64–65, 90
  nature and, 68–81
  personal advantage and, 64–75, 78
  personality, 10, 161
image, 142–144, 146–149
  abstract image, 142
  concrete image, 142
imagination, 29–30, 54–55. *See also*
  daydreaming
impermanence, 11–13, 24–27, 62–64,
  76–81. *See also* accident; change;
  contingency
impression, 142–144. *See also* image
impulse, 10, 11, 51, 51n
indignation, 93–95, 98–100. *See also*
  anger
insecurity (sense of), 28–33, 93–97.
  See also security (sense of)
intellect, 52
  emotion and, 52, 75
irony, 85–87, 155, 169
  dramatic irony, 155, 166

J
Jacob, Robert G., 84n
Johnson, Barbara, 124, 129
Johnson, Bruce E., 62, 80, 140n
Jung, Carl Gustav, 4, 15

K
Kadowaki, J.K., 125
Kamo-no-Chomei, 7n
Keats, John, 153
  negative capability, 153
Keith, Joseph, 8
Kirschner, Paul, 15, 15n, 66, 87
Kyogen, Shikan, 77n

L
Lawtoo, Nidesh, 8, 24, 110
Lester, John, 28
Levin, Yael, 147n
Lodge, David, 142, 144
Lothe, Jacob, 86, 126, 128
love, 89, 114–120
  compassionate love, 114–117
  passionate love, 118–120
Lucas, Edward Verrall, 87

M
Mann, Thomas, 173
Margolin, Uri, 11
Martinière, Nathalie, 30, 30n
Maude, Ulrika, 124, 140, 140n
McCarthy, Jeffrey Mathes, 80n
meditation, 12n, 126, 128
Mencken, H.L., 7
Merton, Thomas, 52
Miller, J. Hillis, 140n
mind, 76, 131–134
  'from the body to the mind',
  128–131
  mind's eye, 131–134
  sailor's mentality, 123, 174
moral vision, 174
Moss, Mallie M., 41

N
Najder, Zdzislaw, 173
Nakamura, Hajime, 168
narrative
  change and, 11
  literal/non-literal, 124–125
Nature, 7, 63–64, 68–81
  artificiality and, 71
  identity and, 68–81
  impermanence and, 63, 79–81
  manifestation of, 76–81
  natural forces, 6–7, 73

INDEX 189

natural world, 67, 173
Noble, Edward, 1, 2, 9, 41, 84, 150

O
Oatley, Keith, 2, 4n, 24, 85, 89
Orr, Leonard, 63

P
patriotism, 75
Peake, Charles H., 12, 12n
Peters, John G., 41n, 67, 71n
Phillips, Arthur W., 174
pity, 55–57. *See also* compassion; sympathy
Poradowska, Marguerite, 16, 25
Prickett, David, 86
pride, 119

R
Rahula, Walpola, 13n
resentment, 91–92
resignation, 91, 121
resourcefulness, 121
Rimmon-Kenan, Shlomith, 112n
Roussel, Royal, 62n
Royce, Anya Peterson, 46
Russell, Bertrand, 176

S
Sachs, Curt, 46
Said, Edward, 39, 53, 80
Sander, David, 5, 89, 89n, 114, 119
Scherer, Klaus R., 5, 89, 89n, 114, 119
Schopenhauer, Arthur, 4, 14, 14n
Schwarz, Daniel R., 128n, 151
security (sense of), 29–30, 34, 93–97, 129–131. *See also* insecurity (sense of)

self-forgetfulness, 68–72
self-possession, 124, 131, 134–135
senses, the five, 128
  hearing, 128
  sight, 128–134
  touch, 128, 130
Shakespeare, William, 30n, 132
  Hamlet, 132
  King Lear, 171
  Macbeth, 30n
Short, Mick, 111n, 112n
Skolik, Joanna, 25
spectacular universe, 175–176
Spinoza, Baruch de, 4
Stape, John, 110, 122
Steiner, Joan E., 132
Stein, William Bysshe, 57
surprise, 89, 89n
sympathy, 55–57, 68, 154–157. *See also* compassion; pity

T
Tanner, Tony, 24, 140–141, 150
thought(s)/thinking, 76, 85, 90–92, 98, 99, 143, 144, 148, 149
  emotion(s) and, 53, 85
  obsessive thought(s), 85, 90, 92, 105
  thought-bound, 76
  thought process, 104–105, 148
  vision(s) and, 103–106
trauma, 56, 97, 102
trust, 27, 35, 155

U
'unexpected (the)', 25–27, 163–164
Unwin, T. Fisher, 9, 26, 176

V
vanity, 118–119

190 INDEX

vision, 32–33, 103–106. *See also* thought(s); words
   as means of thought, 103–106
   as revelatory insight, 32–33

W

Wales, Katie, 110n
Waliszewski, Kazumierz, 16
Warren, Robert Penn, 62
Watt, Ian, 6–9, 30, 41, 42, 62, 124, 125, 133, 135, 173
Watts, Cedric, 124
Wells, H.G., 16

'Why (the)'/'How (the)', 117, 121. *See also* resignation
word(s), 15–17, 94, 157–160, 165–168
work ethic, 43–45
world, 6. *See also* contingency; impermanence
   Nature, 7, 63–64
   spectacular universe (the), 175–176
   'world as a whole (the)', 6–9
   world of contradictions, 85–86

Z

Zemka, Sue, 164

Printed in the United States
by Baker & Taylor Publisher Services